We, Monsters

To Angela with love

We, Monsters

Zarina Zabrisky

VOX NOVA
A NUMINA PRESS BOOK

SAN RAFAEL, CALIFORNIA

ISBN-13: 978-0-9842600-4-1

Library of Congress Cataloging-in-Publication Data

Zabrisky, Zarina, 1966-
  We, Monsters / Zarina Zabrisky.
      pages cm
  ISBN 978-0-9842600-4-1 (alk. paper)
  1.   Suburban life--Fiction. 2.   Sisters--Death--Fiction.
3. Sexual dominance and submission--Fiction. I. Title.
  PS3626.A355W4 2013
  813'.6--dc23

                                    2013037394

Cover Design © 2013 by SAMMY!/IAmSammyDesign.com

A Vox Nova Book
Published by NUMINA PRESS
www.numinapress.com
Printed in U.S.A.

for K.

INTRODUCTION

by Katherine Zubritsky, Ph.D.

The Freudian theory of the unconscious is one of the major scientific developments of the 20th century. It has profoundly influenced our understanding of human nature, affecting modern science and art.

The main tenets of Freudian theory are the existence of the unconscious and transference. The theory of the unconscious postulates that the main forces underlying our behavior (including powerful sexual and aggressive drives in classical theory) are not controlled by our rational mind. Transference refers to the way we are bound to repeat and replay childhood dramas and conflicts in our adult life without being aware that we are doing it. Freud located the genesis of psychological pathology in a conflict between instinctual libidinal and aggressive forces seeking satisfaction, the id, and forces that restrict their access to consciousness.

The latter he called the superego, the fear of parental disapproval and punishment that becomes internalized and largely unconscious. Today, many mental health professionals do not accept the idea of inborn instinctual drives and instead place the genesis of pathology in the area of developmental trauma.

But whatever the cause of neurosis, all modern psychologists believe that our behavior as adults is largely unconscious and repeats patterns acquired as children.

Though today therapy as a method of mental health treatment is widely accepted, most of it is based on cognitive behavioral modifications that do not affect and do not consider the most powerful motivating force of human behavior and the focus of Freudian psychoanalysis – the unconscious. Furthermore, in the past several decades, psychoanalysis has all but been forced out by the aggressive use of pharmacology in psychiatry and short, goal-oriented cognitive-behavioral therapy.

The primary cause of the shift is economic. With the advent of insurance-based health care, mental health treatment, as other medicine, has become motivated by profitability. It is much more cost-effective to prescribe medication and short-term therapy that can be done by a wide range of professionals, such as social workers and substance abuse counselors, than pay for the long-term, expensive services of specially trained psychoanalysts.

The second reason is ideological. Freudian views question the supremacy of rationality and our ability to control our actions and is at odds with many values of western society, especially in the U.S., where rationality and sexual conservatism are highly valued commodities. The roots of American modern mentality can be traced to its Puritan religious culture combined with European scientific positivism of the 19th century. It is not surprising then that psychoanalysis is consistently marginalized and trivialized in U.S. popular culture.

Much as Freudian theory has become caricaturized in our society, in Zarina Zabrisky's novel *We, Monsters*, Dr. Strong is intentionally made into a caricature of a modern Freudian. As a result he is somewhat of an overblown, over-the-top character. It makes it so much more powerful then that in the book the only voice in defense of understanding and depathologizsing the characters' motivations belongs to a half-mad doctor. Our heroine lives in a world where as soon as she ventures outside the prescribed norms of behavior, she becomes "mad," understood only by Dr. Strong. They are both marginalized: she by daring to explore her human nature, he by trying to understand it.

Until we understand the irrational, the unconscious and the history of our childhood experiences, we will never be able to decipher human behavior or learn to have inner peace.

It is dangerous to ignore the most powerful parts of ourselves.

It is irresponsible and unwise to replace the study and treatment of human psyche with profit-based, medication-based health care. Psychoanalysis today is more under attack than at any time since Freud's life. If it is only Dr. Strong who will be left to understand and treat us at our most human moments, we are in trouble. Unless we learn to accept and understand our unconscious, one day we all might find ourselves in Mistress Rose's place when we are frightened and disoriented, terrified that our rational, well-constructed life is just a mirage, an illusion.

July 2013, New York

I WILL BECOME A DOMINATRIX

How do you cook dinner when everything seems to be devoid of sense? How—and why—do you set the table when you know that you are going to die?[1]

"How?" I asked my cat.

She watched a pot of borscht bubbling in the sunlight-drenched kitchen and didn't move.

A six-year-old next door was torturing the piano—as always. Day after day after day, the kids were off to school, my husband was off to work, and I folded clean underwear, paid water bills, and rearranged the flowers—lilies or irises. The sun touched my face and played in the sparkly curtains' folds;

---

[1] I have every reason to believe that Mistress Rose is indeed dead. I had never met her or heard about her until the black envelope appeared at my office desk with a note: "*Institute of Human Sexuality. To Dr. Strong from Mistress Rose. Publish my writing, Mike.*"

My name is not Mike, and I don't know any mistresses.

I'm Dr. Michael H. Strong, a clinical psychologist, and a leading expert on questions of human sexuality. I'm the author of footnotes in this "novel." I decided to publish the material, adding my commentary in footnotes, as I believe it would be of interest to psychiatric professionals, sexual freedom activists, and members of the general public interested in psychology—specifically, Dissociative Identity Disorder.

a fly zoomed by the open window, lulling me toward sleep. Everything went exactly the same as yesterday, and the day before, except for the moment when I sat down at my laptop and Googled "sex work."

A black-and-red website. Fiery letters: *YourFantasyWorld. com*. A leather-clad Asian Amazon squished her heel into the chest of a human ogre; her scarlet lips twisted in a grimace, or a smile.

Reading the small print—red on black—hurt my eyes.

"No sex involved." The mistresses at this dungeon didn't do sex. Only fantasies. No sex.

I closed the window; I even drew the curtains.

I needed this. For what had been five years by then, I had been writing a novel about my dead sister. I wrote, and wrote, and wrote, but I could never capture that final chapter. It slipped away; it was not right. And so, to get it right, I needed to perform the dungeon experiment.[1]

I searched the Craigslist jobs section for "dominatrix." Two ads came back: "Adult Gig: Amazon Ladies: let's have fun!" and "Looking for attractive, creative and open-minded ladies for recreating fantasies. Light switch, friendly team, clean environment. No experience required, will train. Mature welcome. No sex. Send short description and a photograph."

I reread the ad. *Attractive.* I did yoga and Weight Watchers, and at parties men asked my husband about "that tall Ukrainian chick." *Creative.* Ever since I had painted my son's bedroom—green sea, fleecy clouds, white sail—my neighbor Vanessa introduced me as an artist. Plus, I was a writer. *Openmindedness* was my major life principle. *Light switch.* Had to

---

[1] **Rationalization** is a psychological defense maneuver that allows people to provide themselves with a "good" reason to engage in behavior they know, consciously or not, is unproductive or harmful.

research that. And, although I hated to think about myself as "mature," I had to acknowledge it: At thirty-eight I was hardly juvenile. Hey, *no sex involved.*

Little James next door stopped tormenting the piano.

The borscht was simmering, the ruby beets and chopped garlic filling the house with the sharp and sour scent of my grandmother's kitchen, tingling my senses, reminding me of something long gone, long forgotten, like part of a dream hidden just below the surface—but I had no time for such considerations.

I created a new email account, *mademoiselle666@gmail.com*, found a St. Maarten's beach photo taken from afar—my red hair gleaming in the Caribbean sun, my blue bikini shining against my tan—and wrote a note: "*Dear Sir/Madame: In response to your ad...*" My heart was racing, and my palms got clammy, but I shook my head, hit the "Send" button—and jumped at the sound of an explosion from the kitchen.

The borscht shook the pot and spilled over the sparkling white stove, dripping to the floor, a steaming red pool on the black marble. It looked like blood.

I couldn't unglue my eyes from the puddle. It was quivering, and the eggshell walls of my living room jiggled. My wedding photo and the rainbow-hued vase trembled and blurred. That was how my lost time always started: A burst of silver light, a trace of acacia scent, a tang of bitter chocolate, or a gauze curtain fluttering in the draft. A minor disturbance, the shift almost intangible, a miniscule earthquake—nothing had changed, yet everything was different, unreal.[1]

---

[1] Possible **derealization**, a dissociative symptom characteristic of numerous psychiatric and neurological disorders. The external world is experienced as uncanny and unreal. These symptoms may be caused by sleep deprivation or stress.

My alarm buzzed like a fly against the window. I was back in my kitchen. I had to pick up my kids from school. The dull sense of everything around being unreal lingered over me as I turned my car key in the ignition, my fingers numb and tingling, and drove fast, opening all four windows, tilting my cheeks to the breeze, and chewing winter-cold peppermint gum to wake up.

"Did I close all the emails? Did I log out from *YourFantasy-World.com*?"

KIDS

As usual, I nodded to Ms. Jenkins, my son's teacher. She stood in the scattered sunlight in the corner of the schoolyard behind a magnolia tree.

I was afraid of Ms. Jenkins despite her girl-next-door look: pretty and petite, slick hair, shiny forehead and a toothpaste-ad smile. Her narrow face was spoiled only by the deep folds leading from her nostrils to the corners of her always-smiling mouth. Like brackets, they turned her otherwise perfect smile into a little formality before an invasive procedure. I always expected her to say "*however*" at the end of each flattering speech, and she always did.

"Nick is intelligent; however—"

Next to her stood a freckled woman in a washed-out denim overalls, without a neck, and wearing glasses that looked like a pair of binoculars. Her name always escaped me, and I could never remember if she was a parent, an assistant teacher, or both.

"Mrs. Coppola and I were just saying there's nothing like California winter," said Ms. Jenkins.

I waited for her to say, "However, I'm sure you're incapable of appreciating it, you whore," but instead, she said, "Enjoy the day!" and turned her beige back on me. Everything on her was beige: her checked jacket, her turtleneck sweater, her slacks, her boots. Even her always-polished nails, her lipstick, and lightly outlined eyes were beige.

"Someone must have told her that she looked good in beige," I thought.

Nick skipped out of the school doors, green marker and sweat on his chin and nose, and flew past me, straight to the car, screaming, "I want pizza for dinner."

I watched him wiping his nose with his sleeve, wondering, "Will I pick him up just the same? After a shift at the dungeon?"

Next, I pulled the car in front of the junior high. Olga, my middle daughter, ran out hopping like a baby hippopotamus, chewing a cookie and sending air kisses mixed with pink sprinkles into the shrieking schoolyard. A hurricane of doll-blonde curls, sugar crumbs, and quick smiles, she filled the car with a vanilla-and-Coke aroma as she plunked her round bottom into the back seat.

"How was your day?" I asked her.

"Oh My God, Oh My God, Oh My God," she exhaled, her eyes and pink mouth creating three Os on her round face. I looked at her raspberry cheeks and moonlike belly falling over her belt, when Roxanne, my older daughter, showed up, all in black, swirls of mascara on paper-pale cheeks.

"How was your day, sweetheart?" I asked Roxanne.

She sighed and said nothing, while Olga peeled off her Keds—one with neon green shoelaces, the other with electric blue—and threw them into the back of the car, wiggling her toes in Hello Kitty socks, texting and popping gum at the same time. The young smell of healthy, sweaty feet was familiar and soothing, but I couldn't wait to get home, pour the borscht, check homework, and look at my email.

When in two hours I opened my Inbox, I found a note from Luke: "*Honey, late meeting at the office. Will eat here. Don't wait for me.*" An ad from Victoria's Secret. A note from "Margaret": "Regarding the Dominatrix position: *Call me at your earliest convenience.*"

Like an automaton, I muddled through my usual routine: loaded the dishwasher, put the leftovers in the fridge, put the kids to bed, washed my face, brushed my teeth, and went to bed.

FANTASIES

I always slept naked. I loved feeling the freedom of my breasts rolling and the touch of the silky sheets on my skin. I would roll on my side, my back to Luke's—when he was there—blanket tucked in between my thighs, pressing upon my crotch. Then I would close my eyes and scroll through a fancy menu of erotic fantasies and delicacies until I chose the most tantalizing one for the night.

All I ever needed to do was push an invisible button on the remote control of my imagination—I'd squeeze the blanket between my thighs, riding it like a wild horse, and land in the other world, the parallel world of my dreams that I kept hidden in that lingering moment between closing my eyes and falling asleep.

I first found my fantasies in the same place I found everything else in my life—on Grandma Rosa's bookshelves.[1] In the murky corners of oak wood, in the dark creases of book covers, between the pages and lines lay the forbidden world, full of breathless shame and orgasmic joy. More titillating than adult stores in Las Vegas, more criminal than a Hollywood action thriller, more visceral than any of the hardcore porn movies Luke and I had watched together on occasion—that world was always there, waiting for me.[2]

---

[1] Rose lives her life in her imaginary world, the world of her fantasies. Psychologists find a direct correlation between such fantasy-proneness and **Dissociative Identity Disorders**.

[2] Fantasy worlds are **an emotional plumbing system** where both negative and positive emotions are discharged in a safe way. Just like a human body, a mind produces waste: non-digestible material that is often toxic. These psychic odds and ends take the form of fantasies, dreams,

In my fantasies, Leda copulated with a swan, her arms flailing, white feathers floating along the moonlit mirror of the lake. A god-goat raped a pink nymph and turned her into weeping willows. Sometimes I was Psyche wriggling in Cupid's embrace, sweaty and hot. On other nights, I was Esmeralda entwined with the hunchback, my lithe legs around his waist. I could be Catherine the Great: Then I rode the black stallion into the golden fields of grain, snow-white silk velvet and ermine tails soaring behind me, the whip in my hand clutched so firmly that my wrist hurt, and then I walked by the rows of naked soldiers, touching them with my whip and laughing. [1]

I ran this secret theater in my head, and all roles were played by me and anonymous lovers. It never got boring. The scenery and wardrobe were unlimited. The Time Machine worked flawlessly.[2]

---

daydreams, and, frequently, literature and art. Fantasizing provides individuals with an outlet for release of negative emotions and is a function of mind.

[1] Fantasy also serves as **an effective tool to manage feelings** such as pain, anxiety, and anger by replaying real-life events and by providing alternative positive outcomes to unwanted situations, thus repairing them.

A fantasy world is a **training polygon for the human psyche**: replaying real and invented life situations in one's mind prepares an individual for practical life situations. The mind processes real and invented situations in order to find solutions.

[2] The majority of people experience, on average, 7.5 **erotic fantasies** a day, but the quantity of individual fantasies can be as high as forty or more. All-consuming, elaborated fantasies are prevalent in abuse victims and symptomatic in individuals with **Post-Traumatic Stress Disorder** and Dissociative Disorders, and they represent an adaptation to continuous threats to existence. Fantasizing is a function of a normal mind, but overinvestment into fantasy worlds is typical for individuals with a child-

That night I chose the Cleopatra fantasy. I took years to build it up, growing it layer by layer: every glittering hieroglyph, every jeweled braid, every turquoise bead, every golden cup, precise and vivid, bright and alive.

I first dreamed it up after I stole Gauthier's *One of Cleopatra's Nights* from Grandma Rosa's shelf during a long winter vacation, blushing and losing my breath. I hid under the blanket with a flashlight, trembling as I heard footsteps and night noises. I fell enamored with every word, from the name *Théophile* to the azure scarab's wings on Cleopatra's ankle bracelet.

In the Cleopatra fantasy I fucked my slave on the shimmering gold of the bed. The red sun dripped down the lotus-shaped pillars. I breathed in an odor of decaying acacias from the Nile and his sex—honey and musk. His lips grazed the nape of my neck. His rough fingers hurt the skin on the inside of my thighs. I rode him as a wild horse, twisting, squirming and writhing. ...and then I stabbed him with my golden sword[1] and watched his agony in a pool of semen and blood, a whiff of his musky, oily scent lingering in my trembling nostrils.

The Cleopatra Fantasy had never failed to lull me to sleep, but it did that night.

---

hood history of either abuse or neglect. For them, fantasies replace realities that are either too painful or too difficult to understand. It is possible that Rose suffered from serious trauma as a child.

[1] According to a recent research study, heterosexual individuals with no history of deviations experience "normal," heterosexual encounters in up to 75 percent of their fantasies, the other 25 percent being deviations, including **BDSM**, **homosexual**, and **group sex activities**. The usage of swords in Rose's fantasy symbolizes penis envy, as well as her sadistic inclinations.

At two a.m., I was in front of the laptop again. I opened a new file, the blank page yearning. I wrote the story of finding YourFantasyWorld.com. All those details could become a novel one day. Everything could turn into a novel.

LUKE

For our traditional Sunday dinner I made Luke's favorites, Ukrainian *vareniki* (small dim-sum-like pockets stuffed with potatoes or cheese), his mom's secret seven-ingredient lasagna, and an apple pie with vanilla-custard ice cream.

"Feels like Christmas, Honey," said Luke after dinner.

He was comfortably slumped in his favorite place: the sunken green armchair in the living room, an open bottle of beer in one hand, the remote in the other, the *Economist* on his lap, and a football game on. I sat on the carpet by his knee. Our cat Potemkin, a miniature female tabby with delusions of grandeur and a short stub for a tail, settled by his other knee and pretended to doze off.

"Good game," I said. "Honey?"

"Mhm…"

"Honey, I'm working on a new book."

"Sure."

"You want to hear what the book is about?"

"Sure."

"It's—it's about sex workers."

"Sure."

"Did you hear me?"

"Sure. Your book… I'm listening…"

I stood up and screamed into his ear, "Sex!"

That got his attention. Both Potemkin and Luke stared at me. Luke's round, water-grey eyes and fluffy, pinkish eyelashes hadn't changed throughout our fifteen years together, and although he'd lost most of his dull orange curls, he, as always, reminded me of a little boy—over six feet tall—about to go on a roller-coaster ride, curious and frightened at the same time.

"What?" he said.

"Honey, I am writing a book about sex workers."

"Who?"

"God! Prostitutes. About prostitutes…" I said. "A book."

"Okay. Weird. And?"

I wanted to tell Luke that I had spent the whole winter in a freezing library trying to capture that last chapter, that I'd developed carpal-tunnel pain browsing the Web, that the facts I had learned about escorts were the most useless facts ever—for instance, I had discovered that clients often threw cheesecakes at working girls—that I had to write this novel, that I'd been having nightmares every night, and so much more. Instead, I said: "Ehh… It's kind of hard to explain, but basically I need to do some research. I mean… hands-on research."

"What, you want to be a hooker?"

"No, Honey. Just a temporary job, a dominatrix. At a dungeon. Bondage, spanking, that kind of stuff. No actual sex…"

My husband drank some beer and then looked at the bottle as if the answer was spelled out on its green label. Then he looked up at me. Potemkin was looking at me, too. Together they made a tough jury.

"Why, again, are you doing it?"

I should have told him: "Because of my past."

Like a maniac with a razor, the past kept chasing me. It raged in my nightmares and in my daydreams. I would get up, have my oatmeal, and move on. But ignoring the past is ignoring a bomb—no, a nuclear reactor. Ignore it and it might explode.

I could never have told Luke any of that; I didn't know it myself.

Instead, I said, "I told you…material for my book. Why, are you prejudiced?"

Beyond anything, Luke, the former captain of the Tufts football team, valued freedom, justice, and independence. We had assigned shifts for changing diapers and taking garbage out. I was free to go out on Saturday with the neighbors for a girls' night out—if I gave him a week's notice.

Luke stared at his bottle again. I picked a sliver of a cheese cracker from the bluish carpet; the house needed vacuuming. Potemkin scratched behind her ear with her hind paw for what seemed like an eternity. Finally, Luke cleared his throat.

"How about you write about parenting? Lisa just got her book published, you know. Or children's stories, you know, like the stories you tell Nick—about a little crocodile—"

"Armadillo."

"Sure. Those are good. I mean, why hookers?"

"Don't call them that."

I stood up and walked to the window. The street looked empty at first, but then I saw Vanessa, our neighbor, in her eggplant kimono, dragging an oversized green recycling bin out into the street. I forgot it was garbage night. I sighed.

"I don't know what's in your mind," Luke said. "I know you, though. You've already decided everything. You'll do what you want no matter what I say. Go ahead, it's your life."

"Yeah, but it's your life, too. I want you to be okay with it!"

"Like, can I be? Really? But—What am I going to do, divorce you?" He sighed, too. "You're a grownup, a free person in a free country. Can I watch my game now? And would you mind bringing me another beer?"[1]

---

[1] Luke's reaction demonstrates **the unvoiced conflicts in this marriage**. He is in denial or rationalizing; it is possible he has been unfaithful and his guilt is now absolved in the unconscious by his understanding attitude

I got him a beer from the fridge and started to take empty beer bottles and Diet Coke cans out from the kitchen. It was my garbage shift.

That night, I had my usual nightmare. I had had that nightmare since I could remember myself. It always ended with me standing on an empty beach and screaming, or, rather, trying to scream. I could never make a sound or move—like a fish on the beach.

When you have a nightmare every other night, no matter how agonizing, you don't think about it during the day; you think about mundane stuff. I kept thinking about the dungeon job phone call.

I thought it through as I hurried the kids out of the house. Olga was almost twelve, and as usual we all stood waiting for her as she stood in front of the mirror, examining her pear-shaped backside, hands in pockets, woven charm bracelets around her plump wrists.

"Don't call from home," I thought. "Drive far, but not too far. To a gas station."

There was a slit in Olga's brand-new jeans at the place where the butt met the thigh, a flash of tight pink. I pointed at it, saying, "You are not going to school like that! Go change this very minute!"

Meanwhile, I kept thinking, "Find a payphone, get some quarters."

"No way!" Olga stomped her Ked. "Don't tell me what to wear! You don't know anything! You're Russian!"

---

towards his wife's research. He also "buys" himself more freedom in the future—Rose's transgression will justify his own inappropriate or questionable actions and behaviors. Couples often enter into unspoken agreements of this sort; for example, "I will close my eyes to your infidelities, and you will forgive my shopping addiction."

"She makes a good point—change your accent," I thought.

Luke sleepwalked by with the *Economist* in his hand. I wished he would say something.

"Ukrainian. Into the car. Now."

I backed up out of the garage, stopped to get Nick's forgotten water cup, bumped into a trash can and jumped out—to make sure I hadn't run over Potemkin, who enjoyed throwing herself under the wheels every single morning—all while still thinking about the phone call. Like a fly in a locked room, the thought buzzed in my head as we got to Nick's school, two minutes late for his math class, and as I read yet another note from the principal: "Your child has been late to school 33 times during the last semester. Please..."

THE GAS STATION

And it was still buzzing when I put on drugstore sunglasses and Luke's baseball cap and drove a few miles away from home, looking over my shoulder. A black Buick seemed to be following me, but then it turned into an alley, and I made a loop and stopped by a Kwik Stop gas station.

I filled the tank, then stepped inside and asked, "Payphone?"

The Latina attendant smiled and waved her hand. I looked at her purple nails, and headed for the phone.

I couldn't believe I was calling Margaret. There she was, a husky voice in the cold earpiece, roaring with laughter. I covered my mouth with my hand, and spoke back in a huskier voice, roaring back. She had a slight British accent, so I kept saying, "Excuse me? Excuse me?" I exaggerated my Ukrainian accent and rolled my *rrrr*s until I sounded like a Brighton Beach resident on a Manhattan shopping spree. My temple got all sweaty and stuck to the phone by the time I hung up. I landed an interview the following Tuesday.

The gas station attendant smiled and waved again. I hoped she didn't understand English.

I came home and grabbed a peacock feather duster to clean my books. It usually helped me focus. Our cleaner never did it, and I had lots of books. As I ran green-and-blue feathers over the shabby paperback of *The Brothers Karamazov*, I remembered first seeing the book—and Luke. It was fifteen years ago.

"'Tiz for you," said Ivette, a French waitress and my best friend at the time.

She pointed at a redheaded giant in a white blazer—athletic, glowing with health, sipping a latté, submerged in *The Brothers Karamazov*. I had remembered serving him a lox-and-cream-cheese bagel and a non-fat latté with extra foam, our specialty at Eatz, a trendy Manhattan café.

I shrugged. "He looks like a refrigerator."

We had nicknames for our regular customers, and for the men who hit on us.

"Well, Mr. Fridge just ordered his third latté," said Ivette, with a baby-fox grimace. "From you."

After a fourth latté, he asked for a date. I said yes right away, resisting the urge to wipe the foam off his mouth with the sponge clutched in my hand.

After our third date, I stopped calling him nicknames. That was how we knew it was serious. I was so blown away—by his Boy Scout smile, his mix of charming geekiness and non-male-chauvinist attitude, and the raw sex, both wild and sweet—that I didn't notice he never finished *The Brothers Karamazov*.

On our honeymoon, in a four-star hotel in Maui, Luke dug into his documentary books on World War II and said he couldn't remember where he left *Karamazov*.

"Honey, I prefer history to fiction," he said, scratching his neck, melting me with his Boy Scout grin. "You remember my grandfather was injured in Pearl Harbor, right?"

"But in Eatz, why were you reading *Karamazov*?"

He scratched his neck again and wrapped his large arms around me like a blanket.

"To lure the cute Slavic waitress, of course," he said, kissing the tip of my nose. "It worked, didn't it?"

It was too late to change my mind. Luke never finished reading any of my stories.

"Your writing is your religion," he told me. "Books are your fetishes, not mine."

I knew ahead of time that my new book would be of no particular interest to him,[1] despite the raunchy subject. If Luke had any secret interest in prostitution, he kept it to himself. I finished dusting and switched on my laptop.

---

[1] Rose has difficulties establishing reciprocal intimate relationships.

LILAC MIST

First I searched YouTube for "dominatrix" videos. Brunettes—breasts spilling out of black leather—whipped bald men. Double-chinned men licked black leather shoes. I decided I would just be a foot-fetish object.[1] I stared at my feet, anxious they were not dainty enough at size nine-and-a-half. I spent twenty minutes in front of the bathroom mirror, looking at myself from different angles.

Potemkin was sitting on the toilet seat, her narrow pupils fixed on the S-shaped furrow between my eyebrows.

"What are you staring at? I've had it since I was sixteen," I told her in Russian. "You think Margaret will notice?"

I made a Margaret-face, not unlike Queen Elizabeth, scrutinized myself in the mirror and dropped, in a British accent, "You are too ugly, too fat, too old. Please, go home now."

"I'm not intimidated," I told Potemkin. "I'm not a high-school girl anymore. I'm from Odessa. It's only a dungeon."

Potemkin closed her eyes, like a bathroom Sphinx. She was used to me talking to her in Russian, Ukrainian, English, and occasionally, bad French, and she knew my darkest secrets.

"I'm a writer, Potemkin. And, I need a facial."

I pressed my forehead to the cold mirror and stared deep into my own eyes.

---

[1] Rose is deceiving herself. This is a typical **harm-reduction** maneuver. She considers foot-fetishism to be the least harmful activity available and tries to convince herself that she retains control, thus alleviating feelings of shame and guilt.

I saw myself, yet I didn't. I couldn't put together a face out of features that were falling apart. Everything trembled.[1] I was back to being eleven, helping Grandma in the kitchen, cutting greens for borscht.

"I'm feeling strange, Grandma."

"How does it feel?"

She wiped her blue-veined hands over her apron—beet stains on white.

"I don't know, Grandma. Like I'm some other girl."[2]

She gripped me in the vice of her knees.

"Speak!"

"Like I'm flying."

She twisted my head up and spread my eyelids apart with her firm fingers.

"Now, stop your fantasies! Tell me, is it throbbing?"

Her steel-grey eyes were so close I could see yellow dots dancing next to her pupils.

"I see gold glitter, stuck in my eye, it's trembling," I said.

"I don't see anything."

She pulled my head toward her face—a weak scent of lavender mixed with garlic and beets, familiar and dangerous—probed her tongue inside of my eyelid, and rolled it all over my eyeball.

"I don't feel anything, either."

She jerked my head to the side, and peeked into my ear.

---

[1] Rose does not recognize her reflection, which is one of the symptoms of **depersonalization**.

[2] **Dissociative Identity Disorder episode:** The sensation that the individual is going to wake up or become conscious in a different location, city, or country, living a different life under a different name, similar to what would happen if recovering from a coma with total amnesia.

"Nothing. Migrrraine, maybe," said Grandma.

She rolled her *r's* like the French do, and the little thunderstorm in the middle of a foreign word made it sound exciting, like far-away islands and multicolored parrots. It sounded magnificent, but Grandma Rosa was wrong. I never had migraines. The strangeness I felt had no word for it. How do you name something that has no name?

It wasn't true, though, I did have a name for it.

Misty Lilac. Lilac Mist.

The Lilac Mist was the name of a popular Odessa song my Grandpa used to hum and whistle as he sketched nude women in charcoal. Millions of naked women pinning up their hair, leaning on windowsills, stretched on pillows, laughing and waving, swimming and dancing. As he drew curves and smudged sad shadows around women's eyes and hips, he changed the words and the tune each time. I imagined the lilac mist, the purple haze, the green star and the fury of the railway station, tears and suitcases, and a disappearing train. I remembered sitting by his side, drinking in his tobacco, vodka, and paint smell, and singing along, "Misty Lilac!"

"The Lilac Mist, silly, not Misty Lilac!"

"Grandpa, what if life is just a dream?"

"It is a dream."

Charcoal squeaked against the rough paper.

"Then, how do you know which is the dream, and which is real life?"[1]

"You don't."

---

[1] **Dissociative Identity Disorder episode**: Dissociation is a disconnection between a person's thoughts, memories, feelings, actions, or sense of who he or she is. Confusion between dreams and reality is typical in individuals with dissociative disorder. Fantasy-reality boundary management is compromised, resulting in a painful clash between objective and subjective realities.

The silver mirror shimmered. The Misty Lilac swam toward me, shadows of the past weaving out of it. They danced like Grandpa's charcoal women. The only way to deal with the shadows was to write them down.[1]

I didn't remember moving to my desk. I must have opened my laptop and started to write. I just kept writing down everything that happened to me since I found *YourFantasyWorld.com*.

As I wrote my life down, it wasn't me anymore. Someone was living my life for me: someone inside my body. I was just looking from the outside and writing things down. I wish I could have known at that point that my life had by then become a novel, a neurotic Russian novel full of drama, and the ending was approaching with the speed and remorselessness of a surreal train, with the inevitability of my alarm buzz. It buzzed as always; and as always, the Misty Lilac drifted away. It was time to pick up the kids.

---

[1] According to Freud, **writing is a form of sublimation** of innate aggressive and sexual drives: a way of finding a socially acceptable way of expressing her **eroticism, anger and hostility** through relatively healthy activity. It is a category of compromised formation in which individuals find a way to satisfy both the innate drive and societal traditions at the same time. Thus, creative **writing becomes a coping mechanism**.

THERE'S NOTHING TO TALK ABOUT

In front of the school, Mrs. Jenkins was facing the freckled woman in denim overalls. They both nodded and smiled at me. I still didn't know who that woman was.

Olga was crumbling a cream puff and giggling into her cell phone. Roxanne was late, and her mascara was smudged under her eyes. Nick's ears burned like he had a fever.

"Turn on the radio," he said.

"Let's talk instead," I said. "How was your day? What did you learn in math? Olga, get off the phone."

"There's nothing to talk about," said Nick. "It was boring."

"Well, think of something interesting," I said. "I know you can!"

"I have no thoughts to think—I thought them all."

I looked in the mirror. Olga switched to texting, hunching over her cell phone, her poodle curls hanging down, covering her face. Roxanne threw her head back, pale hands crossed on her chest, earphones in, her eyes closed.

"That's why you read books, Nicky," I said. "So you have something to think about."

"Boring! Turn on the radio!"

I pushed the button. The rest of the trip we listened to rap.

At home, I had no time to think about the dungeon job.

"Mom, I don't want no salad," said Olga, stressing her Os.

"I don't want any soup," said Nick. "I want pepperoni pizza."

"I'm not hungry at all," said Roxanne.

"You guys all sit down and eat what I tell you to eat," I said.

After dinner, I watched my kids, slumped next to each other on the couch, blasting the Disney channel, silver-gray shadows reflected on their faces. I couldn't help feeling that they looked like aliens. Sometimes I got this feeling that they were not mine. Sometimes—often times—I had the feeling that I'm not me, and my life isn't real.

"Homework in twenty minutes. You have to do some reading, Nick."

"I hate reading," said Nick.

Luke came home around ten that night.

"Dinner? I'm starving, Honey."

He collapsed on the chair, losing shape, looking small and colorless despite his bulk.

"On the table. Nick was waiting for you. What happened? A revolution in the world of optic fibers?"

"Fiber optics, Honey. Hand me that plate. He's asleep?"

"Yeah, he didn't want a story, or anything. The girls are fine."

Luke opened his *Economist* and crunched salad leaves like a turtle.

I waited a bit, then stepped out into the backyard to smoke one of my Vogue Lights.

An acacia tree hid in the dark corner of the backyard, like a bridesmaid secretly smoking before the ceremony. It was just starting to bloom, and the pearl-like flowers sparkled in the dusk like fairy dust. It smelled like my hometown. Odessa.

The air in Odessa was like condensed sweetened milk: dense, alive. In the midst of a July night you could almost eat spoonfuls of air, and it would hit that sweet spot on the roof of your mouth. I'd searched for that lost taste ever since and never found it.

An amethyst star twinkled through the acacia blossoms. I'd never noticed it before. I knew it was a light from the window across the street, but for a moment I imagined it was a fairy winking at me. I folded my arms and shivered.

Blue evening shadows always made me nostalgic. Nostalgia became a toothache, piercing yet dull and familiar, almost desired.

The smoke rings vanished. I thought about calling Vanessa, my neighbor, to chat, maybe ask her about her new light, but then I remembered her voice—she talked like a duck quacking—and I changed my mind. Besides, I was having lunch with her the next day.

Potemkin was sitting by my foot, gazing into the bushes.

"You're the only person I can talk to, Potemkin. Here. Or there. Anywhere."

I returned inside, and scribbled my to-do list for the dungeon interview.

Nails — acrylic, bright red
Eyebrows — thin, dramatic arch, Greta Garbo
Fake Tan — spray?
Clothes shopping: Goodwill
Sex store: Garter belt, stockings, shoes. Sexy bra. Leather?
Makeup — dramatic, think drag queens

VANESSA THE NEIGHBOR

The next day, I drove to San Francisco to buy lingerie. I wore my shades, stumbled getting out of the car,[1] and almost fell down entering the sex shop called Does Your Mother Know? It was in the seediest part of town, with an out-of-business strip club on the corner and two shrunken people—their gender wasn't clear—in teen miniskirts smoking by a liquor store. Somebody whistled outside and I ducked. A homeless woman, hunchbacked and crooked, covered in a ragged American flag, was pushing a shopping cart up the street, looking into the vast sky and whistling.

In the store, a mustached sales lady wrapped red thongs in pink paper. She looked at me above her square glasses, her eyes transparent and asphalt-grey.

For a moment, I yearned to drop the hot pink package into the homeless woman's shopping cart. I could see tissue crinkling, a scrap flopping in the wind like a flag, the old woman shuffling away, rolling away with all my shame, fear, and queasiness.

Instead I hid the pink parcel in my purse, and drove all the way back home to have lunch with Vanessa. We took turns and did lunches once a month. We always planned on every week, but never had time.

Vanessa met me in her workout pants and a tank top, white Lycra with yellow stripes, two flute glasses in her hands.

"Mimosas," she said. "And Weight Watchers' chicken salad."

"Perfect."

---

[1] Somatic phenomenon. This momentary feeling of disorientation has a dissociative nature.

I was a vegetarian, but Vanessa never remembered that.

"Joe's out of town again. Let's celebrate."

As usual, I saw myself turning away and leaving. As usual I didn't do it. Vanessa happened to live next door. Like me, she had two daughters and a son. Her husband Joe worked for the same company as Luke. We went to the same yoga studio. I always forgot the stifling feeling of those lunches—as if there wasn't enough air in the room. Or as if a dead body was hidden behind the white gauze of the curtain.

"James' gym teacher is a real jerk," said Vanessa.

"And I'm going to be a mistress at a dungeon," I heard myself saying—in my head.

She put mustard-yellow salad on my plate. She talked and talked, and I only listened and smiled. I was busy separating chicken from spinach leaves, anyway. Over the next twenty minutes, she told me all about the gym teacher's crush on Ms. Jenkins, who fancied herself a runway model just because she had won a Miss Alabama pageant at twenty-one, and about James' insecurities when it came to team games. As usual, I didn't listen. I alternated between looking at the chicken strips on my plate and looking around the room.

Vanessa's younger sister, Victoria, laughed from her graduation picture on the mantelpiece: a Peruvian beauty, pink teddy bear squeezed to her golden-brown chest. The photo always worked like a magnet on me: Victoria had jumped off the Golden Gate Bridge twelve years ago, after her fiancé left for India to become a Buddhist monk. Ever since that had happened, Vanessa never crossed the Bay.[1] She never talked about her sister—except on one occasion at a girls' night out.

---

[1] **Gephyrophobia** is an anxiety disorder, an abnormal and persistent fear of crossing bridges. Sufferers of this phobia experience undue anxiety even though they realize their fear is irrational. High bridges over waterways,

"What a beauty," Lisa, our new neighbor, had said.

"Vickie was a bitch," said Vanessa, finishing her fourth chocolate martini. "She thought she was such a princess."

Then her lips shifted forward, so she looked like a duck, and she started to cry.

"They refused to install the safety railing," she said. "Didn't want to spoil the view. Fuckers."

I ate my spinach leaves and imagined Vickie climbing the railing. What was she thinking? I shooed the image away and looked back at Vanessa.

We both had lost sisters; she was probably grieving the way I was grieving. Yet she seemed to me unreal, fake, like a cartoon character, unable to grieve or to feel. Maybe it was her raisin eyes, maybe her puckered mouth, maybe her quacking voice, "Dan's wife looks positively homeless! With all that money, couldn't she do something with her hair? Macy's is having a sale, and Lisa said that at Nordstrom's—"

If I were to jump off the bridge, I thought, I would choose the Bay Bridge. The Golden Gate was too camera-friendly and touristy, too symbolic in its shameless red. The Bay Bridge was naked. It offered no frills. Solid, grey, it shot through the fog like a cannon, the landscape of poetry and disaster, a monument to death and life with no pretense or promise.

"I had to return the bracelet, but I never told him and he never even noticed. I'm telling you—What did Luke give you for your birthday? Sweetheart?"

"Ah? Oh, Luke. A new laptop," I said. "I mean, a new, used laptop."

"Not bad!"

---

or extremely long or narrow bridges, can instigate this phobia. Even the thought of bridges, rather than an encounter with an actual bridge, can trigger this fear.

Vanessa stood up. She ran every morning, did martial arts with her personal trainer, Ed, and went to yoga with me, so her tanned body was seamless and bouncy, as if made of smooth rubber.

"I love art. You've got to see my quilt. I'm just done with this one part—here!"

Butterscotch yellow, purple, and turquoise pieces gleamed in the afternoon sun.

"It's amazing," I said. "How do you find time?"

"Oh, I have tons of time! I'm so bored. Joe's always away, kids are… you know, kids. Blossom's around, but he's bored, too. Come, Blossom."

We both looked at her orange-red cat, Blossom. He looked more like a lion, lying in the middle of the room in a sunny spot, motionless. Only his tail raised and hit the floor, as if he was angry—or really bored. Vanessa walked to the cat, kneeled down, and scratched his back. Her face softened, her flat lips shifted forward, giving her that duck expression that she probably thought was cute. She bounced up, her chest jumping up like two tennis balls.

"Besides, I just love quilting. If you really want something, you'll find the time no matter what. Like I see you at your laptop all the time, you know. Shopping?"

"No, not really. Sometimes," I said. "I'm—I'm writing."

"What are you writing?"

"A book…"

"Oh, I love writing, too," said Vanessa. "I started to write a book, too, when I was pregnant for the second time. I was writing down recipes for stews, and when Brittany was two I wrote this kids' stories book. I almost had it finished, but then I got into quilting. Are you writing for kids?"

I smiled at her and waved one hand through the air. She patted Blossom's belly one more time and grabbed her third mimosa.

"You see, it's all the same. You like writing, I like quilting. We both have hobbies, and that's so awesome." Vanessa never stopped to take a breath. "Oprah says it's critical to keep hobbies and stay well-rounded, healthy for family life, especially when menopause hits. And fit!"

"Yes," I said. "Thanks for the lunch, I'll see you at yoga."

I almost ran to my house. There, I smoked in the bathroom, sitting on the toilet seat, my eyes closed, the orange and purple triangles of the quilt floating before my eyes in a lilac mist. A radio was playing somewhere outside, or in my head—violin or the whole orchestra—a familiar tune I couldn't recognize. Then I remembered to hide the pink paper packet in the bottom drawer of my writing cabinet.

CROSSING THE BRIDGE

On the foggy day of the interview, I started to drive towards the Bay Bridge. I looked out the window. There was something I'd forgotten to do. Something important, crucial—lipstick! I needed new lipstick. I made a sharp U-turn.

I drove to a mall and parked next to a sky-blue SUV. A woman with a wide back lifted a baby girl from her car seat, laughing and blowing into the little creased neck.

"You guys lost a shoe," I said, picking up a white-and-pink knitted slipper from the asphalt.

"Say hello to the nice lady," cooed the mother.

I waved to the baby. A toothless smile. A wrinkled button-nose. A giggle. Her head rested against her mother's formula-and-ketchup stained T-shirt. So protected. So loved. I wanted to be this baby. I wanted to stroll next to them, laughing with them. I wanted to try Gentle Sunset lipstick on the inside of my wrist. I wanted to throw kitchen towels with cockerels or grapevines into my shopping cart. I wanted new champagne glasses with thin stems that would sparkle when I polished them in my sunlit kitchen. I wanted a pleated navy-blue bed skirt. More than anything, I wanted to go home.

I dragged myself along the mall's shop windows. My eyes jumped from discounted ergonomic sandals to zebra patterned leggings to rhinestone hair clips. The medley of stuff waited to fill my clanking shopping cart with the excitement of a plastic bag's flutter, leather and shampoo scents, and glossy and scratchy textures. A swipe of a twinkling credit card and the zebra leggings and coffee-and-cream cashmere sweater would hug me like my nonexistent mother. For an instant, I would feel new and real. The yearning void inside would close.

I stopped, looking at my reflection in the shop window. Was I going to turn into these dead garments made in China? Was I married to kitchen cabinet liners and liquid detergent? No. I was going to write a novel.

I turned around, pushed away an obese teenager, sweat beading on her acne-struck forehead, bubble-gum fury and bulging eyes—*X-cuse me, Maaam!*—ran to the parking lot, backed up my car, and raced to the bridge, and over the bridge, losing my sense of time. Losing all senses.

I was about to take my exit when I nearly got into an accident. A bloody mess in the middle of the road threw up a black and white raccoon paw. I squinted and jerked the wheel. Brakes screeched. I saw the twisted mouth of an Asian driver to my right. Two more cars swerved and beeped. As if in slow motion, I took my exit, my mind blank, hands numb on the wheel. I looked in the mirror and smiled to shove the image out of my mind. My face looked like a Venetian carnival mask—scarlet lips, smoky eyes. I took a few yoga breaths and felt calm, but my hands were shaking.

I got lost, driving in circles past bleak houses in a blue-collar neighborhood. My hands still shook as I rang the polished doorbell of the neat Victorian house, but I faked a sultry smile. I wore old jeans and a sweatshirt as instructed, but slipped on a pair of red stiletto platform shoes from Goodwill. There I stood, balancing at my newly discovered height, six-foot-three, clinging to the cold railing, fighting the desire to run back home.

THE DUNGEON

The door moved. A dark eye glistened at me from the crack. "Hello," I said. "I'm looking for Margaret."

For a moment there was no answer. Then the door squeaked open.

A hunchbacked old creature barely reached my shoulder. This wasn't a dominatrix: shabby, ratty-grey old person, maybe a man, maybe a woman, maybe a broom-riding, man-eating witch from a scary fairytale.

"This has to be the wrong address," I thought.

Fat caterpillar eyebrows crawled up. Beady eyes drilled through me. After a long moment, the mustached upper lip twitched into a grin. A long hair sticking out from the mole on the side of the hooked nose trembled, and Margaret said, in the hoarse bass of a retired sailor, "Come on in, doll."

She shuffled inside, and I followed, staring at her felt boots and lumpy back—my mind moving and stalling in rhythm with her limping: "She's wearing an apron…How old can she be?"

The house smelled of fried grease and fresh paint. With a royal wave of her arm, Margaret pointed at a grey armchair, and tottered into the kitchen, like a human hairball. I heard her whispering loudly, "She's a carrot top."

I looked around. A fireplace with a Walmart art deco vase on the mantel, two aged armchairs, a nondescript sofa, a desk, a computer—all in various shades of ratty-grey. I went straight for the bookshelves.

The best way to learn about people is by looking at their bookshelves. Margaret's bookshelves could have come from my library. One impressive shelf was dedicated to psychology: Freud, Jung, a massive black book with the title **DEVIATIONS**[1] in red, and clinical psychiatry manuals. Next shelf—ornithology: *The Princeton Encyclopedia of Birds, Birds of Prey, Game and Water,* and more bird-lovers' collectibles. A couple of illustrated mythology anthologies, an oversized coffee-table book called *EGYPT*. A faded black-and-white photograph of a pre-teen boy with a stubborn mouth, in shorts and suspenders, in a pink, teddy bear frame.

"When's your birthday?"

Margaret was back, smoking a pipe. She was holding on to the back of the chair, her bowed legs in felt boots planted into the carpet, puffing on her curved pipe. Through the gray smoke I could see her face: Aztec bronze skin, etched with creases and wrinkles. The no-nonsense look of an old pirate.

"Zoe!" she said.

"Coming."

A gladiator woman marched after her, a half-eaten pink glazed donut in her hand. Her baby-doll face, framed by a black bob, mismatched her heavy body, which seemed more fit for an American football team than for a sex work establishment. She reminded me of someone—an actress? As usual, I saw everything that was happening from outside myself, like a scene from a Disney channel vampire movie, the type my daughters loved to watch around Halloween.

"I'm Zoe!" said the big woman in a trumpet-like voice.

She threw herself into the tattered armchair next to me, wolfing down the pink donut as she sized me up with the forthright manner of an ex-Marine.

---

[1] **DEVIATIONS** is my revolutionary study of the nature and origin of "perversions," truly the most comprehensive guide to sexual diversity in the history of psychology.

"Do you smoke?" Margaret asked.

"No," I said. "Yes. Just a little."

"Well, I smoke a lot. You're not allowed to smoke in here, anyway. You go outside, in the backyard."

She puffed on her pipe, "I love my smoke. It won't kill you, and if you don't like it, you can go to hell!"

"I'm here on Mondays, Tuesdays, and Wednesdays," Zoe said. "Thursdays and Fridays I'm in my office in Livermore. I'm an accredited real-estate agent."

I couldn't help but stare at the frosting-white skin—there was an uneven hole in the black pantyhose beneath her jeans—her pancake makeup and million-dollar red lipstick: a security guard, maybe, but a real-estate agent? Lisa next door was a real-estate agent; she drove a Mercedes and wore an Armani scale-silver suit.

"The real-estate industry's dead," Zoe said.

She sounded like she'd killed it.

"You have kids?"

"Yes. Three, actually."

"My son's seven. He's got learning disabilities."

I imagined her lounging in Vanessa's living room, at my girls' night out with the neighbors: a tray with pink donuts, Weight Watchers' chicken salad, complaints about the lack of time and decent men in the world, and a heated discussion of the appraisal procedures of property in Livermore. Except none of my neighbors dressed like a murderess from the musical "Chicago."

"My name is not Margaret," said Margaret. "It's Lizzy."

"Okay, Lizzy."

"But call me Mommy. That's what everyone calls me—perverts, mistresses, neighbors. Everyone but my bloody child."

"What does your child call you?"

"Never mind. She's a Cancer. Nasty sign. What did you say you were?"

"A Capricorn."

Mommy looked at me for a minute, chewed with her lips, then hooted and chuckled, coughing at the same time.

"Good! I love Capricorns. I have faith in them. In us. I'm a Capricorn. You need to stop biting your nails, though.[1] But I do love your accent. Exotic."

I had always considered my accent to be a major handicap.

"Raises your value. Americans love everything exotic. Give them Thai food, Italian dresses, Brazilian underwear models. And Russian sluts."

"Thanks."

---

[1] **Oral fixations**, such as biting nails or sucking on the thumb, are common symptoms of developmental arrest. The child first is fixated on sucking the nipple, and then symbolizes the nipple into a finger or a pencil. The object then attains the same soothing effect as sucking the breast once had.

THE DOMINATRIX JOB DESCRIPTION

Mommy gave me an overview of the job. She had the demeanor of Ivan the Terrible and the charm of Lady Diana. I tried to remember every detail for my research and regretted not having a secret voice-recording device.

According to Mommy, all clients were perverts.[1] They were sick.[2] Statistically, perverts accounted for only ten percent of the general population (bad). However, perverts were obsessive-compulsive,[3] so they kept coming regularly (good). They were overachievers and had high-paying jobs[4] (good); they were under a lot of stress (good) and had no fun in their lives

---

[1] Astonishing fact: in the U.S., there is no common legal term for the range of behaviors generally known as BDSM. The correct medical term for the "disorders" in question is **paraphilias**.

[2] Allow me to quote myself: "Deviant sexuality is not a personal choice: It is a rebellious act against society. Moreover, nonconformism of such magnitude undermines not only social laws, but the basic socially accepted concept of 'natural.' **Freedom is a crime in the existing world order.**"

"'All universal moral principles are idle fancies,' said Marquis de Sade. And everyone knows it." *DEVIATIONS*, Introduction, p. 5.

[3] No connection.

[4] No direct correlation between income status, professional development, and sexual preferences has been established. However, the **prevalence of finance industry professionals in BDSM** is a fact, and can be best explained by a number of psychosociological factors, such as the availability of financial resources; the self-acceptance and broadmindedness associated with higher levels of education; and the anal-retentive organization of individuals selecting jobs associated with money (investment banking, hedge funds, brokers, financial advisors, and so on).

(good). Some of them were a real pain in the ass and really hard to deal with (bad, but what can you do?).

"Just to give you an example," Mommy said. "The same guy wants to be tied up to the same fucking chair for thirty-five fucking years. It bores the fuck out of me."

"I hear you."

"Remember, you're a dominatrix, not a therapist."

She lit her third cigarette.

"Don't cure the clients—even though you could. Keep 'em coming back for more, right, Zoe? It's your bread and butter."

"Yep," Zoe said.

"Most clients think they can take a lot of pain, so we tell them of course they can. They actually can't."

"No?"

"No, but it's their fantasy. We're their fantasy, and we tell them whatever they want to hear. The job is fifty percent psychology. I have a Ph.D. in psychology. It helps."

"Oh, wow… what's the other fifty?"

"Acting, dear."

Mommy's forehead—a Greek tragic mask—her vibrating voice like an old pirate's, her vaudeville gestures and mannerisms, her monkey grimacing and hooting laughter all reminded me of my Great-Aunt Rina, my grandmother's sister, who'd been an opera diva back in Odessa. I wiggled in my chair, regretting my non-existent dramatic talents and miniscule psychology education—namely, sleeping through my college psychology course twenty years before.

"I have a lot to catch up on," I said.

"Never mind, it's common sense," said Mommy. "The clients are perverts, but they want to think of themselves as really nice guys. So we tell them they are, right?"

"Right."

"They're all married, mind you, but not getting along with their wives; of course, their wives could never understand. Take Joe. Dirt-rich.[1] A billionaire—but his wife! He just bought the bitch a new Mercedes, paid for her plastic surgery, got her a membership to the country club—you think she's appreciative?"

Mommy waved her pipe as if it were a scepter.

"No! She doesn't like him having sex with a toilet brush.[2] Of course, he also likes to put a padlock on his balls. Well, he comes here, and I tell him it's fun. Then I let him do it himself. He's happy as a clam. I say, where's *my* fucking Mercedes?"

---

[1] Joe's **coprophilia (love of excrement)**, his ability to make and save money, and his tendency to buy love and sexual gratification are symptomatic of his anal-retentive character organization and can be traced back to his toilet training. Freud was the first to openly state **the connection between money and feces**, although it has been portrayed in folklore and myths since antiquity. "Uncleanliness in childhood is often replaced in dreams by **avariciousness** for money; the link between the two is the word '**filthy**.'"

[2] **Analytic Narrative**: When Joe was four to six years old (pre-Oedipal stage), he played with his feces when put on his potty. His mother reacted strongly by hitting him with a toilet brush and making him clean the toilet with it. This traumatic experience was sexualized and turned into a ritualistic behavior. The magic touch of a toilet brush turned Joe into a gold digger—figuratively and literally.

ROSE

The room was filled with smoke. I looked at the cuckoo clock. Two hours had passed, but no clients had appeared. The black retro phone gleaming in the corner never rang. I tried to imagine Joe the Billionaire and failed. Mommy kept smoking and filling me in.

There were no women clients.[1]

Each dominatrix in Mommy's dungeon had her own specialty. She herself was a bondage expert with thirty-five years of experience, but she could do pretty much anything else. Zoe had a couple of years at the dungeon, and specialized in role-playing: older woman, authority figure, secretary, and, surprisingly, a chauffeur. She was also submissive, so the perverts could tie her up and do things to her. I tried to not think of all the "things" that perverts could do.

"You'll find out your strength with experience," said Zoe.

---

[1] A myth. Yes, according to the *DSM*, "except for Sexual Masochism, where the sex ratio is estimated to be 20 males for each female, the other Paraphilias are almost never diagnosed in females, although some cases have been reported." "Not reported" does not mean "not existent."

Women might choose to become lifestyle or professional dominatrices to release their aggression and sexual drives. The ratio of males vs. females in the sado-masochistic community warrants a high demand for the latter. Married women have an opportunity to play out fantasies by acting as a couple and hiring a third person. Yet another category of women might become frigid or sexually unresponsive. The innate aggressive drive and libido in women are as strong as in men, but the repression, fear, and societal stigma allow for less sexual expression.

"I—I know one thing for sure: I happen to be—well, extremely dominant. No submissive roles for me. I don't think I'd respond well to being tied up."

"That's what you think," said Mommy. "They all think they're dominant at first. You'll see."

"Yep," said Zoe.

"Foot fetish, maybe?"

Mommy grabbed my foot and turned it in her hands as if it were a shoe.

"Size ten?"

"Nine and a half," I said.

"That's fine. Long toes, that's always good. But you have to grow out your toenails, honey. Let me see those babies."

She dropped my foot and turned my red platform stiletto in front of her.

"Stripper shoes. Good choice."

I decided to make another run to Goodwill.

"Can I use your bathroom, please?"

"Sure," said Mommy. "I have some repairs going on in there. I just ripped off the wallpaper."

"Yeah, for the third time this month," said Zoe.

"Nobody asked you," answered Mommy.

At the end of the interview I settled with my feet in the armchair, stopped rolling my *rrr*'s, and confessed to my real age. I was pleased to learn that I could pass for twenty-eight but that it didn't really matter.

"You are paid at the beginning of each session. Seventy-five an hour," said Mommy. "Give the money to me afterwards, so I can keep my cut. I pay you at the end of the day. You keep the tips. You won't get rich, but you can pay your bills. What's your work name?"

"I had a few thoughts," I said. "Judith? Sade? Delilah?"

"Judith's taken. Sade, what's that, a singer? Nah. Delilah—hmm… Anything else?"

"I also like Rose."

I had no idea why I said that.

"You look like a Rose," Mommy said, twisting her mouth.

"Is it a common Ukrainian name?" Zoe asked.

"Yes," I said.

I lied. It was a Jewish name. My grandmother's name was Rosa, I remembered, but it was too late.

"This is it," said Mommy. "Mistress Rose. We'll need a photo, a close-up to put on the web page. Take a look at home. It's *YourFantasyWorld.com*. You are starting next Monday."

Nine-thirty every night was my favorite time of day. As usual, I settled between a three-legged teddy bear and a bold stuffed killer whale on Nick's bed to tell him a story. When Nick was little, he loved stories about the adventures of a little armadillo named Mr. Armstrong, a sassy and invincible young thing. Now, at almost ten, he sometimes wondered whether a bedtime story made him a baby, but almost every night we built a house out of the navy-blue blanket, and whispered in the amber glow of the nightlight.

That night, Mr. Armstrong embarked incognito on a snow-white ocean liner from Odessa and sailed to discover the emeralds and rubies of Atlantis; but despite a tsunami, a strange island with a monster witch and sad cannibals, Nick picked at the basketball poster above his bed and kicked his foot, a question or a thought burning on his lips.

"And then Mr. Armstrong jumped off the skyscraper, but didn't fall, for—What is it, Nick?"

"I know something you don't know!" he sang. "I'm not supposed to tell, but Dad and I just started building a robot! In the garage! Daddy says that robots are better than people. Are robots better than armadillos?"

"No," I said. "People and armadillos are better. Robots don't have feelings."

"Why do you need feelings?" asked Nick.

"You just do," I said. "People do."

He shrugged, yawned, and tucked his stuffed killer whale under his chin.

The girls did not like stories anymore. They preferred Facebook friends in their rooms upstairs to moonlit ponies and transparent unicorns. I sat down at my desk, stared at the empty street outside, and tried to figure out my photo and web-presence situation. My kids browsed the Internet 24/7. Exposing my face on the black-and-red webpage called *YourFantasyWorld.com* with the caption *Savage and Sweet Mistress Rose* was not an option.

After ten minutes of watching Vanessa's cat Blossom hunt for an invisible mouse in a pile of cut branches, I got up and headed for the bedroom. There I unrolled the pink tissue paper and put on the lacy black corset and stockings—I wasn't used to stockings and they squirmed in my hands like two vipers. Trying not to click the red stiletto shoes, I headed for the garage.

Luke was stooped over metallic parts on a piece of cellophane wrap on the floor. He wouldn't look up at me, so I nudged an aluminum tube with my shoe and asked, "An arm?"

He raised his head, saw the stockings, and gave me his big Boy Scout smile.

"Consider abandoning your android?" I said. "I have a better project, Honey."

He stood up, scratched his neck and moved toward me, trying to kiss me.

"Wait, the lipstick," I said. "Hold on, seriously. Remember that digital camera?"

While Luke got the camera, I made margaritas on the rocks—lots of lime, lots of salt—and then we went into the bedroom and locked the door. I rolled on the bed, spreading out on the tiger-print bedspread the way I saw porn stars posing in *Playboy*.

"What's with the face? Relax!" said Luke.

"Here," I half-opened my mouth and half-closed my eyes, like a gay model on the poster in the front of *Does Your Mother Know?*

"Straddle the chair!" said Luke. "Lean back! Stop laughing!"

We ended up with six steamy shots and had sex on the bedspread, right on the floor.

"Wow, you're a sex machine," I said, getting my stockings untangled from the bedside lamp. "We should do this more often, Hon. Will you help me Photoshop a digital veil over my face, please?"

Luke scratched his neck and looked away.

"Not now."

I sat at my computer. My photographs scared me.

Was it really me—these long, white arms and legs, this heavily made-up face? How did I know it was really me? What made me—me? My aquiline Jewish nose? I didn't choose it. I didn't choose the cowlick on my forehead. Why was I stuck in this body—and who was the person stuck in that body, anyway? Rose?

I touched my face, my neck, pinched my earlobes. I didn't feel real.[1] The Misty Lilac turned into a yearning gap in my stomach. I found a piece of stale apple pie in the back of the

---

[1] Another episode of **depersonalization**.

fridge and ate it, then started to write down everything that had happened to me that day.

Time stood still. I wrote and wrote,[1] until a loud crash snapped me out of the Mist. Potemkin knocking over Nick's scooter in the garage? I was back at my desk, my head splitting, and it was four-thirty in the morning.

I climbed into bed, and pressed my body against Luke's, trying to feel real, alive and me again. I closed my eyes, and was counting to a dozen, "One armadillo, two armadillos..." then to a hundred, counting, counting, until finally I drifted into the fuzzy blackness of sleep.

There I stood, at the crossroads, but I wasn't me. I knew I had to cross the chalk line on the asphalt. I looked back, and saw my sister looking at me from a dark forest, waving. I looked down, and realized I was on the edge of a void. I let go and flew down into the black hole.

---

[1] Writing satisfies Rose's **exhibitionism and narcissism**. She needs an imaginary audience, an invisible anonymous observer—in this case the reader—to witness her life and to love her. She creates her identity through the narrative of her life; otherwise, her Dissociative Identity Disorder disallows her from making historical links in her real life and deprives her of a sense of continuum.

APPRENTICE DOMINATRIX

On Monday, Luke got up at five-thirty a.m. I heard him clearing his throat, coughing, and stomping, and then heard the door slamming. I was awake, having just lain down in bed with my eyes closed, listening to the sleeping house. I got up and took a shower, dizzy and weak with sleeplessness.

Then, I sat Turkish-style in the living room, a yellow leather scroll in front of me. Worn and warm in my hands. I unwrapped it and patted the sunny moiré silk lining and my makeup brushes. Like tails of strange animals and feathers of mythical birds, those brushes were magic. They reminded me of Grandpa's palette. Like him, I set out my glittery boxes with cloudy powder, rosy blush and dusky shadows on the bluish carpet and started to paint. Grandpa painted blue horizons and misty ocean; I painted my face in the moonlight mirror.

I learned the art of makeup from my older sister.

"Let's make our faces," she used to say.

She knew many tricks: how to make eyes sparkle and play like Fabergé Easter eggs, fill them with luster, turquoise, and dreams—or how to make men give you anything you want.

Our last makeup session was only two weeks before she died. She spit into the toy box of shoe polish-black paste and shoveled a tattered toothbrush into it.

"Angle it to your lashes," she said. "Like this."

She held her mirror close to her eye, framing it like a jewel. Her eyelashes grew and grew like the wings of a bird with each stroke of the brush.

"Now."

She opened the eye wide with her fingers. A thick sewing needle sparkled next to the eye. With one slow, melting move she slit the eyelashes apart. I remember thinking that if I pushed her elbow she'd lose her eye.

"Here."

A clod of mascara hung on the tip of the needle like an ant.

"Keep this needle."

Her eyes looked like horizontal teardrops.

"And now, Little Bird, you can't cry."

She always called me "Little Bird"—it was Grandma Rosa's pet name for both of us, but she only used it for our birthdays, or when we were sick.

"'Cause if you cry, it runs."

She laughed, her eyes not moving.

"So, when you feel like crying, put mascara on."

I'd been making my face every morning ever since. Luke never saw me without my makeup. My kids never saw me without my makeup. I wore it to Labor and Delivery and re-applied it one hour after giving birth. I never went anywhere without my palette. Over the years, I'd bought glossy books on makeup and learned tricks from catwalks, but I still used Oksana's needle.

I was setting up bowls of cereal and milk for the kids when Luke shuffled in. He wore a drenched Tufts sweatshirt, baggy red shorts, and beaten-up sneakers. His face was flushed, sweaty, and distorted with pain. A bluish vein pulsated on his left temple. His dull orange curls were soaking wet and stuck to the sides of his square head. He collapsed into his chair, still huffing.

"What happened?" I said.

He never ran in the morning—nor in the evening.

"Training for a marathon."[1]

---

[1] Luke's **desire to run** is a common reaction to internal

Potemkin jumped into his lap and started to purr.

"Good girl," said my husband, scratching the cat behind the ear.

It sounded more like a reproach to me than praise for Potemkin.

And thus my dungeon apprenticeship began.

---

conflict. The internal need to escape from this conflict, to "run away," is translated into physical action. It is a common example of the psychological defense called **externalization**. It never quite works, because the person runs away from internal discomfort while behaving as if it is external.

MISTRESS SUSANNA—THE EGYPTOLOGIST

I drank lots of coffee again. I normally drank black Indian tea from a Russian grocery store, with milk and no sugar. For my new job, I needed espresso if not cocaine. My heart was racing as I arrived at the dungeon with two bags of Goodwill clothes stuffed full as sausages.

Mommy opened the door, pipe in the corner of her mouth, and rushed back to the kitchen without greeting me. The stench of fried fat made me nauseous. I left my bags in the living room and followed Mommy into the kitchen, gasping and holding my breath. Zoe was sitting by the table, her back rounded, a donut in her hand, like a wrestler preparing for a match. The kitchen, with its polished cabinets and fake-marble counter, looked like a furniture-store display or a funeral parlor. Mommy in her worn apron stooped over the stove, a greasy butcher knife in her hand. A sprig of bacon oozed and wriggled in the frying pan. Mommy was poking at the bacon, and closing and opening the fridge and staring at empty shelves. I imagined dismembered corpses in the oven and the freezer.

"I could eat a dozen of these babies!" said Zoe. "I luuuhv my food!"

She gave me a broad smile and started her second donut. Neither woman paid attention to the little TV set on the table. It was on mute. The History Channel was on. The black-and-white Auschwitz documentary flashed skull-like faces, shrunken chests, protruding ribs, sunken eyes, endless lines to gas chambers and mounds of dead bodies.[1] I quickly looked away; I could never stand the sight of pain and death.

---

[1] Note how Mommy is literally replaying the worn-out

"I started remodeling this kitchen three years ago, and it never ends,"[1] said Mommy.

She tossed her bacon on the frying pan, threw it on a plate and bit into it, munching and chewing on it. "I've gotten so engrossed in the process I've confused all the dates. I just realized Sunday is Easter—Bloody Hell!—No time to go to the butcher shop!"

"Easter was three weeks ago," said Zoe.

The doorbell rang and I ran out of the kitchen to avoid the stench. A slender young woman in a bicycle helmet walked in. With the elegance and grace of a ballet dancer, she put down an oversized bag, and with the same precise and flowing movements took off her helmet. Her pearl-blonde hair flooded over her shoulders.

"Susanna," she said, with a smile worthy of Mona Lisa, and offered me her delicate hand.

I couldn't help but stare. Her olive-green top matched her childlike eyes, and with the same color corduroy pants and flip-flops and no makeup, she looked like a model for *Eco-Green Lifestyle Magazine*. She slid on a pair of nerdy glasses, and I imagined her at a Berkeley café doing her calculus homework. I could not imagine her doing anything I had seen in YouTube videos.

---

tape of her childhood: **the war horrors**.

[1] **Remodeling and cleaning** are coping mechanisms commonly used to control anxiety and reestablish the illusion of control over one's environment.

THE BOUDOIR

Mommy, still gnawing on her bacon, beamed up at Susanna with the gentleness of a cannibal.

"Did you bring pot?" she said. "Good girl. I'll pay you at the end of the day. Will you show Rose around, darling?"

"I've got the pot," said Susanna. "Follow me, Rose."

She opened the door to the adjacent room.

"The Boudoir."

First, I saw my puzzled face reflected at many angles in the mirrored walls; the morning light crawled through the lacy coffee-and-cream curtains. My daughters used to play with a Victorian dollhouse; the Boudoir reminded me of its jewel-box bedroom. With a twist.

"Touch," said Susanna.

She sat on the edge of a low queen-sized bed in the middle of the room. The black bedspread felt cold under my fingers.

"Vinyl. Easy to clean."

I looked around: A high cross with metal handrails gleamed on the ceiling. Chains and ropes hung on a wall like giant cobwebs. Boxes of latex gloves glowed white on tables, stools and by the bed, like in a physical exam room.

"Here's the closet for cross-dressing," said Susanna.

I ran my hand through the silky rows of gargantuan old ladies' dresses, pleated skirts and flowery slips, and marveled at the boxes of high-heeled Payless shoes, size 11.[1] The inside of

---

[1] **The female wardrobe** offers unlimited possibilities for a number of deviations, such as **Fetishism**, **Transvestic Fetishism** and **Sexual Masochism**. These deviations are typically formed when daughterless mothers playfully dress their sons in girls' clothes, or older sisters or female cousins involve a boy in a dress-up game. The experience is then sexually charged and turned into ritualistic behav-

the door had a rack with more ropes, chains, and leather straps. Susanna—a black whip in a small hand, close cut fingernails on the harsh leather—was a perfect character for my book. While I listened to her instructions, I tried to commit her to memory: Pearl hair around a gentle forehead, the innocent smile of a child, a flowing walk and a siren voice.

"The drawers of dildos are organized and labeled by size and color. We do inventory. Mommy has rules, you'll remember them."

"Neat," I said. "I might not remember all this right away."

"It's easy. Everyone loves the blue dildo. The black dildo is for John only."

I looked at a tire-black dildo the size of my arm. Susanna reminded me of the Odessa Art Museum tour guides, lovely but distant. I had problems asking any questions about dildos. I started to stutter.

"Do you... ehhh... treat... the clients to these?"

"Oh yes, most of them. You should use Vaseline—to your right, red label—and condoms—to your left, yellow label. On the coffee table, we have a collection of makeup, and small tools like clothespins and safety pins. You can see candles— those are used for hot-wax torture. Occasionally, they are used as dildos. Please take note: This red candle has a typical curve. Please follow me."

Susanna glided to the corner, bent over with the grace of a big cat, and lifted what appeared to be a trapdoor to secret stairs leading downstairs.

"Down to the Dungeon."

---

ior. These deviations are observed in both heterosexual and homosexual males.

THE DUNGEON

We climbed the spiral steps down, almost falling into mushroom-smelling darkness. Susanna turned on the dim light. I lowered my head and remembered the temples of Angkor Wat.

Luke and I went to Cambodia for our tenth anniversary. He had lots of frequent-flyer miles, and found a great deal on the hotel. I hated the ruins: The low ceilings in the place of worship were designed to keep the mortals intimidated by superior power. They reminded me of municipal buildings in the Soviet Union.

Mommy's Dungeon designers used the same architectural trick as Cambodians and communists. My face, frozen in a polite smile, was multiplied by the mirrored walls alongside the rows of ropes, collars, handcuffs, leashes, chains, crosses, slings, whips, and other torture devices. Visual tricks and multiple images à la pop art seemed to be another theme well-liked by the Dungeon interior decorators. Everything in the Dungeon was black and red.

"This is our golden-shower place.[1] We don't do brown showers.[2] You have to clean the room after a water-sports session."

The golden-shower place turned out to be a black vinyl apparatus, oddly reminiscent of both a guillotine and the wading pool in Vanessa the neighbor's yard. From my research I knew

---

[1] "Golden showers," "water sports" — **urophilia,** or love of urine. The sexual energy is channeled into the act of urinating or smelling, feeling, or tasting urine, as well as urinating on someone or being urinated on.

[2] "Brown showers" — **coprophilia,** or love of feces, similar to urophilia.

that those golden showers had nothing to do with Titian or Rembrandt. Other than diaper-changing accidents and toilet training my children, I had no exposure to water sports.

"You don't have to do it. You don't have to do anything you don't want to do," Susanna assured me. "However, you most likely will end up doing it. They tip well for it."

A vertical suspension cross was hanging from the ceiling, like a *Jurassic Park* dinosaur about to attack. A table in the corner with adjustable stirrups reminded me about my overdue ob-gyn appointment. Susanna opened another built-in closet.

"Dildos."

"More dildos?"

"Oh, yeah," she said. "Many more! Hungry?"

We climbed the stairs, returned to the kitchen, and sat down to lunch. Susanna took small bites of her tofu spinach wrap, thumbing through a thin book about documentary films. I settled across the table from her, set down my container of leftover *vareniki*, and stared at her. I knew I had rich material for my novel.

"You like the book?" I asked.

Susanna sighed, and set the book aside, reminding me of Olivia, my daughter's best friend, a straight-A student and teachers' pet who always offered to wash dishes on pizza night while the other girls watched a chick flick.

"Not really—it's for my job. I work as a motion picture producer's assistant, part-time."

"Is that what you want to do?"

"No, no, it's just to support myself through school. Grad school's expensive, you know. I've been working here for almost four years. I tutor kids here and there, and I take some other jobs, too."

"What's your major?"

"Egyptology."

Susanna pulled a piece of tofu out of the wrap.

"Egyptology?"

"Yeah, I'm working on my Ph.D. now."

"Why Egyptology?"

"Why not?"

Susanna swallowed her piece of tofu and laughed. Her laughter sounded like a vintage music box. I didn't know what to say, so I put a *varenik* into my mouth and smiled back.

"Did you make those?"

She pointed at my container.

"Yes, it's my grandma's recipe. Here, try some."

"No, thanks. I'm a vegetarian."

"It's potato."

"Fascinating. I love international cuisine, especially sushi. I love everything Japanese. I do ikebana for fun."

"This is Ukrainian. What's ikebana?"

"The art of flower arranging."

Mommy shuffled into the kitchen, puffing on her pipe.

"Susanna's the artist in the family. How's your Portuguese going, dear?"

"I couldn't keep up. Too much work, Mommy. I've started nude modeling at the Art Academy."

"Work, shmerk. Your client's almost here," said Mommy. "Get ready."

THE OUTFIT

"Rose, you get dressed, too," muttered Mommy. "They need to see you…"

She slammed the door to the only bathroom in the house. As I stood in the middle of the living room wondering where to go to change my clothes, Zoe marched in and pulled off her jeans, demonstrating a pair of impressive cottage cheese-white thighs and a powerful backside. There was something cubist about her, as if she'd just stepped out of a Picasso canvas.

Soon the living room turned into the communal baths of my childhood. Everyone was stripping. Susanna—all lines, angles, and curves—undressed, and her skin shone like living porcelain. That is, until I noticed that Susanna did not shave— at all. Coarse black hair covered her chiseled calves and slim shins; hairs sprouted from her armpits like spiders. Her pubic hair reminded me of a bearskin on an ivory wall in a medieval castle.[1]

Nobody paid any attention to me, and jumping on one foot, I pulled on a red-and-black garter belt and my viper stockings. As I polished my stiletto heel with the sleeve of my sweatshirt, Susanna picked up the other shoe and weighed it in her hand.

"Nice shoes," she said. "Mine are getting too shabby and cracked. Foot fetishists wear them down fast."

"How?"

---

[1] Susanna is fixated on her body, its functions and state. She attempts to take control over it, reclaim it, and re- cover from a childhood trauma (possibly, an acute illness or hospitalization). Her libido is invested into her own body.

"Licking. This one guy always wants me to stick my heels into his balls. And then he wants brand-new soles!"

Susanna smelled her stockings and laughed at my gaze.

"To see if they're sweaty. Pantyhose have to be smelly—don't ask!"

Zoe squeezed herself into a black, ruffled bodice—lard-like folds of flesh piled over the stiff lace—and stamped her shiny go-go pump into the carpet, "How do I look?"[1]

"Like a Cirque du Soleil elephant," I thought, and said, "Fantastic."

We both layered on streetwalker-style makeup, standing side by side. I lost touch with reality. I wasn't me. I was a loud, bright woman, spots of red and black, a circus performer on a bad day.

Susanna wrapped a floor-length cape—or a burial garment—around herself, see-through black lingerie underneath. Her skin glimmered, blood-red lipstick making her mouth look mournful, like that of a dead virgin.

"I'm stepping out on the porch," she said. "Smoke, anyone?"

"Such a pothead,"[2] said Mommy, laughing and coughing. "But a great mistress. Rose! Bad hair."

She inspected my teased do, her lips twitching.

"Take it easy on the spray, Hon. What are you, 'Married with Children?' Clients need something touchable, like goose down. They want glamorous, but real-life. They are not allowed to touch their wives' hair, as not to ruin it. Wives can

---

[1] Zoe needs external validation. Her emotional state is determined by other people's reactions to her behavior; she lacks internal self-structure.

[2] Susanna did not internalize self-soothing mechanisms, and she turns to external substances such as marijuana, alcohol, and opiates that depress the central nervous system in order to calm and reassure herself.

be so dumb. Sometimes they understand what their husbands want, but rarely."

She started to pull on my hair. It hurt.

"I remember this nice couple, and they wanted to live their fantasy, so they came here and brought a lot of patent leather and had a party—coke, weed, pills and stuff. They were in their eighties. She tried hard, but she kept throwing up. He was tiny, and kept saying: 'Will you suck my pecker, please?' And she kept saying: 'But sweetheart, what would they say at church?' So I told them: 'You need a plan. I will tie him up to this chair, you will wear this corset, I will whip him, and you will suck his pecker...' Here, Rose, that's better."

"Hey, she looks like—like Cher in Las Vegas," said Zoe. "I love Cher."

"And careful with the lipstick, Hon. Don't leave traces on their clothes."

I ran into the bathroom and couldn't make myself pee for a long time. My stomach was all knots, and I couldn't feel my hands.

"Where's the client?" I whispered to Zoe, back in the living room.

She was slouched in the armchair, popping chewing gum, and pointed at something behind my back.

THE FIRST CUSTOMER: THE BEST BOY

The Boudoir door opened softly, and Susanna swam out like a Day of the Dead vision. She was holding a leash. On the leash, behind Susanna, crawled a monster.[1] For a moment I forgot all about my writing. I wanted to go home.

A hybrid of a grizzly bear and a werewolf, its bulging eyes crossed, rolling in their sockets; its chest and back sprouting patches of gray wool; its behind wiggling, the thing in the middle of the neat living room did not look human.

"Say 'Hi' to Zoe and Rose," cooed Susanna. "Oh, he is the *best* boy."

"The Best Boy" crawled toward me and licked my shoe. Then he kissed my hand. His lips felt like slugs. I shivered. I had never encountered a man that gruesome that close.

"Hello, Mistress Rose," uttered the monster.

"Oh well hello, the Best Boy," I heard myself saying.

"Would you like to come with us and spank our Best Boy?" asked Susanna, her voice calm and bright, like sunlit, icy water.

"But of course!"

It wasn't me talking anymore: Some force took over me, lifted me from the chair and carried me to the Boudoir.

"Our Best Boy is ready for a good inspection, isn't he? And if he isn't good, we are going to have to punish him, aren't we? We'll give him a spanking, won't we?"

Susanna and the Best Boy swam into the Boudoir like a circus trainer and her tamed bear. Susanna glided in front, every move in sync with the classical music pouring out of the hidden speakers—I tried to remember the tune and couldn't,

---

[1] The Best Boy is a masochist; he is sexually excited by humiliation and verbal abuse.

although it was really familiar, an opera maybe.

There Susanna sat on the edge of the bed like a fallen angel, the Best Boy's beastly head in her lap. She pointed at his hairy behind.

"Spank gently!"

I closed my eyes and spanked the Best Boy. Then Susanna put on latex gloves.

"Kneel on all fours."

We bunched together like kids playing doctor. Barely touching the Best Boy, Susanna put her index finger to his genitalia. The man had no penis whatsoever. Just tiny balls. I had never, ever seen such a small penis in my life, for real or in movies.

We looked at each other, and she shrugged.

"He is the *best* boy," she purred. "He can't read or write, can he?[1] He can't even talk or move now, can he?[2] He is our house slave… You need to go back to the living room now, don't you, Mistress Rose?"

"Oh yes," I said, promptly leaving the Boudoir.

I ran to the bathroom and spent the next ten minutes scrubbing my hands, soaping, rinsing, drying, and then washing and washing and washing over and over again.

Zoe walked into the bathroom, exploding with her short laughter, "Mistress's hands… You'll wash your hands right off your arms, you'll see. Get a nice hand lotion, honey, the skin gets so dry after a while."

I smiled, dried my hands, and felt like taking a shower.

---

[1] To reach sexual satisfaction, this individual needs to re-gress developmentally.

[2] **Analytic Narrative**: As a small child, "The Best Boy" watched his nanny putting his severely mentally and physically handicapped brother to sleep by patting his genitals and calling him "the best boy." He replays this scenario in the dungeon.

MISTRESS ROSE — SMART AS A WHIP

In the living room, I found Mommy smoking a joint and working on my web page. Mommy took a drag and squinted at the photograph of my red vinyl-clad backside against the tiger-print throw.

"Dear, are you sure you haven't done this before? You look professional," she said.

I did not answer.

Mommy crossed her legs, her felt boot swinging, and read aloud from my erotic resume:

"What the fuck is this? 'Rose's Eastern European high cheekbones, her innocent and slanted blue eyes and an avalanche of long red locks give her an exotic air.' Who the fuck cares about your cheekbones? Forget the avalanche. Who do you think you are? Dostoevsky?"

"Um, no."

"'Black lace, scarlet velvet, gentle satin and silk accentuate her creamy skin.' Ha!"

"It took me two hours to write it."

"Well, you are not a good writer."

She deleted part of the text, and started to type with her index fingers only, murmuring to herself, "Mistress Rose is a redheaded blue-eyed exotic Ukrainian beauty, 6'3" in heels."

"This is not too … original, though, is it?"

"No one needs your originality. Screw that. Plain and simple, I say."

The final text read: "Mistress Rose is savage and sweet. She loves slutty dresses that hug her slender body like a glove. Rose has long shapely legs, and is addicted to sheer stockings, high-heeled pumps, pointy-toed Italian stilettos, strappy sexy sandals or thigh-high boots. She takes great pleasure in a good foot massage."

"Rose is smart as a whip, sensual, and playful. She lives for role playing. She can be your wicked psychotherapist, strict nurse or capricious hypnotist. Rose is dominant and strong, and will give you a whipping session to remember."

"Some of that crap might work," concluded Mommy. "You have to learn to write clearly."

I agreed and wondered if I could ask Mommy to edit my future novel.

The door to the Boudoir opened. A respectable middle-aged man walked out, swinging his patent-leather briefcase. With his dark-navy suit, sunglasses, and neat goatee, he looked the perfect gentleman. I couldn't help gasping. He took a gallant bow.

"Goodbye, ladies."

"Have a great day, sweetie," said Mommy.

Susanna, stark naked, walked the transformed Best Boy to the door. I noticed a red mystery imprint on her marble-like buttock. She then gave Mommy a roll of bills, and Mommy shoved it inside her felt boot.

WEIRD JOHN

The phone rang, and Mommy announced: "Weird John. For you, Zoe."

Zoe pouted.

"Why is he weird?" I asked.

Instead of answering, Mommy handed me a black catalogue box with library-type cards arranged in alphabetical order. Each customer had a card: *Name, age, first visit date, preferred mistress, type of perversion/fantasy, personality type, notes made by mistresses.*

I pulled out a random card: *Don. Straight-A type—likes to be tied up to the table and tortured slowly. Pins, rat traps. Look, don't look. Do not pull on the balls. Doesn't tip much.*

I found Weird John's card under "J" and discovered that Weird John was a plumber, a flasher, and liked to walk out of the Boudoir whipping his penis around. I read aloud: *"Brings tools (rulers, syringes, plumbing pipes).[1] Fantasy: a doctor's office, the doctor and nurses out for the day, you are a secretary (or two or three). Perform a physical examination, prescribe shots, give shots. Into his penis. Use a flashlight. Excessive pre-come."*

"Well," I agreed. "It does sound a bit odd, and really gross, but then look at this card: *Elf Paul. Fantasy: He is a lesbian butch elf. Two hours verbal session. Thinks he is nine inches tall; send him*

---

[1] **Analytic Narrative:** Weird John equips himself with a **Giant Penis** by using **pipes** and other tools as a **penis extension**. He might be a latent homosexual with negative resolution of his Oedipus complex. Cleansing excrement and dirt from pipes is an oxymoronic attempt to both cleanse himself and get dirtier. Weird John's **Internal Morality Police** punishes him for being "dirty-minded" and wanting his father. By choosing this exposure to feces and submerging in "filth" on a daily basis, Weird John satisfies his coprophilia.

down your toilet pipes to clean them from shit and piss; he is the shaft of a screw-driver that goes down the pipes.[1] *Talk to him in detail about your boyfriend pissing into his open mouth. Jerks off, can come up to four times during two hours.* Isn't that pretty bizarre, too?"

"Never mind Paul, he was fine. He was so into it, he visited every day for a two-hour session, but then he had a triple-bypass and died."

"Here?"

"You ask such idiotic questions, Rose," said Mommy. "Why? Not here. Paul just never came back, poor guy. The strange thing about him was that he never noticed when the whole interior had changed after the remodeling—the walls, the doors, the bed, the curtains, I mean everything. He said he was color-blind and his wife always picked out his ties. He was all right."

"Okay, but I mean—no offense—they're all pretty weird, aren't they?"

I studied a stack of cards.

"Look at this one: *Virgin James. 60 y.o., technically a virgin. Fantasy: a fetish for red satin dresses. You walk around in a red satin dress. He jerks off. Very submissive.* Is he really a virgin?"

"Oh, not a big deal. Of course he's a virgin! Pretty straight-forward case. It's clear that he wants to be fucked by his father.[2] Lot of guys do."

---

[1] **Analytic Narrative:** The pipe takes on a new meaning in this case. Elf Paul is aroused by a **pipe**, a powerful sexual symbol. To Elf Paul, the pipe represents a **vagina**, and cleaning the pipe represents intercourse. Like Weird John, Elf Paul feels "dirty" because of his sexual desires. Hence, the vagina is extremely dirty, and Elf Paul must clean it. By swimming down the pipe he becomes dirty, too; he is inside the birth canal and is swimming back toward the comfort of the womb. His "elfism" is his desire to turn back into a fetus.

[2] **Analytic Narrative:** Another fascinating case of un-

I blinked at Mommy.

"Why? I mean why is it clear?"

"He can't do any penetration, that's why. But at the same time, he wants his older sister—that's what the dress stands for."[1]

"Hmm. I see."

I really didn't.

"How is Weird John weirder than Virgin James?"

"You'll see. You ask too many questions. There is no way you can do him on your own right away. This other new girl tried and never came back to work."

---

resolved Oedipus complex. Virgin James desired his mother, but he could not "have" her due to the social taboo of incest and the fear of his rival, the father, castrating him. Due either to genetics, anatomy, hormones, brain development, trauma, or a combination of these factors, his psychological growth was sidetracked, and as a result Virgin James never successfully identified with either his mother or father. He is suffering from gender identity ambivalence. In "normal" development, a male child identifies with his father and re-channels his sexual energy from his mother to other women. Instead, Virgin James had identified with neither his mother nor his father, and a part of him identified with his mother and desires his father, while another part has identified with his father and desires his mother. He cannot penetrate or be penetrated, and hence Virgin James is destined to live and die as a virgin with a wardrobe of satin dresses.

[1] **Analytic Narrative:** Virgin James had an exposure to **"primeval scene"** and witnessed his father penetrating his mother, perhaps after a house party. His mother was wearing the red satin dress, and she later punished the boy for his voyeurism by spanking him. He developed a fixation on satin and the color red. The inspiration for this interpretation is obviously Sacher-Masoch himself, the author of *Venus in Furs*, who witnessed his aunt having sex and was whipped by her afterwards. He invested her furs and horsewhip with libido and eventually immortalized them in his artistically mediocre but psychologically outstanding work.

Zoe looked up from filing her nails.

"Well, she was eighteen," she said.

Eighteen.

I shuddered. I intended my novel to promote the freedom of all adults to make medical, reproductive and other decisions about their bodies, including selling body parts. I believed it was a human right, and no God, no government, no society, no authority should take over that right. Just like athletes sell their arms and legs and scientists sell their brains, sex workers should be able to sell their sex organs without any moral constraints.

But… eighteen. My past was knocking on the door again. And, I thought of my daughters. Did I have double standards?

"Stop biting your nails, Rose. Yep, he's sick to his bones," Mommy went on. "The sickest one of them all…"

I reached into my purse for my nail file.

"What about Mike?" asked Zoe.

"The Motherfucker?"

"The who?"

Mommy winced.

"Never mind. I won't even talk about that one. To hell with him… You'll meet him pretty soon anyway, mark my words. Oh, but you know who else was weird? What's the name of the guy who invented computers?"

Before I could answer, she snapped her fingers.

"He died, too. Oh, don't look at me like that with those big blue eyes, Rose; he didn't die here—no one died here, for crying out loud!"

She closed her eyes for a second.

"This one kicked off at home, of old age. The guy invented a bloody microchip in his garage. Those geeks play with parts in their garages, and then come here to play with themselves. If he were here now I would spank him for inventing the computer… Computers drive me nuts. But Weird John is *weird*."

Mommy kept mumbling, reminding me of that crazy homeless woman by the porn store.

Weird John arrived with a suitcase of tools as promised. I expected to see a monster, but he looked average, normal, the sort of guy you'd see in the store buying milk and would never remember later, except for maybe the blank look in his eyes. That look reminded me of Bobby, Lisa's son, the mentally handicapped child next door, except Bobby didn't have a goatee.

"Godzhaningmishbushzhazina," said Weird John.

"Pardon me?" said I.

"He's deaf," said Mommy. "You get used to it."

The whole scene was staged: Mommy minded her own business polishing the stove; I stood idly next to her like an inexperienced secretary. Mommy and Zoe had outfitted me in a worn pair of soccer-mom jeans and a loose polka-dot blouse that in its drab periwinkle blue belonged more to the seniors' section of a Dress for Less store than either a dungeon or a medical office.

"Now you'll see," said Zoe.

Naked, Weird John came out of the Boudoir, strolled down the hall, burbling non-stop, his lips moving like two worms. Attending parent-teacher conferences and Christmas Eve parties at the Wartons' would never be the same after watching him. I would never look the same at Mr. Blansky, the girls' Science teacher; Joe, our neighbor; or Dr. Noodleman, my kids' dentist.

Was the idea of "normal" people a gross misconception?

"Paranoia," I told myself. "I'm turning into my grandma. Soon I'll start looking for enemies of the people at Bloomingdales."

Weird John paced around the kitchen.[1] He pulled on his penis, as if he wanted to tear it off. He bent it and swung it as if it was a plumbing pipe. Transparent liquid dripped all over the place. I thought he was having an orgasm. I recalled the victim of a forty-eight-hour-long orgasm from *Everything You Always Wanted To Know About Sex But Were Afraid To Ask*. Luke and I liked Woody Allen

"No, it is not come," explained Mommy when he stepped back into the Boudoir for a moment. "It's just lubrication. Some guys are like that."

She kept scrubbing the walls and the kitchen cabinet. Weird John was back and walked around me in circles.

"Is she going to be here all the time? Is she a secretary?" he mumbled.

"Yes, she's a secretary. She's taking some phone calls now, see?"

I gagged on the phone, pretending to handle a business inquiry and paying no attention to the nude man pacing in front of me.

"Come here, new girl," said Zoe. "We have an injection session."

Zoe, a giant syringe in her mighty latex-gloved hand, greasy hair falling on her baby-doll face, her nostrils flared, brought back traumatic memories of my childhood hospitalization when my tonsils were removed, or rather snatched out with no anesthesia in Spartan-minded Odessa People's Hospital.[2]

---

[1] Weird John is anticipating the reaction of fear and disgust from "the new girl." His sexual arousal depends on the degree of her response. In a typical masochist's manner, Weird John exposes Zoe, Rose, and Mommy to his humiliating exhibitions and painful "procedures," and thus humiliates and inflicts pain on them.

[2] It is possible that the tonsillectomy without anesthesia was the root of Rose's trauma. Up to 98-99 percent of in-

There was some beating with a metallic ruler, some fussing with measuring various parts of the patient's body and other quasi-medical activities.[1] I watched Weird John's face. By that point it was devoid of any expression, but his lips kept twitching.

Weird John wanted only half a session, and thirty minutes went by fast. "Good to see you, hon. Come back soon," said Mommy.

In the bathroom I bumped into Zoe, and we washed hands for a long time.

"First time I did him I took three showers," boomed Zoe. "And ate a whole apple pie."[2]

---

dividuals with **Dissociative Identity Disorders** have by age nine experienced traumatic events (accidents, natural disasters, sexual abuse, invasive medical procedures, or wars.)

[1] **Analytic Narrative:** As a child, Weird John suffered a traumatic experience at a doctor's office, most likely involving an injection into the gluteal area and being restrained by a tantalizing nurse, perhaps with a secretary looking on or helping out. The fear was sexualized and bred this particular deviation, possibly complicated by his strict upbringing, physical handicap, and low-self esteem.

[2] Zoe uses external substances for self-soothing—in her case, food—just as Susanna uses marijuana.

MISTRESS ROSE, A NATURAL TEASE

We returned back to the kitchen where Mommy kept polishing the immaculate stove, chatting away.

"I wish I could go to the movies... They just don't make good movies anymore... Zoe, stop stuffing[1] your face and pass me the soap. When I was little they had all the war movies; war, sea battles, uniforms. Mmmm, I love me a man in uniform. I once had a cop for a boyfriend."

I tried to imagine Mommy with a boyfriend.

"Or, there was this serial, 'The Perils Of Pauline.' When I was eleven I used to go watch it on Saturday mornings with Timothy. The silly boy clapped and cheered whenever poor Pauline was getting kidnapped and tortured... One day after the movie, I chased him down... he was ten and of course he could run faster than me, but he didn't... I dragged him down into the laundry room in the cellar, dark as hell, and tied him to the wine rack with clothesline, just like in the movie..."[2]

Mommy chuckled and coughed.

"I blindfolded him, gagged him with my handkerchief and tweaked his nipples with clothespins. He had to pay me all the money he had saved for movies before I'd set him free."

She laughed so hard she almost cried.

"Who's Timothy? Your brother?" I asked.

---

[1] Zoe's non-stop eating is her coping mechanism developed in childhood. She is caught in a vicious biochemical circle in which serotonin abnormalities contribute to dysregulation of appetite and mood and impulse control, as well as obsessive-compulsive behaviors and depression.

[2] Depictions of aggressive acts against others might trigger deviant sexual explorations in individuals with fixations on previous traumatic events.

"No. Timmy was my buddy. He died from meningitis the following winter. Boy, did that kid love Westerns, 'cowboys and Indians' movies...[1] They just don't know how to make movies these days..."

The next customer was for Mommy herself and arrived wearing a uniform—a goatee, glasses, and a suit. So far, all our customers looked like employees of the same corporate structure. Conservative, middle-aged, reserved, and dignified, every one of them struck me as a quintessential American character. That is, until they removed their clothes. Of course, in my suburban reality, quintessential American characters never removed their clothes. The fear of running into Mr. Dorson, Luke's boss, or Joe, our next-door neighbor, got stronger with the entrance of each client.

"He's a partner in a law firm," said Mommy. "Good guy. Come down to the Dungeon after about fifteen minutes. Put on the red vinyl and platforms."

Mommy's crooked body was transformed. Clad in black—a miniskirt, all leather and spikes, a mesh top and nylon stockings—she looked like a German sausage served at a Halloween party.

In fifteen minutes I walked through the Boudoir, smiled at Susanna and Zoe, who were taking turns spanking[2] somebody's scrawny butt[3] with a fly swatter, and stumbled down the steep stairs into the Dungeon, afraid of breaking my neck.

---

[1] This childhood trauma fostered deviations in Mommy's sexual development. She replays the games invented with Timmy to soothe her sense of guilt and loss.

[2] During a corporal punishment session the brain releases opiate-like endorphins that not only serve as natural painkillers, but also create pleasurable sensations.

[3] Buttocks are a highly eroticized zone, and for men especially the behind is connected to **fantasies of being**

The customer was transformed, too: He was spread-eagled on the ob-gyn table, modeling a playful flowery dress and pink old-lady panties.[1] Like a shaman, in slow, sticky motions, Mommy tied him up. She put on handcuffs, ropes, and straps; she made and unmade knots, moving with a hypnotic quality. As I took small steps around the ob-gyn table, watching the scene reflected in the mirror, I realized that bondage required a dexterous ability that I lacked. I looked in the mirror: a hunchbacked witch, pins in her mouth, creepy skin of her cleavage spilling out of her mesh top, and a tall red-vinyl Amazon—was it me? Unsure of my role, I touched various parts of my body in a provocative manner. I did and undid my shoe straps. I licked my venom-red lips. I sighed. I didn't feel real.

"You are a naughty, naughty girl," said Mommy to the customer.

"Naughty," I repeated in a guttural voice.

"We are going to punish you…"

"Punish you…"

"You are going to be in so much pain…"

"Pain…"

Mommy then attached a clothespin to his left nipple.[2] I attached another clothespin to the right one. It was really hard to find his nipples. She then twisted her clothespin a lot. I did the same. It had to hurt. I expected to see some reaction

---

penetrated by the father or a **phallic mother,** as well as with fantasies of regression and infantilization.

[1] This is a case of **transvestic autogynephilia,** a deviation in which the man's sexual arousal is associated with the thought or image of himself as a woman.

[2] Nerve endings that sense pain or pleasure and transport the electrical signals to the brain are located throughout the body and are concentrated in "erogenic" zones: lips, nipples, penis and clitoris.

from the customer: wincing, grimacing, some sign of life of a human in pain.

The customer was just lying there like a lump. He looked dead.[1] Mommy blindfolded him, and in an instant, her solemn air was gone. She winked at me—a playful pirate, tossing chains, grunting and clicking her heels. She was goofing around, grimacing and pointing at the clock.

Then, there was a knock on the window.

I froze. I imagined cops with guns, arrests, my semi-nude pictures in the San Francisco Chronicle with the caption "Thirty-eight-year-old mother of three caught torturing the CEO of Midwest Bank." My knees gave in.

Mommy just grinned, raised her knotty index finger and led me to the window. She lifted the black-leather curtain, grinned wider and pointed at a bluebird sitting on the windowsill, pecking on the shutter. Mommy beamed like a child, wiggled her ugly finger at the bird, and returned to the torture table.

My knees were shaking so bad I almost fell off my platforms. Mommy readjusted the clothespin on the man's nipple, scratched her head and dismissed me with a royal gesture.

After the session, Mommy changed back into her grey rags and felt boots and announced: "The new girl is a natural tease."

I smiled and shook my head.

"She's just like me."

Zoe frowned.

---

[1] This individual may have lapsed into a **"sub space"** — a trance-like, euphoric state that for the short term blocks the ability to think or act rationally due to the excess of endorphins, the opiate-like chemicals produced by the body in reaction to extreme pain.

"You should have seen her! Prancing around. The way she touches herself![1] You slut!"

"Thanks," I tried to avoid Zoe's stare.

"You go, girl. You can get really good. Just figure out the psychological part. After all, remember: They're here for the psychological in the first place, or else they would go to escorts. They need the suspense, helplessness, mystique; they want to feel special. You tell each one of them that he was your best client ever and that you had tons of fun. But at the end of the day the whole hour is all about—? Girls? It's all about—"

Her caterpillar eyebrows crawled up and she squinted at us like a schoolteacher who hadn't had her breakfast, as if saying, "All together now, children!"

"The clients?" I asked.

"Their dicks," said Zoe.

"Mm-hmmm," said Mommy. "And aren't those bluebirds just adorable? Look at them."

She then looked at her appointment book, "Susanna, you have a new customer. Carl the Shit Eater."

Zoe winked and whistled. Susanna offered me the box of cards, the way Dr. Winston, our pediatric dentist, offered Nick a box of rainbow colored pencil sharpeners and giraffe shaped rubber bands after cleaning his teeth, "Take a card."

"No, thanks."

They both looked up at me.

"You don't want to be here, do you?" asked Zoe, putting her donut down. "You think you're so cool, and we're all just—"

---

[1] The tease appeal is tracked to a Tantalizing Mother scenario. A **Tantalizing Mother** is the Mother that seduces but never satisfies. Typical or "normal" sexual development results in the interest in striptease prevalent in both heterosexual and homosexual males.

"You're wrong, Zoe," I said. "I actually like it here. I like you guys. I really do."

Susanna kept looking at me from behind her book, but said nothing.

"Do you care for the rest of your doughnut, Zoe?" I asked.

I didn't really want it, but Zoe and Susanna watched me, and I took a bite, trying hard not to cringe. As my teeth sank into its spongy softness, a whiff of sweet powder shot up my palate and filled my nostrils, the back of my mouth, and my head with the memory of the cotton candy I used to have at the Lanzheron Beach, back home, in Odessa. Hot yellow sand burning my toes, bleeding red cherries smudged on a white page of *The Three Musketeers*, transparent seagull shadows in white-blue skies. I didn't realize how long it'd been since I'd had anything sweet—years, maybe. I didn't realize how home-sick I was, how much of a foreigner I was—here.

"Thanks, Zoe," I said. "This is a good doughnut."

HEAD TO TOE BEAUTY

On the way back home I turned on Madonna, and blanked out. Crossing the bridge was like crossing a border: The past was behind me, the future was... now. High winds shook the skeleton of the bridge. The steel railing of the upper deck trembled. I could hardly see in the fog, the car swerved, and I had the eerie feeling of being in a different dimension, as if my heart was a violin and an invisible hand pulled on the strings.

I thought about Vickie, Vanessa's sister, and imagined her climbing the railing, imagined being her: dizzy, out of breath, as if I were about to give a public speech—in English. Like Vickie, I lost myself. I lost my native language. I lost my native land. I was a lost grown-up child, all alone on the bridge over the churning ocean.

I still had an hour before the kids got out of their after-school program. I pulled by Head to Toe Beauty.

The salon was almost empty, with only one woman having long artificial nails affixed to her fingers. Her black hair glistened as she looked back, and I recognized the Latina attendant from the gas station. She smiled, and cried, "Hola, hola!"

"Choose color, lady," said a Buddha-like woman, bowing to me with her head only.

The counter looked like a tropical forest, with fat-bellied bottles perched on it like exotic poisonous frogs and birds. A Lucky Cat nodded its orange head.

"Purple," I said, smiling back at the gas station woman.

"Good," she said.

"Pretty," said the Buddha woman.

In an instant I was crucified on the spa chair, water bubbling around my swollen feet, three small bird-like women slumped over my hands and feet. I closed my eyes and thought that the dungeon clients might feel as relaxed, idle, and helpless as I did. The women kept chatting in their abrupt, musical language, and laughing, and I knew that I was no more to them than a client on a torture table was to Mommy, or the robot in the garage to Luke. We didn't exist in each other's dimension.

I opened my eyes and looked at the face of the Buddha woman. She was squinting, slapping a tiny brush with purple poison on my nails, turning my hand this way and that way, like a piece of wood. Her crinkled face was worn like her nurse-like blouse; wrinkles carved her forehead right above her painted eyebrows—not a single hair, just two penciled arches. She looked up and gave me a smile, the missing front tooth making her look like a baby.

"Pretty. Pretty lady," she said.

The name tag on her blouse read, "Lizzy."

"I have friend named Lizzy," I said, thinking of Mommy.

"Not real name, work name." She kept smiling her toothless smile.

"What's your real name?" I asked.

"Difficult. Americans don't know," she said. "You call me Lizzy."

"How did you get here?" I wanted to ask her. "What was your life like back in Vietnam? Do you miss your home? Why did you run oceans away?"

"Thank you," I said.

The gas station woman got up.

"Work," she said, waving her nails to me—this time they were blood red.

What destiny pushed her here, to a gasoline-reeking booth in California? Was it the same force that led an elderly Vietnamese woman to Head to Toe Beauty, to cut the nails of an anxious Ukrainian housewife who had spent her afternoons adjusting clothespins on a lawyer's nipples? Why were we all here? Was there any meaning to it at all?

"You dry now. Twenty four dorrars," said Lizzy.

At school, Ms. Jenkins and the freckled woman in the denim overalls were standing in their usual place, underneath the magnolia tree. As usual, they looked like they were taking a smoke break, only they didn't smoke.

I noticed Ms. Jenkins's beige pumps and tights, and felt goosebumps crawling up my arms.

Did she moonlight as a dominatrix, too?

I looked at her slick hair and shiny forehead, at her lipstick. How could I not have noticed before? Mistress Jen, the sexy librarian, would punish you with her favorite pointer.

"Hello."

"Hello, sweetheart. So good to see you."

I could see her with a whip in her hand, one foot on a vinyl bed, perfect smile on her beige lips, saying, "However—"

At home, Potemkin had killed a mouse. Following her instinct, she first tortured her victim, meowing as if she were possessed, devoured shiny intestines, dragged the tiny carcass to the inside of the garage door, and placed it on the straw mat as a gift. She then curled up at a distance on her favorite rag, proud, purring away with happiness, and waited for us to appreciate it. I called Luke to clear the mess, as I never could touch or face anything dead, not for a million dollars. A steel clutch gripped my stomach and I could not breathe. I could feel the mouse's horror and pain. I was one with the mouse. I was the mouse. I was the Vietnamese browless woman. I was the naked lawyer on the torture table. Death was waiting for me, fluffy and ruthless. I felt the Misty Lilac coming over me, covering me, leaving me empty, robot-like and vacant, and fighting it, I picked up my phone.

"Vanessa?" I choked. "I—I—I need help."

"What happened? Nick—"

"No! It's about me."

"You're sick?"

"I'm—I'm addicted to sleeping pills."

I dug my nails into my palm.

"Phew!" laughed Vanessa. "I thought you were having an affair! What pills?"

"Ambien."

"Oh, that's fine, honey, I take it sometimes, too. Just start breaking the pills in half."

"Thanks," I said. "Really. I'll talk to you soon."

My heart was beating so hard, as if I was about to make a public speech at a PTA meeting: Last time I had tried, the whole room turned to me the moment I opened my mouth. "Do you need a translator?" asked Ms. Jenkins, straightening her beige skirt.

REAL ARMADILLOS NEVER CRY

I forced myself to heat frozen chicken-apple sausages from Costco, steamed rice, and opened a can of tomato sauce. After dinner Luke went to the garage, and I followed him and stood by his workbench in silence, looking at the robot's body parts. He repositioned metallic wires in a plastic box like his life depended on it. I picked up a hair-thin wire and twisted it.

"Aren't you going to ask me about my day?"

"Naah... Maybe later," he said. "Give me that."

At bedtime I held Nick's feet firmly, clipping his nails.

"Mr. Armstrong was tough and he never, ever cried, even when his claws were being trimmed. Armadillos always hide behind their armor, and that is why they are invincible."

"But I want to cry when it hurts," said Nick.

"Don't," I said. "Real armadillos never cry."

That night, Mr. Armstrong the Armadillo wrecked his lifeboat on a deserted island trying to get to the enchanted lighthouse, fought big, bad monsters, and turned them into people by using ancient Armadillo magic.

"Here, I'll show you the lighthouse."

I opened the curtain, and pointed at the amethyst light flickering in the dark.

"Did Mr. Armstrong kill all the monsters?"

"No. Real armadillos never kill. He put a spell on them, and they all became good."

"Why didn't he kill them? With a gun?"

"Because killing is bad. No one should kill or hurt others, Nicky. Remember that."

Nick put his thumb into his mouth.[1]

"What's this? You haven't done that since you were a baby!"

He shrugged and kept sucking on his thumb.

I almost fell asleep next to Nick, Potemkin purring on top of my leg, but made myself get up and move to the living room. There I pulled a smoky green volume of Dostoevsky from a shelf, patted the shabby cover, was about to open it... and stopped.

Every night I curled up in Luke's green chair with a book, Potemkin in my lap, a steaming cup of black tea with milk balanced on the arm of the chair. Words burned inside, just like tea, both hurting and soothing, and I read and cried. The kids were in bed and Luke was in his garage, so it was okay to cry.

When I was little, my sister and I would sit in Grandma Rosa's lap in our nighties and listen to fairy tales. I remembered my sister's sharp elbows hitting me in the ribs as we pushed each other, fighting to open the volume of Brothers Grimm's tales. I remembered the translucent wax paper rolling, uncovering the faded-out illustrations. Grandma's weak lavender scent mixed with the smell of the ancient book—sweet dust. Dried rose petals fell out from between its weathered pages and floated down through the air as if time had slowed down or as if we were transported into a different dimension, a world of dark secrets, hairy monsters, dismembered bodies, and wheat-haired princesses.

"Read about the sorcerer," I would say.

---

[1] Nick is reacting to Rose's emotional distress; sucking on his thumb is a defense mechanism. It is quite common for people to regress during times of stress or frustration to earlier stages of childhood development, such as the oral stage. When infants turn away from the breast, they suck their fingers or pacifiers; later, it might become nail biting or hair chewing, for example.

"Oh maybe not, Grandma, I think I'm afraid of the sorcerer," my sister would say, covering her ears.

Grandma would smile at me—a rare occasion.

"Bring the book, Oksana, it's just a story. And Gogol is a fantastic writer. Now listen..."

The scariest story we ever heard from her was about a sorcerer who wanted to marry his own daughter. In order to do that, he turned himself into a good, old man. The worst part, the part that sent goose bumps running up my arms, was at the very end, after the sorcerer was captured and doomed and thrown into an abyss where dead giants—his ancestors and children—were gnawing on his raw flesh till the end of time. My sister always whimpered at the end, and hid her warm head in my lap. I felt triumphant—I was younger, but I didn't cry.

When I grew up, curling up with a book became my way of escaping reality. In my Odessa apartment, I devoured classic novels, pages and pages of trials and suffering: fallen women and tortured counts, students torn by their criminal obsessions, grumpy old women exploiting innocent beauties, the world of masters and slaves, villains and victims, the world of passion and pain.

In that strange, bodiless world, neither heroes nor murderers ever had an urge to empty bladders. Their intestines convulsed, but they never sat on a toilet. They could have killed for love, but their genitals never appeared and no one ever copulated. People were devoid of bodies in My Fantasy World. Enveloped by Misty Lilac, my only true friends were nothing but spirits. Ironic, I thought. I lived in the dungeon of my life, feeding on fantasies—just like Weird John or Elf Paul—only my fantasies never crossed over the covers of the books or the bones of my skull. But in a way, we were the same.

I used to read and cry, read and cry, read and cry, and I would forget all about being alone, being an orphan, being scared.[1] And then, I would write, too. I would write down my musketeer and grande dame fantasies, and also the smells of the sea—salt, decaying dead dolphins and acacias trees melting in the air. I tried to pour their ephemeral being into the heavy, pulsing, visceral life of my body, feel it, sense it; and as I wrote, I forgot the pain of my own existence, because I was a part of the Universal Pain.

When we first met, I tried to tell Luke about it.

"What pain?" he said. "Listen, life is short. I don't want any pain. When my shoulder hurts, I ice it. Or, if it's really bad, I take Vicodin. You've got to relax, Honey."

I was still holding Dostoevsky as my eyes fell on the *People* magazine Olga had left on the green carpet. A blonde with impressive cleavage winked at me from the cover.

"Do you want to cry now?" she seemed to be saying. "Or do you want to read about the latest summer trends in Paris? Relax, Honey."

Potemkin gave me a harsh stare. She looked like my grandma. My grandma never relaxed.

"Fine!" I said.

---

[1] "Getting lost" while reading is another example of dissociation. By submerging herself in an imaginary world, Rose loses awareness of her immediate surroundings.

A WRITER'S DIARY

I curled up in the chair and opened Dostoevsky. *A Writer's Diary*. Great. Potemkin jumped on my lap and started to purr.

"Suffering is the essence of Russian morality—the endless suffering in everything, even in joy…"

I shut the book.

"Screw it…" I told Potemkin, patting her silky back. "You like to suffer?"

Potemkin closed her eyes and started to knead my thigh with her paws—first one, then another, like a kitten sucking milk.

"You're weird," I said to her.

"Mrrr…" said Potemkin, digging her paws into me.

I sank further into my green chair, the hot heaviness of Potemkin's body against me, the gas heater buzzing lightly in the background, but I didn't read. I felt like talking to someone, telling them about Dostoevsky and suffering.

"Here's your tea, Honey," said Luke. "It's cold."

He stood in the doorway holding my favorite purple mug.

"It's okay," I said. "I don't want it. Thanks."

I watched him disappear from the doorway, stooping, and heard him heading to the garage.

"He's building a robot," I told Potemkin.

In response, Potemkin pierced her sharp claws through my jeans and right into my skin. I pushed her off my lap, and went to my computer. I was typing fast, making more typos than usual, my fingers slipping off the keyboard: I was writing down everything about the dungeon, and the kids, and the mouse, pouring it all out of my brain and onto the all-enduring white of the page.

A few minutes into it, my computer stalled. The unsaved file disappeared. It occurred to me that what looked like a page wasn't even a page, it was a fantasy of the page, ready to collapse and disappear at any minute, dissolve into the cyberspace abyss. Even writing, which normally made me feel real, wasn't real anymore.

"No way," I told my mother's picture.

And slowly, taking pauses and saving every two minutes, I rewrote my life—only the words didn't feel that light any more, they dropped down like rocks, like the overripe cherries of my childhood, like blood dripping on the paper.

At four I slid back into bed, next to Luke, and fell into a maze of vague nightmares. Then as I sank deeper, I had The Nightmare: chestnut trees, Odessa boulevards, the deserted beach, the lost voice. At the very bottom of darkness, I saw my sister, crying, mascara smudged all over her cheeks. I woke up and turned to Luke, my eyes still closed.

"Honey, I'm scared," I whispered. "Something really bad will happen."

I reached out my hand: Luke wasn't there, just a cold pillow. I opened my eyes and saw him, the running gear on, lacing his shoe.

"I'm off. Do some yoga, Honey," he said. "You'll feel better."

THE PEST EXTERMINATION

Still groggy, I poured Friskies into Nick's breakfast bowl.

"Mooo-om!" he screamed. "Gross! And what did you do with my soccer shirt?"

Potemkin just sat by her empty dish, looking hurt.

I fished Nick's soccer shirt out of the unsorted laundry.

"I'm staying over at Angie's tonight," said Olga.

"Oh, no, you're not," I said. "That is *so* not happening. No midweek slumber parties."

"Angie's helping me with my science project," Olga started to weep. "I'm—"

"Which part of 'No' you don't understand? Sweetheart, why did you just change into your old jeans?" I asked Roxanne.

She just gave me the look of a dying unicorn.

"You look slender," I said. "You are beautiful. Please wear your new pants."

I drove across the bridge, trying to suppress the same feeling, disturbing and dull. Like a piece of gum stuck to a shoe sole. Like the invisible dirt on my hands that I couldn't wash off no matter what. The ghost of Vanessa's sister was hovering over me when, from behind my car, catching up with me, and then getting ahead of me, came another Subaru Forester.

Trancelike and steady, it swam forward in the fog, same quagmire hue, same FasTrak sign in the top, right corner of the windshield, same small crack in the back bumper. It was identical to my car, but then I saw the driver.

The woman behind the wheel was me.

She had long, wavy red hair that was screaming for a brush, a grey sweatshirt, sunglasses of the same deepwater-diving shape. I had a sudden pang in my stomach—I saw me driving away from me, peeling away, leaving me behind. The disturbing feeling of splitting apart, dividing like a cell made me squeeze the wheel harder, clench my teeth, bite them into my lower lip. The pain made me feel grounded for a second, but as I watched the car disappearing in the distance, I knew that I had departed from myself forever.

I almost crashed into the railing. I arrived at *YourFantasyWorld* almost happy to smell Mommy's morning bacon. This morning though, a sweet, almost syrupy odor blended with the hardly exhilarating bacon-and-smoke aromas of Mommy's empty kitchen. I looked for Zoe's Starbucks Java Chocolate Chip Frappuccino Coffee or a monster peanut butter marshmallow cookie, but Zoe was outside on the porch.

"Do you smell this shit, Rose?"

"What is it?!"

The kitchen space was heaving with fat, black flies the size of hummingbirds. They buzzed by like mini-helicopters over a battlefield, bumping into the kitchen window, cabinets, and women; they swarmed and murmured and swirled around in fuzzy streams.

"A freaking dead rat, that's what it is."

I instinctively pulled my feet up onto the chair and held my breath.

"I've been trying to get hold of someone since seven this morning. Sick of it! Rose, here! An assignment."

Mommy dropped the brick of the Yellow Pages into my lap. It was open at the Pest Control section. Dealing with dead mice around the clock certainly was not the pastime I had imagined for the characters of my novel. I spent the next hour calling pest extermination companies with names like "Clear Skies Pest Elimination," "Ratbusters," and "Capable Exclusion," and having conversations like the following:

"Hello! *Capable!*"

"Do you remove dead mice?"

"We provide animal carcass removal service, Ma'am."

"How much?"

"Initially we do a premises inspection in order to evaluate potential damage to the property..."

"How much?"

And so it went until I finally found "Bow Wow Meow Pest Control," which had proudly served the area since 1941. Their motto was "We're Not Happy Until You're Happy," and they "gladly" gave "phone quotes." Bow Wow Meow stood up to their promises, and I succeeded in bringing over "Doctor" Phil, whom I first mistook for one of our clients. There was a difference, though: He wore navy-blue coveralls instead of a navy-blue suit. "Doctor" Phil shut himself in the kitchen and after some intense pounding and puffing returned to the living room with a full black garbage bag. He wiped his forehead.

"Yep. You had a cemetery in your kitchen vent, Ma'am. Don't know what did them in. Looks like some bloody rat massacre... This one bastard was particularly large... and you know what? They were hanging out there, dead, for at least two weeks."

"How do you know?"

"Oh, that's how long it takes for the larvae to develop into flies. Be careful of the traps I've put out around back there for any potential vermin-development situation. You have a nice day, ladies."

The next hour was spent fussing around the kitchen, flapping the flyswatters from the Boudoir closet, shooing the flocks of scavenger flies out to the porch. They bobbed and weaved, absurd in their black, fat realness.

Those flies were more real than me. Mist obscured my vision, and I saw myself sitting at a narrow oily-yellow desk at Odessa State University, listening to Professor Zavyalov: "In this little-known Dadaist staging of a Chekhov play, the socially challenged bourgeois characters clap their hands in the air chasing non-existent insects, thus symbolizing the historical impotence of the distinguished-yet-doomed Russian intelligentsia circa 1900..."[1]

It all turned around. I was a non-existent character, clapping my hands in chase of bigger-than-life, death-black, vibrating dung flies. My life was nothing but a useless metaphor. Mommy, as usual, was quicker to the point.

"Hey, a dead rat is better than a dead man," she giggled. "Easy disposal! Did you write down Phil's number?"

---

[1] Flashbacks are **somatosensory**, **auditory**, and **visual hallucinations**. Traumatic memories are stored in a different part of the brain than ordinary declarative memories of events, people, and objects. The same part of the brain is also responsible for experiential memories; thus, traumatic memories have the vividness of reality. They include smell, sound, and touch, and contribute to Rose's feelings that she is actually reliving her past. Due to her history of trauma, Rose's memories are mixed, her time sense and continuum are lost, and she cannot differentiate between real and fantasized events.

THE DOCTOR

The flies were still buzzing when the phone rang. Mommy answered and beamed at me.

"Rose, good job with the vermin doctor. Now you can take Doctor Rob. Look up his card. Oh, and mind you, we'll have no racism here. You have a black client, you take a black client."

I assured Mommy that I would take any client. Race did not concern me. I reached for the card:

"Name: Rob. Occupation: Emergency Room Surgeon. Fantasy: a woman-lesbian.[1] Me or him?"

"Both, Honey."

"Wears a skirt and two condoms. Tell him you'll pee on him, but don't do it. Sometimes wants cameo with third girl and some toys. Real germaphobe.[2] *Never touches girls. Wear gloves throughout session."*

"A popular fantasy," explained Mommy. "Most of our perverts are secretly gay.[3] The truth is: They all want a dildo up

---

[1] Males presenting with autogynephilia sometimes imagine themselves as women sexually interacting as lesbians.

[2] Note how the Doctor is terrified of **germs and blood** but still opts to be exposed to them on a daily basis! I had a client with a similar sexual deviation who worked at a mortuary, and in addition to wearing three condoms during sexual intercourse was a compulsive shower-taker, which in turn led to a painful skin condition. As a boy, he was afraid to sit on a grown-up toilet due to the extreme fear of germs that he associated with disease and death. His older sister had died of diphtheria, and the mother practiced ritualistic cleansing behaviors.

[3] Yes. And no. Many heterosexual males are sexually aroused by the thought or image of themselves as females. The medical term is **autogynephilia**. Freud's **womb envy** concept, though bitterly criticized, is a highly com-

their ass, but can't accept that that's what they want. They're scared shitless. So it's easier for them to think that *they* are women, being fucked by women."

I put on heels and lipstick. Suddenly, I didn't feel like a human being. I felt like an animal.[1] No, not an animal. Animals are alive and have names. I turned into a thing, an accessory. I turned into a helium balloon floating aimlessly, with no weight, no sense, no purpose, about to disappear into the vast blue sky and stop existing. I observed my own face in the mirror with cold curiosity. It looked like a mask. A mask with a strange, red smile superimposed on my quivering lips. It wasn't me anymore. It was the dead girl. It was my sister.[2]

I closed my eyes and opened the door to the Boudoir.

The Doctor waited for me, dressed in a pink gauze tutu, the type of ballet skirts my daughter wore for her recitals. He talked like my ophthalmologist. His head was shaven. He examined my body carefully without ever touching me.

"Turn around. Lift your skirt. Will you pee on me?"

---

pelling explanation. The idea of anxiety felt by a man over women's ability to give birth causes so much denial that it is probably correct. However, in some cases the desire to be with prostitutes might reflect a latent homosexuality. It is a compromised formation where a man allows himself to be as close to another man as possible—without actually touching him—through a woman's body.

[1] **Heels and lipstick** signal a transformation into a sexualized persona. A woman wearing a uniform is perceived as a part-object: the personality is reduced to only one part, the sexual self, while all other parts are ignored, denied, or not allowed. Slowly, the sexualized persona takes over because it is the only one being mirrored or seen.

[2] Rose does not recognize her reflection, which is one symptom of **depersonalization**. It is possible that she is developing an *alter* personality, morphing into her deceased sister.

"Oh, yes, I will pee on you..."[1] I exhaled.

I didn't think I could pee on a human, but maybe I was wrong. Maybe I was wrong about a lot of things that I could and could not do, would and would not do—wrong about everything I knew about myself.

The Doctor lay down and invited me to stand on the bed right above him. I crawled on the bed, not sure of the procedure.

"Dance!" ordered the Doctor.

The soft surface slipped under the stripper shoes, and I almost fell down. I went through the dance moves like an automaton, without a thought or any idea of time going by.

Then his cell phone buzzed—like a fly, I thought.

Before I knew it, the Doctor was up, dressed in his suit. He placed the money on the cabinet between the curved candle and the one-dollar lipstick.

"I'll be back to see you, sweetheart. Sorry. Work emergency. Have to go."

"I'm not happy until you are happy, dear. Come back soon! You're my favorite," I told him.

I went back to the living room, thinking role-playing wasn't that hard.[2] Mommy took the money and shook her head.

"Ah, he gets that a lot, poor guy. One time he had to leave the session because a patient had a chandelier stuck in his anus.[3]

---

[1] The Doctor gets excited by teasing others and being teased, creating the titillating sensation of walking the line without ever crossing it.

[2] Rose accepts being reduced to a sex object in the dungeon because this transformation guarantees that she is seen and heard, even if only as a part-object. In her real life she is invisible to both her husband and children.

[3] The Doctor is **a sexual sadist,** hence his choice to become a surgeon and work in an emergency room (symptomatic of his highly aggressive tendencies). The Doctor

He's a nice guy, though, loves gardening. We were exchanging rare cauliflower plants last year... Most of my clients love gardening."

---

is excited by the possibility of inflicting tissue damage, and being exposed to illness and violence.

THE PUPPY

The card for The Puppy read: *Fantasy: a puppy. Rolls on the floor, kisses feet, licks feet (stockings). Throw him a shoe, brings it back in his teeth. Scratch behind his ear. Put your feet on his back. Loves to massage your feet. Commands: Obey! Sit! Play dead! Good puppy!*

The Puppy, like all clients, looked like he was manufactured at the same pervert-making mass-production factory as the others:[1] a middle-aged, beer-bellied, goatee-wearing man. Off the invisible conveyer belt and into the Boudoir he marched, undressed, folded his gray pants and white underwear in a neat pile, took his glasses off and placed them lenses-up on the vanity table. His clockwork moves proceeded to the beat of a silent metronome.

"Hi, Sweetie, I'm Mistrrrez Rrrrose!"

I threw my shoe in the corner and whistled, thinking about Potemkin's annual vet appointment at the Cats and Dogs Spa. The Puppy barked with joy, rolled on the floor, growled, and hid in the corner with my red stiletto in his teeth.

"Bad puppy, bad puppy!" I said.

I imitated the overweight gasping woman talking to her trembling Chihuahua at the waiting room at Cats and Dogs.

---

[1] Creating a collective image of a "**Big Monster Man**" allows Rose to dehumanize men and generalize negative attributes to all males. As a little girl, Rose had no male role models. As an adult, she never learned to see men as individuals; generalizing them allows her to avoid intimacy with men and to perceive males as perverts, "bad" people with no feelings of their own and no human connection. Alienating men allows Rose to hurt them and minimizes the guilt.

"What are you doing, my little puppy?"

The Puppy turned his back to me, took a few gasps and satisfied himself[1] while I got a hot towel for cleanup. He wiped himself, and turned back to me, "What's the capital of Ukraine?"

"Kiev."

"My grandfather was from Byelorussia."

He pulled his pants on and got the money out of the pocket.

"I'll be back soon, want to have more fun together?"

I looked at his bald head, took the money and thought it was as much fun as the automatic car wash last week.

"Loads of fun, and you know what?" I said.

"What?"

"I'm not happy until you're happy. You're my favorite client."

The Puppy laughed. "How do you say good bye in Ukrainian?"

"*Do pobachenija.*"

"Pobobacheeneeya!"

Mommy was sitting on her porch, smoking pot and contemplating her garden, a shady oasis full of green ivy, creamy roses, and crystal-clear birdbaths.

"Done with The Puppy? Good job. Mind you, he will not tip, nor will he come back for you again. He needs a different

---

[1] **Analytic Narrative:** This deviation is rooted in a childhood experience involving a **canine**. Children under the age of three do not differentiate between animals and people, and watching Mommy or Nanny kissing the dog passionately possibly led to sexualizing an animal and further identifying with it. The imprint formation took an atypical development, and the sexual energy was channeled unconventionally; the sexual preference persists during adulthood.

girl each time," commented Mommy. "Look, look!"

She pointed at a hummingbird hovering over an ivory rose, and then buried her nose into her *Cambridge Encyclopedia of Ornithology*. I wondered if she had a secret longing to turn into a bird and fly away.[1]

I stepped back into the living room, my mind blank, and pulled the *EGYPT* coffee-table book off the shelf. Its glossy butter-yellow cover felt smooth on my fingers. The dead face of the Sphinx, eyes half-closed, a hint of evil smile in the corner of her lips reminded me of my Golden Fantasy. My fantasy world was as far from the dungeon living room as another galaxy.

"Egyptians for Dummies?"

Susanna appeared behind my shoulder, rubbing her hip and wincing.

"I'm scared of mummies," I said. "When I was a kid, I had a nightmare about a Russian mummy."

"I didn't know you had mummies in Russia."

Susanna stretched out on the carpet, naked.

"Lenin, in the Mausoleum in Moscow. I saw him when I was twelve. He was all yellow. Scary, really. It's in the middle of the city. Like the White House here. I mean, the mummy's there now, as we speak. "

Susanna gave me a blank look.

"I loved mummies. I told you about my hamster."

She was still massaging her hip.

"No, you didn't."

"Oh, my dad gave me a hamster, Toto, when my parents were getting divorced, and then I got really sick. I couldn't eat

---

[1] A good example of Rose's tendency to project her own thoughts onto others, in this case, Mommy. Rose herself attempts to escape her reality through writing and the dungeon job.

anything, except for applesauce… I still hate applesauce. My Dad couldn't bring me anything yummy, so he brought me all these picture books and read to me about mummies. And then Toto died."

"And?"

"And I mummified him," Susanna said, laughing her waterfall laugh without a smile.

I felt close to Susanna. I took in lots of air, and felt myself blushing, but kept talking, "You know, I have this fantasy—"

I heard a barking cough, and saw Mommy standing in the doorway, frowning.

"Cleopatra killed men after sex," I said.

"Bloody Hell, no," said Mommy. "Not here. Where would you keep the bodies?"

"I say give me your money and split," boomed Zoe, stomping into the room and collapsing into her armchair.

"Don't die on my carpet," said Mommy, coughing.

She shuffled to her computer, put on a metallic pair of reading glasses and opened her website, reading emails and mumbling, her lips moving, which made her look like a big rodent sniffing. Everyone stopped talking. Zoe and Susanna had their eyes closed. I had the physical sensation of life departing me, of becoming more and more engrossed in an absurd madman's play, and I closed my eyes, too.

I was falling asleep, and I saw Lenin's wax mummy, its almost transparent nose and grey wrinkles. Lenin opened his eyes and stared at me.

A NEW GIRL

"That bitch!"

Mommy jumped off her chair, and slapped the desk.

"Who?"

"Mistress Xenia."

Mommy pointed her crooked finger at the fierce little Asian in the home page photo of *YourFantasyWorld.com*.

"The little bitch quit. She finally had the courtesy to send me an email."

Susanna stood up and, her back very straight, walked to the porch.

I turned to Zoe.

"Why is she upset?"

"I think they were doing it," said Zoe. "Anyway, they were always together. Studied Portuguese together, read the Kama Sutra. Boy, was she annoying. Walked the Appalachian Trail and never came back."

Mommy paced the room, almost screaming.

"That bitch, she was so good. Asians have such a good work ethic. Plus, she was such eye-candy! A lifestyle dominatrix. Almost as good as that other bitch, Zena, the one who moved to Hollywood. Bloody Zena ended up marrying a producer of the "Matrix" movies, a sicko in need of a 24/7 live-in dom. Ah, to hell with them both! These girls, they're worse than the customers. You know what Zena did for fun? She carved hearts on her slaves. With her Swiss Army knife. Then pinned the hearts with safety pins!"

"Where?"

"Anywhere! Mostly, to their own bodies... You guys are mellow, you could never replace those bloodthirsty gold-diggers. I have to place another ad on Craigslist!"

The responses to the ad poured in at a startling pace.

"Look, we are competing with Fantasy Makers, but they're not really our competition. We're an intimate, personal, hands-on, friendly dungeon. Those bastards had twenty-nine girls last time I checked, and they're open 24/7. The girls have to take a whole training course there: 'First they are submissive for one year, and they must attend Bondage A-Go-Go every Wednesday. Only then they can work as dominatrices.' What is it, a fantasy production factory? A med school for doms? I'm telling you, it's like we're Joe's Sweethearts Local Bakery, and they're Starbucks. We are definitely better."

The first resume came from someone named Utopia with the email address "braidyourhair," and the second from a fifty-six-year-old housekeeper named Jesussita.

"No. That will never work. Miss Utopia Braidyourhair is black, obviously."

I admired Mommy's ethnic radar. A lot of things that were obvious to her were obscure—to say the least—to me.

"I don't give a shit, black, white or green, but my white clients do not have black women in their fantasies. I once asked a regular client about it and he said, 'Mommy, I didn't play with little black girls when I was growing up.' Bloody racists."

"What about the cleaning lady?"

"Nahh. Latina. Latinas never end up working out—too Catholic. They freak out when they see a dick coming. Remember the Mexican girl I paid with tomatoes, Zoe? At the time I had bushels and bushels full, and she was delighted to have them…"

Next, there was a girl from the Lithuanian-Czech Republic. "Where?"

"Lithuanian–Czech… whatever. Probably speaks Russian. Look, 'Work experience: barista, language instructor, swimming teacher. Education: M.A., Comparative Religion.' Holy shit! 'Volunteering experience: substance-abuse teen program' (a junkie, clearly). 'Objective: to enhance my office career. Summary: results-oriented decision-maker with a proven leadership record.' Is she nuts or what? Slavic is good, however. No inhibitions. You guys are pretty lax when it comes to morals, eh, Rose?"

"Well…" I hesitated. "We have… *some* morals. Just different. It's cultural, you know. Depends on the family, too…"

"Did you have strict parents?" asked Zoe.

"My mom—she wasn't around. My father emigrated when I was three.[1] We were really raised by my grandma, and she was like an officer. Used to hit us a lot, especially me. She always liked my sister better, but she wasn't really mean, she did it because she loved us."

"Did your grandma make you go to church?" asked Zoe.

My grandmother Rosa did not go to church, but she surely was religious. Her religion was Literature. She taught Russian and French literature at a secondary school for fifty-five years.

Grandma Rosa was a woman of tiny stature and steel will.

Her nickname at school was Battleship Potemkin. It was hard to find out how and why students, teachers, and even

---

[1] **Analytic Narrative: The root of Rose's trauma!**
Her father abandoned her as a child, and her Oedipus conflict was never resolved. She longs for her father and his penis, but as a result of reaction-formation develops a deep hatred for men. She experiments with the dominatrix job under the pressure of the suppressed incestual drive. Generally, the loss of one parent deeply affects the sexual development and the resolution of Oedipus conflict in all children.

librarians had started to call her that. My guess it was her stern look and steel-gray suit, and her dry cough exploding like gunshots. She hated the nickname, but even she knew that when she focused her eyes at you, you felt under the cannon. Like her namesake, Grandma wouldn't hesitate to rebel against the whole world. I was ashamed to admit it, but I named my cat after my grandmother. As soon as I saw that miniature wiry body at the pound, I knew I was on to something, and after a week at home, her omnipresence and aloofness—along with her razor-sharp claws—confirmed that she was a reincarnation of my beloved grandma.

I felt like telling Zoe that we *lived* in a church. We shared our communal apartment with five other families, in a building that had been a Catholic church before the Communists came to power. It was turned into a homeless shelter and eventually into an apartment complex. My grandparents, my sister and I all shared a water-green matchbox room that was overtaken by shelves and shelves of books, and portraits of white-bearded, angry-looking men—Russian writers. One wall by the window belonged to my Grandpa and was occupied by a paint-stained easel and sketches.

My first memory was of reciting, "On seashore far, a green oak towers..." at three, balancing on a shaky stool amidst clotheslines hung with giant striped underwear and cauldrons of boiling borscht.

The only way Grandma Rosa could survive in this world of rotten potato peels and urine-smelling toilets was by escaping into her fantasy world. The fantasies and miracles were canned and stored on her bookshelves, the same way watermelons were pickled and stored in glass jars by our neighbor, Aunt Ludmila. Grandma Rosa married Grandfather, enamored with his Parisian starving-artist sparkling eyes, suede beret and burgundy scarf, convinced that he was the next Chagall, and the fantasy kept her sane while dealing with his drunken stupors and reeking socks.

I grew up believing that material possessions came and went, people died, and daily preoccupations were futile and transient. The only meaningful things were literature and art. Despite everything the Communists told us, there was life after death. It was in books. *This* was my grandmother's religion, and she passed it on to me. And that is why I kept writing. Or so I thought. I did not tell Zoe that. I had learned never to talk about important stuff. I never trusted anyone enough.

"We had no church. Communists are atheists, you know," I said.

"Are you a communist?"

"No."

Mommy shrugged.

"Whatever. Anyway, Russians and other Slavs are a good fit here. Zoe, remember the Croatian girl? She came right in the middle of the war. Her two brothers were missing... She was so pretty—with her clothes on. But she was a real skeleton. We had that customer, he was Polish, got really excited about having a Slavic girl, but once he saw her undressing he ran away. She was an artist, and drew me a crystal ball for my newspaper ad... Some people are just so gifted. Too bad she was so skinny."

Mommy was scrutinizing the Slavic leader's picture.

"Big boobs: good. Too fat: bad. Middle Eastern guys like big women,[1] but how many Middle Eastern guys do we get in here? Oh, forget it, look at her birthday. Why did she even

---

[1] These ideals of beauty are based on fertility signs. Furthermore, in some cultures "big," "fat," and "well-fed" are synonymous to "rich," and therefore are desired sexual qualities.

put it here? She's a Cancer. My daughter's a Cancer. Cancers are too sensitive for this job: I remember a Cancer, she quit because she thought jerking off was bad karma."

Mommy interviewed a triple-D-chest massage therapist; then, a former Las Vegas stripper with "Maneater" tattooed on her butt in rouge red; and finally, coughing, and waving her pipe, she said: "Got it. Arriving on Monday: Mistress Greta."

CAMERA OBSCURA

On Sunday afternoon we went for a walk by the beach.

"Why do we always come here?" whined Nick.

"Because I like it. And because you need fresh air. Look at you, you're so pale."

"I'm not pale," said Olga.

We all looked at her raspberry cheeks.

"You need exercise," I said.

"Are you saying I'm fat?"

The corners of her lips dropped down, just like they did when she was five and wanted a new Barbie.

"No. No one here is fat, but we all need exercise. We're going up the hill for a change."

We walked up and stopped by a yellow-and-blue booth at an empty vista point. It looked like an alien spaceship had just landed.

"Is it a lighthouse?" asked Nick. "Like Armadillo's?"

"No, can't you read, Wabbit?" said Olga. "'Camera Obscura is a rare device dating from the 15th century'.... Bo-o-o-ring!"

"Not at all," said Luke. "It's designed by Leonardo da Vinci, and it's a scientific device meant to—"

"Boring!" confirmed Olga.

I read the rest of the placard. "'Spectacular Live Images. Experience the Camera Obscura Effect today. Don't miss it!' I want to see it."

"No way," said Olga.

"Me, neither," said Nick.

Roxanne was silent, her eyes half-closed, her cheeks chalk-white. She chewed gum.

"World famous Giant Camera, kids," said Luke. "We're going."

He walked to the window with TICKETS over it, but quickly returned, scratching his neck.

"Honey, it's four bucks apiece, and those guys are really not into it. Why don't you go, and I'll just watch them while you're in there?"

I paid four dollars and walked into a dark, empty room. A large bowl-shaped antenna—or what looked like a satellite antenna—sat in the middle of the floor.

"Like a giant eye," I thought.

Inside the dish I saw monotonous rocks, plastic-like seals, the endless horizon, the rolling waves: all moving slowly, dreamlike, like a snail crawling up a window. The camera rolled over Luke's rigid hand on Nick's angular shoulder, over Olga, her doll curls trembling in the wind, over the charcoal zigzag of Roxanne's lowered eyelashes, over the empty space where I stood next to them a few moments ago.

Everything in the clinical whiteness of the dish was real— more than real, it was meticulous, precise like a painting by a mad artist, like a glossy photograph of the underwater world; yet, despite its precision, there was nothing real about it. My children, my husband were just images, the mirrored images from the upside-down, floating, drifting world of my mind.

The giant alien eye kept rotating, focusing on the desolate beach. It wasn't the world outside of the booth anymore. This vast cold space with its eternal loneliness, this recurrent beach of my dreams swam at me like a hallucinatory swan—a stage prop, a backdrop tipping forward to reveal its flatness.

For an unreal gravity-free eclipse moment, my inner and outer worlds overlapped, like interlaced fingers, and the shards of light falling through them were like puzzle pieces, like brain contractions of recognition, of primal understanding of the ineffable, the understanding beyond words and beyond mind. I lingered on a threshold of discovery, the eggshell of the dish cracking.

I closed my eyes, turned around, and left.

Just before bed, Luke turned to me and grunted. Then he scratched his neck.

"Yes?" I said.

"Honey. Do you want to stop? The dungeon?"

"Maybe, I do." I rolled away, my knees to my chin, hiding my face away from him.

"Well, stop, then," he said after a while.

"Leave me alone," I said. "No."

THE TRAP

Monday morning, I arrived at the dungeon like a zombie, going through every step without knowing where I was. The world—random objects dislocated in the vast indifference of space, unconnected, devoid of meaning, suspended in time like pieces of a mobile under a glass ceiling—seeped away. I was alone, invisible in the darkness, observing it going round like I had never exited the Camera Obscura: Mommy frying her bacon, Zoe chewing her donut, Susanna smoking her joint and a hummingbird hovering over the ivory rose—again, and again, and again.

"The new girl is here," whispered Zoe, licking her fingers. "A psychologist."

Mistress Greta stepped out of the bathroom and smiled.

She reminded me of a cow. A beautiful, robust cow. I could almost smell steamed milk in the air, despite the obvious fact that every effort had been made to conceal her barnyard association. Her large teeth were bleached, but her double-processed blonde hair retained a honey hue, and the way she moved her jaw and that mouth—chewing gum, talking and bulging coffee-and-cream eyes at you—brought back memories of sultry summers in a fishing village by the Black Sea, the lazy scent of the barn and the merry sound of frothing warm milk hitting the bucket. She said she was thirty-six. The wrinkles around her eyes made her look kind and grandmotherly.

"One of my daughters is a special-needs child," she said in a hushed voice. "And I'm a single mom."

"Hey, Sweetie, who isn't!"

Zoe almost high-fived Greta. "And, my son is ADHD, too!"

"My situation might be a bit different," said, almost whispered, Greta. "My child is severely handicapped. I'm here because I have to provide for my children."[1]

She sighed, and her chest billowed like a pillowcase drying on a sunny, windy day.

"You think I'm here for fun?" asked Zoe.

She shrugged her athletic shoulders and dug into her purse, her brows forming one unhappy line across her low forehead. Her cheeks turned tomato red. I caught myself biting my lip. I was here to write a novel. Greta and Zoe had no other choices in their lives. Or did they? My fingers felt numb. I heard buzzing in my ears. Sounds around were muffled, as if reaching me from far away or as if I were under water.

"Stop biting your nails, Rose. You weird me out when you get this blank stare of yours. Everyone is 'special ed' or 'special needs' these days," said Mommy. "All they need is a good old spanking... My mother used to cure all those learning disabilities, no problem. You misbehave, Bam! You wind up across her lap, bottom up... Worked really well... Actually, it felt good!"

"How often do clients call?" asked Greta.

The telephone was dead silent.

"It's the day before Mother's Day weekend," said Mommy. "Always slow. Holidays are horrible for us. All our clients are with their families."

I settled in the armchair, pulling my feet in, trying to focus my eyes on Greta.

"What are you reading?" she asked Susanna.

"*Kama Sutra.*"

---

[1] Another example of rationalization. Rationalization here allows Greta to deal with the conflict between her impulses and the prohibitions of her **Internal Morality Police**.

"You're reading that shit again?" asked Zoe. "Indian porn."

"It's classics," said Greta.

"Educational porn," said Susanna, laughing. "Do you know that you can grasp a penis with your vagina, like with your hand, and masturbate it to orgasm?"

"No, I didn't know that," said Greta. "I don't think I can do it."

Susanna laughed her musical laughter again and stretched.

"Wait, you're not saying...?"

"Yep. Done. Xenia learned it first. She was... She was hot," Susanna sighed.

"You only can pull that shit if you never had kids," said Zoe. "Try and pop out a couple of brats, and you won't be grasping anything with your vagina."

Greta laughed, "Well, you'd have different concerns."

"Yeah, like not peeing in your pants when you're laughing," said Zoe, giving Greta a sullen look.

Greta stopped laughing, "That, too."

"I don't think I'll have those issues," said Susanna. "You can train yourself to do whatever you want, it's just a matter of practice. You're the master of your body."

"The Mistress," said Mommy. "You're a moron, Susanna."

"I've thought that, too," I said. "There's nothing you can do about certain things. Like stretch-marks."

"Or droopy boobs," said Zoe.

She was looking at the caramel shadow in the V-shaped cut of Greta's soft sweater.

"How do you do it?" I asked Susanna, to change the mood. "The vagina trick?"

She raised her hand and clasped her fingers in a fist. Everyone laughed.

"So, you're a psychologist, Greta?" asked Zoe.

"Yeah... a Ph.D."

"Wow. So, didn't work out that well for you?"

Zoe kept staring at Greta's pillow-like chest, her muscular arms crossed. Greta folded her arms across her chest and chewed her gum faster.

"Well, I'm still carrying the school debt. I studied forensic psychology first, then family and marriage counseling—a good field, everyone needs it. Then I got divorced. By the time I pay for childcare, the only money left is for the rent."

Greta licked her lips.

"I had my private psychotherapy practice in Sacramento," Greta continued faster, "but again, you have to pay for the lease on the office space, and you work like a slave with no breaks, and still have no money left. And then there are the clients, and they are needy. And then you come home, and the family is there, and they are needy, too. It's always about them, never—ever—about you…"

"She's either a compulsive talker, she's really anxious, or maybe she just drank too much coffee," I thought.

"You think it is about you here, honey?" laughed Mommy. "Here, it's all about their dicks."

"Here and pretty much everywhere," said Zoe. "It's never about you. At least here we don't pay taxes. Do you know how much I made last year as a real estate agent? Nothing. I made no money. Real estate sucks. And, I had to pay the taxes on my nothing, anyway. And this makes me mad. All I want to do is open my bakery, bake some cupcakes, but no, I can't make more money—'cause then they'll take more. It's a freaking trap!"[1]

---

[1] Zoe externalizes responsibility and places it on circumstances, her environment, and other people, rather than within herself. Her life is a trap because she has never developed a strong enough belief in her own agency and ability. Despite appearing aggressive, she is extremely passive, detached, and fatalistic.

"Life's a trap!" I thought of saying. "I'm a writer, but for years I haven't completed anything because I'm either pregnant, breastfeeding, or remodeling. I wanted to write novels, but all I've done was change diapers and drive between soccer and cheerleading practices. That's a trap. Family and art are incompatible. Unless you are a Tolstoy and have a submissive Russian wife..."[1]

I opened my mouth... and then I heard my grandmother's voice ringing in my head: "Die, but don't whine." She valued dignity above anything. I looked at Zoe's round face and Greta's folded arms, and closed my mouth.

"Yep," said Mommy. "We're fucked. But so is everyone else."

The phone was still dead silent. Greta was talking about refinancing her house. I tried to read *Princess Spider: True Experiences of A Dominatrix.*

I bought the book on Amazon as part of my research. But I simply could not read it. It made me sick.

Books written to amuse, according to Grandma Rosa, were bad books. The language was torturous. Words were like clothespins attached to the brain. They left a metallic aftertaste in my mouth: *"I like a laugh too. That can help to keep the atmosphere at the right level, or reduce the tension. I'll be caning someone, stop and say: 'Does your mother know you're here?' ... I will attempt to accommodate disabled clients whenever I can. I know a lot of mistresses will draw the line here, but physical needs are physical needs."* Good Lord!

I craved good old Dostoevsky or Fitzgerald or Faulkner the way Mistress Spider's choking clients craved air—besides,

---

[1] Rose also rationalizes her inability to accomplish a novel by externalizing her fear of failure.

I needed something to distract myself from the nauseating emptiness in my throat, the *something-bad-is-about-to-happen-soon* feeling. Book therapy was the only therapy that had ever worked for me.

FORTUNE TELLING

I ventured to explore Mommy's bookshelf. First I browsed through *The Secret Lives of Common Birds: Enjoying Bird Behavior Through the Seasons.* "Why do birds build nests? Why do they sing? Why do they stop singing in a cage? What is cage life like to a bird? A wildlife photographer observes birds' behavior..."

I looked at Greta and Zoe. They stopped arguing about mortgages, and looked at me. I looked at myself in the mirror. My face wasn't mine.

"I like your hair color," said Greta.

"Do you like mine?" asked Zoe, combing through her heavy bangs.

"That's a nice style. You have lipstick on your teeth, Hon."

I thought, "Do the birds know why they fly? Do they know why they sing? Do they know why they're here, cruising those clear skies? Do we know why we are here? I am an observer eating worms and molting feathers..."

I put the book back, and pulled another off the shelf: a seriously damaged volume of Zola's *Nana*. I felt a chill going down my spine: déjà vu. I knew I'd held this book in my hands before.

My sister and I used to tell fortunes by opening books at a random place and reading a line. Sometimes she would tell me the number... I opened the book. The page was dog-eared, and one word was marked by a sharp nail: *"bloodstain."*

Frozen, I read the passage: *"This bedroom had become a veritable public place, so many boots were wiped in its threshold; and not a single man was stopped by the **bloodstain** barring the way. Zoe was still preoccupied by this stain; it had become something of an obsession with her, for it offended her sense of cleanliness to see it* *always there. In spite of everything her eyes would constantly turn in its direction, and nowadays she never entered Madame's room without saying:*

"'It's funny how it doesn't go.... And heaven knows there's enough people come in here....'"

I shut the book and shoved it back on the shelf. The bloodstain on the carpet reminded me of the bloody mess on the Bay Bridge, the black-and-white paw reaching for the skies. The memory added to the annoying anxiety that never left me, buzzing in my ear like an invisible fly. Zoe's name repeated. Was it an omen? I needed a different fortune.

I pulled off the shelf a small book called *The Uses of Enchantment: The Meaning and Importance of Fairy Tales.* That sounded promising. I opened it to the very beginning and pointed my finger at the bottom of the page: *"monster."*

Great. I kept reading: *"There is a widespread refusal to let children know that the source of much that goes wrong in life is due to our very own natures—the propensity of all men acting aggressively, asocially, selfishly, out of anger and anxiety. Instead, we want our children to believe that, inherently, all men are good. But children know that they are not always good; and often, even when they are, they would prefer not to be. This contradicts what they are told by their parents, and therefore makes the child a monster in his own eyes."*

A monster... I remembered my elementary school teacher Ludmila Ivanovna, her polka-dotted grey dress, rabbit teeth, and cobra stare: "You are such a good girl! Why are you being so bad?" I did not know why—at eight or at thirty-eight. I turned the pages... Did this book offer the solution? Did any book offer the solution? Grandma Rosa thought so, but I'd started to doubt. Could books in general offer any solutions?

I read on: *"The dominant culture wishes to pretend, particularly where children are concerned, that the dark side of man does not exist, and professes a belief in an optimistic meliorism…"*

The book would have passed Grandma's censorship. It suggested that in the best tradition of saviors and saints, literature *could* offer relief from the existential predicament by allowing access to deeper meaning. I needed the relief, but I was not sure anymore if there was a deeper meaning. I put the book back. A bad day for fortunes.

I decided to go for a third and final book. Three was always a good number for me. A black book with the blood-red title, ***DEVIATIONS***, by Michael H. Strong, PhD—the tome looked like a haunted house.

This time I took precautions. I whispered the page number and the line to myself.

"Page twenty-six—my birthday, line nineteen—her birthday—from the top."

I counted the lines, my heart beating. My red fingernail stopped by the black word: *"death."*

"Terrific," I whispered.

"Everything has happened before and will happen again. Therefore there is no end or no death. There is only the end, or the death, of an individual human brain. Death of an individual human is imminent but is nonexistent at the universal level. If you understand this infinity, you are immortal."

I slipped the heavy brick of ***DEVIATIONS*** into my purse and felt the heaviness inside my chest. Oh, if I only knew how true that prophecy was and what was to happen soon… How little do we know! How blindly we read the books of our lives. Life is more twisted than any fiction, more logical than any science, but its logic is its own.

Ms. Jenkins and the freckled woman in her denim overalls hovered in their usual place, smoking their imaginary cigarettes. There was something disturbing in the fact that they were always standing there, as if it was staged, unreal, as if an invisible director had placed them like plastic animation figures in the background of a primitive cartoon.

As I waved to them, I had a detailed, painfully realistic vision of stumbling and falling, my purse skidding across the chalked asphalt, spilling out my black lacy underwear, rolls of cash, two bottles of French perfume, **DEVIATIONS** and *Princess Spider: True Experiences of a Dominatrix*, ruby silk gloves, and Vogues.

Ms. Jenkins would stare at it, and then at me with her bracketed smile and say in her ATM voice, "We do love Nick; however—"

A wide smile, brackets sliding apart, "However—and it's too bad—you are a slut. Your sister was a slut. You are a hooker, a shame to our school community. You shouldn't be around children. We are going to take your kids away from you."

Ms. Freckle next to her would bulge her binoculars at me, and hoot, "Get out of the schoolyard, you dirtbag. You can't even remember my name, or who I am. You don't belong here, it's not a place for you or your type, you stupid bitch."

For dinner that night, I made the Ukrainian version of hamburgers—*kotlety*. Nick loved *kotlety*. Grandma Rosa taught me to cook everything from scratch, and I could never buy ground beef at a grocery store. I avoided looking at the pieces of raw meat as I stuck them into the food processor. I wanted to distract myself by plotting the next chapter of my novel. But the Misty Lilac didn't come, and I couldn't see anything.

All I could see was a sinewy mass of meat in a bowl. It seemed to me that it trembled and moved. I almost saw maggots. I put the bowl in the fridge and peeled an onion. Slowly, layer by layer, I took off the brown peel, and the first layer.

Nick wandered into the kitchen, dancing and scratching.

"I want a cookie," he said. "Mom, are you crying?"

"No, sweetheart, it's just onion."

"I want a cookie, too!"

Olga grabbed the last cookie from the box. I took a butcher knife and cut the onion into quarters.

"You look like you're about to kill somebody!" Olga said.

"Throw away the empty box, and go do your homework," I said, shoving the pieces of onion into the food processor.

"You can at least smile," said Olga.

Through my tears, I could see my distorted reflection in the curved side of the food processor. A Russian peasant woman. Kitchen slave. I looked at the butcher knife in my hand.

"Next time I'm just going to buy the ground beef," I told the reflection, looking up to save my mascara.

I had no appetite. All I could make myself eat was an apple, and I never finished it. Before bedtime, Nick recited a poem about Mr. Armstrong:

> "'He went on a rollercoaster as tall as the sky
> and into the outer space he did accidentally fly
> and then he dipped so low
> that right to the other side of the Earth he landed—Oh!
> The end.'

Do you like it?"

"I love it."

I patted Nick's wiry sandy-red hair. I was born a redhead, too. I purred into his ear:

"There was a little girl
And she had a little curl
Right in the middle of her forehead
When she was good,
She was very, very good
But when she was bad she was horrid."

"I am not a girl!" said Nick.

I turned his light off and went to the living room to write down everything that had happened that day. Instead, I picked up my wedding picture in its mother-of-pearl frame and looked into my own eyes. I ordered the photographs in black-and-white, and the staged scene looked vintage. Was it really me? These were my elongated eyes, my mouth stretched in a perfect bridal smile, my gloved hand clutching on Luke's stiff hand. Yet, I looked like a lifelike doll, a broken doll in a white satin dress. Then, I looked at the unfinished apple on my desk. It was floating like a bloody sun in the ocean of quivering fog.

MOTHER'S DAY

Sunday was Mother's Day, the same as many Mother's Days. On Mother's Day, I did not make *vareniki*. Instead, I was treated to breakfast in bed.

I smelled something burning in the kitchen, but didn't get to eat for a good hour. My stomach was grumbling, and I went to the bathroom and put my mascara on while waiting.

"Mom, where are you?!" shouted Olga. "Back into the bed!"

She dropped a plate with steaming waffles on the blanket.

"Wow, look at this shape! I see the USSR map," I said. "Thanks!"

Roxanne followed with runny eggs on the red ceramic tray she'd made herself, and Nick carried strawberries with puffs of whipped cream and a handmade card with an armadillo family portrait in green crayon. The card read: *"Dear Mommy, Thankyou for all you doo for me. I love you."* Luke brought a rainbow-hued vase with lilies and roses, and a flower dust fragrance mixed with the burnt waffle scent. He pecked me on the cheek, his lips cold.

"We have a surprise for you," he said. "But eat first."

"I love the armadillo mama," I told Nick. "She's chubby."

"You are chubby," said Nick, eating the last strawberry off the plate.

He started jumping up and down.

"Eat faster! Let's see the surprise!" he sang.

With my mug in my hand I went to the garage, followed by everyone else, all of us still in our pajamas. In the corner I saw an object the size of Nick, covered with a salad-green tablecloth.

"Guess what it is!" said Nick.

"A real armadillo!"

"Better! A robot!"

Nick pulled the tablecloth off and stood next to the robot, his ears crimson-red.

In the fake daylight of the garage, the robot looked like a monster. It had a tank for a base and the body of an alien. Its metallic skull was grinning at me, and made me think of the *Terminator* movie.

"You like it?" asked Nick.

"It's pretty cool," I said, walking around it.

"Boring," said Olga.

"You're boring," said Nick. "You have whipped cream on your nose."

"Stop it," said Roxanne. "It's Mother's Day."

Potemkin came over to the robot and sniffed it.

"Look at her tail," said Olga. "She hates it."

"Mom, push this button."

I pushed the red button and the robot jerked and moved forward. Potemkin hissed and jumped away.

"I just love my robot," said Nick.

Luke patted him on the shoulder.

"It's you and me, bud," he said to Nick. "Girls don't get it. Even Potemkin."

"We get it," I said. "Let's go."

It was my choice of activities, and no one could argue: we were to go to a museum and then for a walk.

"You not taking a shower?" asked Luke.

"I took one last night," I lied.

I didn't wash my hair. I didn't even brush it. I just reapplied my lipstick.

We went to the Academy of Sciences, a new building—all glass and light. It was drizzling, and fragile Chinese ladies in the amphitheater in front of the museum danced with fans to a long sad song. The sound lingered in my ears as we entered the enormous building. Then it died away, crushed by the thousand voices screaming and bursting underneath the cupola roof.

"Mom, did you know that they made the insulation from recycled jeans?" asked Nick, jumping up and down on his right foot. "Ms. Jenkins told us that. She said we could collect cardboard and shopping bags, and—"

"Boring! Can we go to a café?" asked Olga. "I want a brownie!"

"You didn't come to a museum to eat," I said. "Go look at seahorses."

"Why seahorses, Honey?" asked Luke, smiling.

I shrugged, "Why not?"

"I want to see the white alligator," said Nick. "Daddy, daddy, let's see the alligator."

"You go," I said, "I'll look at the seahorses."

Only instead of the aquarium, I went into a traditional diorama room. It was empty. No oddities. No overweight preteens taking pictures with their cell phones. I was alone in the room, surrounded by stuffed dead animals. Gorillas, zebras, leopards, lions froze behind glass, shredding each other to pieces, drinking out of a plastic lake, stretched in a jump, swinging from a palm tree. Their unmoving glass eyes fixed on me from every direction, and I felt a draft coming from the door, cooling the back of my neck.

Still, I felt better in that room. Life was captured here, like in a snapshot. It was simple. I could see every eyelash on the prehistoric cow's eye, and every hair on the Neanderthal man's knobby head, every wrinkle on his flat nose. A lifeless landscape, miniscule seeds on the barren ground, two prehistoric ants dragging a black stick: death was soothing and easy.

Another diorama pulled me in: a man with the same flat nose and protruding jaw, his long yellow teeth sunken into a chunk of red flesh—perhaps, the leg of a butchered cow. There was something familiar in his soft yellow penis hanging between his hairy legs, in the veins bulging on his short neck, in his stooping shoulders.

"Well hello, Best Boy," I said to the Neanderthal.

"Hello!"

I looked back. Ms. Freckle in her denim overalls stood behind me, the binocular glasses in their metallic frames steaming. Two red-haired girls Nick's age pulled her by her hands and out of the hall. They also wore denim overalls, and I thought of the insulation made of blue jeans. The woman waved her hands as if drowning and disappeared in the doorway.

"Happy Mother's Day," I muttered after her. "You're always around."

"Mommy, did you see Lucy? Lucy and Gina Coppola?"

Nick skipped into the hall, and the entranced space disappeared.

"I hate Lucy! Come look at what I found in the store."

"Where are the girls?" I asked Luke.

"In the café," he said. "I think. I gave them five bucks, for both of them. It's such a rip-off here."

I joined Nick in the hallway. He was skipping and hopping over the map of China.

"I found a robotic bug," said Nick. "Daddy's going to buy it for me next time!"

Afterwards we went for a walk in our favorite place, Lands End.

The cypress and eucalyptus aroma mixed with the salty air; the glittery expanse of the ocean, the gray indifferent rocks and lustful, lonesome screams of foghorns and ship sirens—for a few moments I was back in Odessa, breathing in the Black Sea.

"What are you staring at, Mom?" cried Nick. "Let's go!"

I was looking down at the wooden steps going down to the Sutro Baths ruins, but I was seeing different steps.

Odessa Steps.

The Sutro Steps were like the Odessa Steps, and yet not.

I looked down, and saw a trail of ants on the ground. The ants fussed around in a frenzy, one carrying a stick, another carrying the carcass of a dead bug, two more fighting over the body of another ant. I crouched and watched their orderly life, their chores and calamities, tiny victories and failures. Clueless, oblivious to being watched, sad and brave in their determination and phony sense of purpose, they were frightening in the meaninglessness of their little lives.

I straightened my knees and looked up again, at the wide expanding landscape swallowing the world, seeming even bigger than it was. I heard voices in my head:

"Who am I?"

"Everything is so unreal."

"Am I dreaming? Or am I someone's dream? A dream within a dream?"

The beach at my feet evoked the haunted beach of my nightmares. I saw ant-like figures here and there along the water line, and then made out Luke and the kids in the distance, but I couldn't see their faces. Their features were vague, as if they were present, yet absent.

Roxanne silently appeared behind me. She was looking at the steps, too.

"In Odessa we had Potemkin Steps," I said.

"Potemkin, like our cat?"

"Yes, and like a ship called Potemkin. I'll show you this old silent movie one day. *Battleship Potemkin*. One day, when you grow up."

I thought that maybe I wouldn't. For me, The Steps were all about my sister, and her Steps nightmare.

She was eight and I was six when Grandfather took us to the movies. Despite Grandfather's suede beret and burgundy scarf, it was a hot and steamy July night. Bottle-green flies buzzed around melting ice-cream cones. The door to the movie house was propped with a beer cart to let in fresh air. I fell asleep in the lazy murkiness of the hall, but my sister watched *Battleship Potemkin*. Grandma Rosa was convinced that the scarlet fever my sister came down with that very night came from the ice cream and the draft in the cinema.

We had a dark, oval mirror over the couch. I remembered looking up at it, catching a glimpse of Oksana's red face, sweat beads on the bridge of her nose, colorless strands of hair glued to her cheeks. She was rolling in her bed, lisping, whispering, screaming, crying, asking to save the baby, catch the baby, stop the stroller, stop the soldiers, stop the stairs. I half-sat, half-lay next to her, holding her hot wet palm, and cried, taking quick looks at the mirror when she stopped.

"You will never take her to the movies again," said Grandma, holding a vinegar-soaked towel to Oksana's forehead, fanning her with the PRAVDA newspaper, and trying to pour water into her mouth with a silver spoon, her grandmother's monogram glistening in the dim light.

Grandfather never took us anywhere else. He died that same year, in October, fell off a scaffolding. Every year he was commissioned, along with a team of bearded artists, to paint a palace-sized portrait of Lenin for the November military parade. Grandfather died, suede beret and burgundy scarf on, a brush in the tobacco-stained fingers of one hand, and a bottle of vodka in the other, without having finished Lenin's eye.

Oksana used to have this nightmare for years afterwards.

"I'm there, running the stairs, running up when everyone is running down, and the stairs are moving, like in the metro, it's moving down and down... The very worst part is not the baby, and not the maggots in meat, it's the mother running down the stairs alone after her boy had been shot. She forgets—and I can't reach the top," she once told me on an early foggy morning, just before she left us.

I didn't tell Roxanne any of that. Instead, I said, "I loved standing on top of the Steps. If you looked down at the landings, they melted like a sour cream honey cake, all layered, you know?"

"Fantasy cake?"

I nodded, "And the funny thing is, you only saw the landings, not the steps. It looked so short."

"I'm cold," said Roxanne.

I put my arm around her, and thought how small and slight her boyish body was, how fragile and angular were her shoulder blades, as if she were growing wings.

"Come here, my little bird," I said, and we stood there looking down.

"But, you know, when you went down, and looked up," I said, "you only saw steps, and no landings. It seemed endless."

"Why?" whispered Roxanne, looking up at me.

"An optical illusion. My Grandpa used to explain it to us. False perspective. The bottom stairs wider than the top ones, so it creates the illusion of endlessness."

"Why did they do it?"

We were whispering, although no one could hear us.

"It was designed by an Italian architect. He wanted to do something different, I guess."

She shrugged.

"Maybe he felt that life was an illusion," I said. "I sometimes feel that way."

I ran my eyes over the limp shadows, over the rocks devoured by the ocean, over the pelicans perched on the rocks far away, then over the stairs.

"You know, I used to imagine my life like the Odessa Steps."

I hugged Roxanne, and kissed her ink-black hair.

I thought that when she's grown up, I'd tell her about the night after my sister's funeral. That night, I went down the stairs and I knew it was all wrong. The pink-and-gray granite lay still underneath my boots. The landings were empty. As I reached the bottom of the stairs and looked up at the endless steps, my whole life felt like an illusion, a nearly constant hallucination.

"Mom, I want a tattoo," said Roxanne. "On my wrist."

"Let's go already," screamed Olga. "Really!"

"Coming," I heard myself saying.

In the evening, we all settled on the couch to watch *American Idol*. Nick brought the robot in from the garage, and Luke balanced his beer bottle on its square head. Potemkin settled on the other side of the couch.

I rarely watched TV, and instead of watching, I looked at my children, entranced by the cheerleading voices of their idols. Olga sprawled at the couch, sugar cookies in her lap, chatting about her crush on the fifteen-year-old singer with slick brown hair and a Michael Jackson hip swing. Roxanne was not saying much, just bit her black-and-blue nails, but two uneven rose clouds appeared on her cheeks, and she smiled, which made her look like a sad raccoon with braces. Nick settled in my lap, fidgeting, mimicking the performers, and bombarding us with questions.

"Why does that guy in pink talk like a woman?" he asked.

"He's gay," said Olga. "Too bad, he's so cute!"

"What's gay?" asked Nick.

"When man marries a man," said Olga.

"Why?"

All three kids stared at me. Olga giggled. Luke took a sip out of his beer bottle, and started to read the label.

"Well, people can be attracted to men or women, it doesn't really matter. Some men are attracted to women, and some to men. Like this guy—"

They kept staring. Olga rolled her eyes and made a farting sound with her full lips.

"He's sick, that's why," she said.

"Oh, no," I said. "It's not that."

"Maybe, he liked his Daddy too much," said Nick.

Luke stood up and went to the kitchen to get himself another beer. Potemkin followed him.

"Hey, this girl looks like Olga," said Nick. "Only she's not fat."

"Don't speak like that about your sister," I said. "And don't point, it's rude."

Olga slapped Nick's sticking-out ear, and he kicked her.

"Stop," said Roxanne, without a smile. "She does look like Olga. I want her tattoo."

"Shh, listen," I said, raising my finger.

A blood-chilling guttural scream was coming from outside.

"A baby?"

"There aren't any babies on our block. And it's not crying, it's howling."

"Maybe it's a ghost," said Nick.

"Yeah, a vampire," said Olga, giggling.

Nick jumped off the couch and ran to the window.

The sound was swelling into a siren.

"I only see Vanessa."

"Maybe Vanessa turned into a vampire. She's always alone," I said.

I joined Nick by the window. Vanessa was struggling with her green recycling bin.

"You're not too kind, Honey," said Luke, staring at the TV. "She's by herself on Mother's Day."

"What, you want to invite her?"

We all looked at Vanessa. Every week—year round—on garbage day, Vanessa in her eggplant kimono dragged the green recycling bin to the driveway. Like an ant with a stick, I thought. A giant purple ant with a green stick.

"It's Sunday, right? Boy, they produce a lot of garbage," I said. "What is she going to do next week? Start a recycling plant?"

"She can make insulation out of it," said Nick.

Luke came up to the window, too.

"She's just planning ahead," he said. "Her house is pretty clean."

I looked at him, but he didn't look at me.

The howl resumed. Vanessa stopped, her ducky mouth half-open, and was listening, too.

"There," shouted Nick. "It's not a ghost. It's Potemkin. And Blossom."

He pointed at two spots gaping in the dusk: orange and dark, darker than the night.

"Don't point."

I saw four sparks—the eyes. The cats sat close to each other, not moving, and howled. I noticed that the amethyst light glowed behind them like an unknown star.

"They sound worse than *American Idol*," I said.

"How long are they going to do that?"

Vanessa blew us all an air kiss and walked back to her house, bouncing like a rubber duck.

"She must have been drinking alone again," I thought.

"Look, look! They're fighting!"

Slowly, Potemkin stood up. She arched her back, her tail fatter than her body. She opened her mouth and hissed, but we didn't hear it, just saw it.

"Kill!" said Luke.

Then, as if nothing happened, Potemkin turned around and strolled away, swaggering like Vanessa, with her signature indifferent walk, short tail sticking up like an antenna. I thought that Potemkin was like a spy from an alien world. She was here at hand without honoring us with her actual presence, without disclosing her secret self to us, or to anyone.

Blossom, probably, felt the same as he fixed his unblinking eyes at the exclamation point of her posterior view, at her neat and scornful butthole. He looked lost: the object of his fury was moving away slumber-like, drifting out of the arena, just as he prepared for the fight.

"Bravo, Potemkin," I said. "Never stoop down to your opposition's level."

"Who won?" asked Nick.

"Technically, Blossom," said Luke. "He stayed in his territory."

"It's impossible, Potemkin's invincible. It's just a maneuver," I said. "She's above the fight."

After the kids left to get ready for bed, I looked at Luke. He looked into my eyes, his water-grey eyes wide, like two lakes, and I almost asked him, "What's the meaning of life?" when Luke looked away, scratched his neck and said, "Honey?"

"Yeah?"

For a moment, I thought we were feeling the same way.

"Honey, I hate to ask, but what do you do with the money?"

It took me a minute to understand.

"Oh, that. There's hardly any money left after the pedicures and skin care," I waved my red nails in the air. "What, you want me to pay the mortgage with dungeon bucks?"

He shrugged. "Just asking, that's all."

"How do people talk to each other?" I thought.

I went into Roxanne's room and settled on the bed by her feet.

"What did you do back home for Mother's Day?" asked Roxanne, hugging her toy black cat.

"We didn't have Mother's Day, sweetheart. Only the 8th of March, International Women's Day. For all women. A kind of celebration of all women."

"For what?"

I paused.

"Good question. Just... for being women, I guess. After all, it's not easy, is it?"

We both sighed.

"And you know, my mom died when I was so young, anyway. I'm glad we didn't have Mother's Day."

"Tell me about her, Mom."

Roxanne was the only person I could talk to about my mom.

"Well, you've heard this story a hundred times. We were in the car… This truck ran into us. She died right away. I can't remember her at all, Sweetie, I was only three years old. I kept imagining her but I can never get her face, all's covered with mist—"[1]

"But you say I look like her!"

"You saw the pictures; I think you do. She was very beautiful. Just like you. Good night, Sweetie. Thanks for a great day."

"Mom. Tell me something," she whispered, looking away.

"Yes, Sweetie?"

"Did—did your mom leave you?"

I hit her. My hand missed, and struck the pillow behind her. A small feather flew up and floated in the air. I watched its snowflake descent, then closed my eyes. Roxanne didn't look at me and didn't move. I took her black cat, and patted it. Then I took her hand in mine, and touched a fake blue tattoo on her wrist: an angry cobra, forked tongue out.

"I'm sorry," I said. "I would never leave you."

I thought, "Why, how did my mom leave me? Was I that bad?"

Olga was on the phone.

"Hold on a second," she said into her phone, and covered it with her pink hand. "Good night, Mom."

---

[1] It was difficult, but possible, to understand her father's betrayal and be angry with him; but it was unthinkable that her mother was neglectful or abandoning. Deeper into the analysis, this seems to be **the major trauma of Rose's childhood!** Rose cannot remember her mother, who only exists in her memory as an idealized creation. Like most children whose parents die at a young age, Rose idealizes her mother to protect herself from the tremendous pain of her loss. The developing psyche is incapable of understanding and accepting death.

I kissed her on her hot damp forehead, brushed her weightless hair back, and left, listening to a quick whisper behind me.

Nick was asleep, lying across the bed, with one foot dangling over the edge.

"Nick," I whispered.

No answer.

"It's me, your armadillo mama. On the rollercoaster, Nick, all alone... between outer space and the underworld."

I pushed him to the middle of the bed, his arms thrown open, and he kicked me with his foot, and mumbled in a faraway voice of a deep sleep. I kissed his little seashell of an ear, pulled up the navy blue bedspread, and tiptoed back to the living room.

I went to my desk and looked at my mom's only surviving photograph.

I never really looked at it. She was flying on the swings, her strong but not thick ankles crossed, hands clasping the chains—like a lock, hanging on for dear life, I thought, smiling with only the left corner of her mouth, forehead forward, like a bull, her braids and floral dress floating behind her like a flag. I never found out her exact age in this picture, but I liked to think that she was sixteen—clueless, careless and, it seemed to me, cruel.

I wondered if my mother had ever leaned over my sleeping hot body, tucking me in, pushing my bangs from my eyes, burning with the same intense desperate desire to cover, hold and defend, and aching from the tragic inability to do anything but wave and blow an air kiss into the monstrous ocean of the future.

Potemkin came over and rubbed her ear against my leg.

"Hey, girlfriend," I said. "Good girl. Good job with Blossom."

She started to purr.

"You know, Potemkin? You do, you know everything, without knowing anything—"

I looked into my mother's face, trying to imagine the color of her eyes, the shape of her nose, the texture of her skin. The picture was black and white and unfocused, and I could only see her in a haze. I didn't know what color her eyes were—sea-blue-green like mine and Oksana's? Steel gray like Grandma Rosa's? Washed-out hazel like Grandpa's? I'd never know. I'd never know anything about her.

Everything I knew as a child was a lie. She didn't die in a car accident, as Grandma Rosa told us for years. My cousin Inna told me the truth, when I was twenty.

My mother killed herself. She overdosed on sleeping pills and vodka. A hung-over janitor found her body on the empty Odessa Steps on a Monday morning, a week after our father left her. We were three and five at the time; she was twenty-six. I couldn't think about it for more than a few seconds before my head started to split and the Misty Lilac hung before my eyes. I put the photograph down.

Potemkin purred like a tiger.

"You are so full of yourself, Potemkin. You think you are... The Cat. And you are. My only buddy."

I scratched her ear.

"Although, you know what? Don't be jealous. I do have some new girlfriends now. At work."

CLEANING THE DUNGEON

Monday was my turn to clean the dungeon. I organized the rattraps and mousetraps next to the clothespins. Susanna sat next to me on the cold vinyl of the bed, almost touching me with her arm, and tossed a box of Clorox wipes between us. She picked up a mousetrap, making a clicking sound.

"These are good to scare clients… Click-click…"

She started to wipe it, and then put it down and said, in her usual aloof way, "You know, on Saturday I actually used it on a client for the first time…"

Her calm olive-green eyes were close, and I looked at them, but not through them. She hardly blinked.

"You look… you look like a cat," I said. "An Egyptian cat."

"Really?" she laughed, still looking right into my eyes. "I always considered myself a bird. An ibis."

"No, no, you are not a bird at all. I'm a bird. You're a cat, you have… catness."

Susanna clicked the mousetrap and meowed.

"You're like my cat. Her name's Potemkin."

Susanna and Potemkin. Diehard confidence in every move, from licking the tail to biting into a sandwich. The secret knowledge of their realness. The lack of doubt in their existence. I sighed. Never, ever had I had such security.

"So, do I get to catch you?" she asked very calmly. "You're a bird, right?"

She was very close; I could hear her even breathing and smell her clean scent—like fresh laundry, *Free and Clear*. I moved a bit, and looked down at a mousetrap.

"Why did you use it on a client?" I said, blushing. "And, how?"

"Oh."

She paused.

"Well, you know the mousetraps that the pest control guy installed in the kitchen? Six little mice got caught alive, and Mommy and I are the only ones working Saturdays—it's actually nice, so peaceful—and she's squeamish, and I'm a vegetarian…"

"Me, too."

"So this lawyer client helped out. Do you want to know how he did it?"

"Not really."

"Well, he 'asphyxiated' them—one by one… That's what he said. He said he did it before—at home for his wife. He was laughing. Jerk. I took one huge rattrap and gave him a good CBT session. Imagine. And I'm practically a vegan…"

I methodically arranged the dildos by size and color in the labeled drawers, taking yoga breaths and hoping my nausea would calm down.

"Do not mess this up. Mommy is a self-proclaimed neat freak."

Susanna weighed a transparent purple dildo in her hand.

"Psychedelic," she said. "Love the color."

"Do you—use anything like that?" I asked her.

I felt myself blushing again. I hadn't blushed so much in years.

Susanna narrowed her eyes.

"I used to," she said. "Recently, though—I guess I didn't, no, not for a while."

We kept wiping dildos for a while in silence.

I coughed and started to say, "Yesterday, on TV—" when Susanna spoke up, too.

"I used to have those daydreams all the time. My mother wouldn't let me close the door to my room, and I was afraid to masturbate, but then I figured out how to do it quietly, and also during the day, when everyone thought I was reading. So I'm kind of used to my own devices."

"It's all in your head," I said.

"And your hand," she laughed her musical laughter.

Talking to her felt all hot inside. I saw gentle rose spots on her cheeks.

"Not mine. I—I can't touch myself there," I said. "Feels funny."

"You're kidding me. You had kids, right?"

"Doesn't matter."

"So, what, you never masturbate?"

In her mouth the question sounded as innocent as, "So, what, you never drink coffee?" but I felt myself blushing again, this time crimson red. Susanna used the word with ease and elegance, the way she folded towels and pulled on stockings, but I felt like a bear in a china shop, and had the feeling that someone was standing over my shoulder, listening to our conversation and shaking her head in disbelief.

I nodded. I had a hook and a chain in my hand, and was cleaning them with a Clorox wipe, so I pretended to examine them. Susanna reached for the freshly dry-cleaned lacy curtains.

"What is this?" I asked, picking up a sharp metallic object in a shape of a question mark.

"Come on," she laughed. "I asked you first."

"I do," I managed to say, finally. "In a bathtub, you know, or there's always a blanket—"

Susanna looked at me and laughed, and I started to laugh, too.

A SPY FANTASY

"C'mon, girls, how many mistresses does it take to hang curtains? We have clients to work with here! The Spy for Susanna and Rose! Hurry up!" grumbled Mommy.

"Fun," smiled Susanna. "Read the card."

The card read: *Name: Gene. Fantasy: He is a foreign spy. Two girls grab him by his arms, kick him behind the knees, make him fall to his knees, and look for money that he's hidden.*[1] *Commands: "Bring more!" "Kneel down!" "Take it here!" "Put it there!" "No I don't want it!" "Slow, torturous death... You are going to die."*

The session was held in the Dungeon. The spy turned out to be a fragile, red-faced man in his seventies. He had the radiant blue eyes of an iconic saint and an infectious laugh. He offered us a bottle of Moet champagne and two glasses.

"It's a bribe,"[2] he chuckled.

---

[1] **The money is the equivalent of feces**, and Gene's deviation is rooted in a possible arrest at the stage of toilet training. Sex is purchased, similar to the bargain of his early childhood: "You go potty and Mommy will love you. You don't go potty, Mommy won't love you!" Feces are the first "gifts" or "savings," the first creative expression of oneself, the first power act that a child can give or withhold.

[2] **Analytic Narrative:** Gene is not just buying sexual services from a professional dominatrix; he is purchasing them piece by piece, bargaining, negotiating. This strategy follows the pattern of the stock exchange and illustrates the anal-retentive character of his personality. Gene might have suffered from constipation as a child; his mother was preoccupied with his bowel movements and controlled him through elimination. She gave him medication and a "bribe," "tortured" Gene to produce stool (locked in the bathroom until he is "done") and watched him. Thus, the toilet training turned into a power play and his first experience of **purchasing love**.

I hesitated, but Susanna gulped hers down, so I followed her example and soon felt all bubbly and lightheaded. As we tumbled between the ob-gyn table and the golden-shower tray, Susanna transformed.

Her angelic face twisted, she scowled; her pupils widened, making her olive-green eyes almost black. Her upper lip twitched and raised and for the first time I noticed her sharp, uneven teeth, like those of a small rodent—a squirrel, maybe. Her gentleness was gone; she'd turned into a wicked, bloodsucking witch, and once again reminded me of Potemkin, Potemkin the Huntress, a dying mouse hanging from her bloodstained teeth.

"We are mean! Nasty! Baaad!"

Her voice was bubbling, like the champagne we were drinking. I felt adrenaline rushing through my veins and my heart pulsing.

"I will *torrrturrre* you in a KGB way! You will *forrrget* your own name!"

I caught a glimpse of my burning face in the mirror next to Susanna's; all we'd need in order to fly was two brooms. Susanna cursed and spit and grunted. We were shouting, hitting, kicking, fighting, hurting,[1] and it felt breathtakingly sweet. We drank more champagne, and pushed the old man around on the floor. He was laughing like a baby and shoving dollars into our thongs...

---

[1] **Analytic Narrative:** Gene grew up during World War II and played "war" and "spy" games with other boys. He experienced his first erections during these romping and wrestling childhood games. In his adult fantasies, the "torture" of these games and the "torture" of toilet training are united. Women in the dungeon are substitutes for both the Big Monster Mother and the strong boys of his childhood.

As we were on top of the old man I felt Susanna's hot soft belly pressing to my hip. Something inside me moved quickly. I looked up at her, and for a moment our eyes locked. I felt her hand sliding down my leg, and her finger touching me there, and felt her sour champagne breath on my cheek. My head went round. For a moment I was dying to melt in her arms, kiss her glistening lips, pull down her silky thong. She smiled and moaned—and then the old guy turned underneath us, giggling, and I quickly jumped to my feet.

"Give me *yourrr* money, or I will cut off *yourrr* balls and stick them in *yourrr* mouth," I said.

Still looking into my eyes, Susanna reached her hand down, between Gene's legs.

After the session was over, Gene tipped us generously.

"You are my favorite client," I whispered to him at the end.

I avoided looking at Susanna.

Upstairs, we found Mommy standing on her kitchen counter, puffing on her pipe, painting the wall. I went to the bathroom and took a long time lathering my hands with lavender soap, my feet, my face, my ears, rinsing them with freezing water. I zoned out and lost all sense of time.

When I finally stumbled back to the waiting room, Mommy was still painting the kitchen.

"Where's Zoe?"

"In a session, with Greta observing. They need to get on better terms."

Susanna was stretched out on the floor, her eyes closed, her face back to angelic. I tiptoed across the carpet and settled as far away from Susanna as I could, still jittery with champagne, adrenaline, and shame.

"Am I sick?" I thought, and, to distract myself, opened **DE-VIATIONS**.

The first page was a full-page headshot of a burly man in a peony-pink shirt opened to the chest—a bit too seductively for a scientist. An ornate signature in black ink—dots and loops—flew across the lower-right corner of the page: Michael H. Strong, Ph.D.

"He looks like a client," I thought. "Oh, well. They all look the same after a while, really."

Dr. Michael H. Strong rested his goatee on his disproportionally small fist, a sparkle inside his plum-brown eyes, hypnotizing the readers, or maybe tempting them.

I browsed through the introduction: "Through flagellation, cross-dressing and excrement play, the BDSM underworld rebels against the predetermined path of mindless existence." [1]

I dozed off, and had a brief dream of many men sprinting through Mommy's house. Some of them were naked, some wore office suits and ties, some wore coveralls, some were dressed in military uniforms—and some were dead, just skeletons wearing nothing at all. One of them was Michael H. Strong, in his peony-pink shirt and no pants.

---

[1] Rose leaves out an important part of the Introduction to **DEVIATIONS**: "Like great Zen masters, deviants explode the bondage of reality and break free from the chains of the everyday life. They are the Masters of their lives, and Slaves only to their passions."

"The real slaves are the mediocre majority, blindly serving the established clockwork mechanism of survival and procreation. **The only way to become truly human is through freeing our energies, rising above good and evil and becoming what we are.**"

When I woke up, Mommy was back, smoking a joint, mumbling: "This is not red. It's pussy-red... Got to change it. It's my bloody bedroom, not my bloody pussy! Ah, Rose! Listen. Mike the Motherfucker is coming for you at four. He's tried every single girl I've ever hired. Now this guy—he's a psychologist himself, and he plays with your head. I don't like him."

She took a drag, and did not speak for a while.

"I told him you're not ready, but he really wants you and no one else, Rose. I don't know, though, if you can handle him. You've got to be careful. If he wants to get on the cross, put him there and put a rope around his neck. He will pull on the rope, and play dead. Whip him, but watch him. Like a hawk, hear me? He might faint on you, he gets off on it..."

"Why 'motherfucker?'" I wondered.

I found the card. It was brief, made in a handwriting I hadn't seen before, and had a somewhat mysterious note: *"lots of pain. 'Motherfucker.' Ask him: what did you do? Fantasy: varied. Autoerotic asphyxiation.*[1] *Be careful."*

"The bitch was so scared she never made the card right."

"Why was she scared?"

"Don't know. She was a nervous type. She quit right after that. He said or did something... off. Never mind, just watch him carefully and call for help if you need to. Call him 'motherfucker,' he likes that.[2] Give him his pain, but take it easy. And stop bothering me with questions."

---

[1] **Autoerotic asphyxiophilia** involves the reduction and/or cutting off the oxygen supply to the brain. It can result in loss of consciousness, brain damage, and death.

[2] Most likely Mike has a history of **childhood asthma**. His mother could have slept in bed with him until an unusually late age (ten or eleven) in order to be able to care for him during night occurrences of asthma attacks.

Mommy went out to the porch and slammed the door behind her.

Susanna sat up, wide awake.

"I don't know about that one, Rose," she said. "I heard from one girl he's a scientist and that he experiments on us, sort of like lab mice; that he actually does this for his research.[1] But another girl heard he was either a former FBI guy or a foreign spy and had survived torture. Somebody else thought he was a prince in some Arabic country, or an assassin or something."

"Assassin, or prince?"

"Oh well, you know. He certainly looks both. Xenia told me that he was a famous writer. She played his favorite sister and otherwise didn't want to say what he did to her... And I know he used to make Mommy play his mother, but she stopped seeing him."

She looked away.

"What about you? What did he do with you?"

For a moment her face took on a squirrel expression again, her pearl teeth showing.

It is not unheard of for mothers of asthmatic children to tie them to the bed to prevent suffocation. If that was the case, little Mike suffered the triple pain of the following: nocturnal erections linked with the need to urinate; the paroxysmal breathing blockage of asthma attacks; and the intense sense of loss of his mother. At puberty, Mike might have associated the paroxysmal discharge of orgasm with the paroxysmal breathing blockage of his asthma attacks, and masturbated excessively to soothe his anxieties.

[1] If this dungeon legend is correct, and in the unlikely event that Mike is an actual scientist, his "research" is a compromised formation. Like the emergency room surgeon, the plumber, and the mistresses, this "scientist" chooses his occupation because it allows him to deal with his conflicts.

"I smoked so much pot after that session, I can hardly remember him."

She looked at the bookshelf.

"Susanna? Please?"

"Fine. With me, he was my Daddy. I was his little girl. We lived in a mountain hut in the snow, far away from the world, and I had to sit on his lap. And then he put my nightie around his neck and played dead," she said. "The guy is seriously troubled. They say strangling makes orgasm better, but the strangling would be the easiest thing about his session."

She closed her eyes, but kept talking: "Don't believe anything he says. Half the girls quit after a session with him... It's a test."

"It would be okay to fail that test," I said.

"What do you mean?" asked Susanna.

She opened her eyes and looked at me with a blank expression.

"I... I don't like to inflict pain," I mumbled.

"Then you're in the wrong place, Rose," said Susanna.

"Maybe I am," I answered.

I decided I could quit that day. The Motherfucker could easily be my last customer. I had enough material to write a novel about a prostitute, actually enough material to write about a dozen of them.

"I'm writing a book, Susanna," I said. "I am writing a book."

She raised her eyebrows, "So? I want to write a book, too."

"It is *me* who is writing my book. Not some motherfucking character *in* my book."

"I don't get you."

"I don't want to be a character in some other motherfucker's book, you know?"

For a moment I stopped. A quick succession of thoughts flashed in my mind: What if I was a character in somebody's else novel? And the author was yet another character in a novel on a universal scale? I shooed the thoughts off and said, "And I didn't plan on becoming a dominatrix, to be totally honest. I can't stand pain, and I'm scared."

Susanna crawled to me. She didn't get up, didn't raise her body at all, just slid over the carpet to me, one hand forward, one knee forward, then another, like a soldier or a stripper. Then she wrapped her arms around me, and gave me a full kiss on my mouth. Explosive, hot, French kiss. I felt her small smooth teeth, her tongue like an eel, swimming in me.

I forgot to close my eyes, and watched her transparent blue eyelids trembling, pearl eyelashes fluttering. I forgot to put my arms around her, but I returned her kiss. Everything was unreal, I was dreaming. Or was I in someone else's dream? A dream within a dream?

"You taste like cherries," whispered Susanna.

The doorbell rang.

"Good luck," said Susanna.

MIKE THE MOTHERFUCKER

I would never forget Mike the Motherfucker. He was the most common-looking man imaginable, yet everything about him was peculiar.[1] A billiard-ball bald head, a dark goatee, an Armani suit, and an iridescent tangerine silk scarf sticking out from the open collar of his shirt like a tongue. I could see both an assassin and a king: his slightly aquiline nose and the sensual mouth of a spoiled child seemed too aristocratic for his pudgy face, and yet he was probably stopped by the airport security as a terrorist suspect. He charged forward with force and bounce, like a firefighter on a mission, almost scaring me, and yet I couldn't help staring at his moustache and beard, which were trimmed with the precision and care of a designer rose garden. His expensive French perfume filled me with a long-forgotten memory of Odessa. It smelled of acacias.

I was wearing my signature Rose platform stilettos, standing six-foot-three, but as we walked into the Boudoir I noticed in the mirror that he still towered over me, even though he was stooping. I had a mind-splitting déjà-vu feeling; something about him bothered me and made him seem unreal, but then everything seemed unreal most of the time. I knew I had seen him before, and quite recently.

I still felt the minty taste of Susanna's kiss. Mike looked at me with such attention, intensity, and warmth that I took a step back. For a split second, I imagined he knew about the kiss.

---

[1] For reasons unclear to me, Rose is unable to generalize her stereotypes of men onto Mike and to turn him into **the Big Monster Man**. She is noticing him as an individual and seems to be attracted to him.

"Sit down, Rose," said Mike in a low velvety voice. "Can we just talk? You seem so different from everybody else here."

He articulated each sound and paused after each sentence, the way actors and literature professors do, yet there was the vulgar ease of a midnight taxi driver in his speech.

"Aren't you going to undress?" I asked.

"No. I just want to talk to you. Here's the money. Relax. Sit down."

He sat on the chair in front of the toilet table, and I sat on the bed.

"I want to learn more about you, Rose. What are you doing here?"

"Working, motherfucker."

I said it quietly, just because the card had instructed me to do so, and I doubted if I'd gotten the wrong card for him.

"No, Rose, not now. None of that. Not necessary."

Mike smiled and blinked. His smile was a mixture of sadness, innocence, and wisdom; Lenin's smile, from the glossy portrait in our kindergarten canteen.

I used to have a secret fantasy that Lenin was my missing father. The gentle wrinkles around those knowing eyes shone with kindness, showered me with love, and made my heart ache as I stalled over my mashed potato and *kotlety*. Then Lenin had killed my grandfather, and as I missed Grandfather's wheezing breath and radio-deep voice, I learned to fear and hate Lenin, but I never forgot my first love. Grandpa Lenin, like Mike the Motherfucker, gave you the feeling that he understood you, or wanted to understand you, and loved you no matter what. A little girl in me longed to see those loving eyes, and I forgot all about Susanna, the minty kiss, and everything else.

"Your accent... Russian?"

"Ukrainian."

He nodded.

"What a great culture. I love Gogol... Reading *Dead Souls*—divine indulgence."

I stared at him in disbelief. No one I had met in America ever read, let alone indulged in, *Dead Souls*. And absolutely not a soul knew that Gogol was Ukrainian. Mike laughed softly, as if he'd read my mind.

"I'm a bookworm, Rose. You?"

"I... like to read."

"Of course you do. Your eyes brim with intellect. And pain. Flaming eyes. You speak other languages, right?"

"Not many. Ukrainian, Russian, French... Some."

"French..."

Then Mike the Motherfucker did something astonishing. He stood up in the middle of the Boudoir, stretched out his right hand so he looked like a revolutionary leader on an armored train, closed his eyes, and recited:

> *"Ô Mort, vieux capitaine, il est temps! levons l'ancre!*
> *Ce pays nous ennuie, ô Mort! Appareillons!*
> *Si le ciel et la mer sont noirs comme de l'encre,*
> *Nos coeurs que tu connais sont remplis de rayons!*
>
> *Verse-nous ton poison pour qu'il nous réconforte!*
> *Nous voulons, tant ce feu nous brûle le cerveau,*
> *Plonger au fond du gouffre, Enfer ou Ciel, qu'importe?*
> *Au fond de l'Inconnu pour trouver du nouveau!"*[1]

---

[1] *Oh Death, old captain, it is time! Weigh anchor!/ This country bores us, Death! Let's go! / The sky and the sea are black as ink, / But you know our hearts are overfilled with light! To revive us pour us your poison! / Our brains are burning, we want / To plunge into the depth of abyss, Hell or Heaven, who cares? / Into the depth of the Unknown to find the New!*

Baudelaire

How did he know? My grandmother used to read that to me. He rolled his *rrr*'s like she used to. I'd known this piece by heart since I was ten. Something shuddered inside of me. I forgot where I was. This man spoke my secret language and he gave me the magic word, an order, my Open Sesame, and it worked. Like a safeguarded vault to a secret code, I opened to him. He couldn't have been a mere mortal; he must have been a heavenly messenger from my forbidden world, open only to the chosen.

"Talk to me, Rose. Tell me about your pain."

I did not notice how he moved to the bed and lay down next to me. We were looking at the mirrored ceiling and talking like two siblings that had just gotten back together after being apart for years. He felt like my soulmate, like I'd waited for him all my life. Words poured out. I told him everything.[1] I told him stuff I'd never told anyone. I told him about writing. I told him about my sister.

---

[1] Rose is incapable of "telling everything." Even when she opens up, she chooses to disclose only part of her personality.

OKSANA, MY DEAD SISTER

Oksana was almost two years older. As kids, we were inseparable. We looked alike, only she had an ethereal quality that made her a true beauty, the rare type that makes people stop in the middle of the street and gasp.

Maybe it was her lazy eye. It always ran away and gave her a somewhat sleepy, mermaid look—her sea-green eyes were never focused. Maybe it was her smile, the smile of a child lost in a daydream. Sometimes I thought it was the Z-shaped scar that went across her forehead like lightning—thick and uneven, it almost turned her ugly, but ended up making her more beautiful. She fell from a cherry tree when she was five, picking cherries for me, shortly after our mom died. I still remembered her blood on my index finger, mixed with crushed cherries.

Whatever it was, men did stop when she was walking down Deribasovskaya, the main street of Odessa. She owned the street. I remember sudden fireworks of carnations, tulips, and roses at her bronze sandaled feet: a Georgian man in a white hat bought all the flowers from a gypsy on the corner and threw them at Oksana, as we were drinking hot chocolate from tiny porcelain cups under a chestnut tree. She was twelve. I had crushes, boyfriends, and short-lived romances, but I never broke hearts the way Oksana did, without even noticing them.[1] She did not care about hearts.

---

[1] **Sibling rivalry** and competition for parental love causes children to direct their aggressive impulse against their sibling.

It is possible that, as Rose was so murderously envious of her sister, she later felt guilty and responsible for Oksana's death. Envy causes fear and an impulse to destroy. This, in turn, can cause persecutory anxiety as the envied

Her dream was to be a prima ballerina, a star. Although she was way too tall for classical ballet, she danced the Snow Queen and Princess Aurora at school ballet productions and told me she was going to Moscow to dance professionally. She never did.

After Grandfather died, we all lived on Grandma's meager salary, and Oksana had to get a temp job as an ice-cream sales-girl the summer of her high school graduation. I remember her laughter ringing beneath the chestnut trees as she whipped up pistachio, strawberry, and crème-brûlée ice cream concoctions for dolled-up little girls and boys in sailor hats with *Battleship Potemkin* printed in the front, on the boulevard by the Opera Theater.

A stocky old man with a meaty face started coming in to buy ice cream. I remembered the first time he bought me a pistachio waffle cone, shoved it toward me with his sweaty crablike hand—fat, red fingers with short, almost non-existent fingernails—and told me to go away in a high-pitched, wom-anly voice. I hid in the cool shade of a street umbrella, invisible to them, and watched her laughing while he slowly licked his vanilla ice cream, his swine eyes fixed on her neck, no expres-sion on his face.

"I have never seen anyone more beautiful in my life," he told Oksana, and she just laughed back, like a movie star. I felt like we all were playing parts in a movie.

After work, he would pick Oksana up in a foreign-made emerald-green car and take her to Metropol, the most expen-

might discover the aggressive drive and avenge it. Rose attempts to repair her guilt by naming her first-born daughter after her sister and sending her to ballet classes, basically cloning Oksana and choosing her as her favorite child in order to fix the imaginary damage caused by her envy.

sive hard-currency hotel and restaurant in Odessa. He fed her chicken Kiev and poured her sparkling sour champagne, and she never stopped laughing.

In three weeks, he rented a four-bedroom apartment for her—antique chairs with lion paws, crystal chandeliers and midnight-blue velvet curtains—right on Deribasovskaya.[1] My grandmother marched there to claim Oksana, and I followed her, hiding behind taxicabs and chestnut trees. I would never forget her face on that day. Grandma Rosa never cried, not at her husband's funeral, not at her daughter's funeral; her colorless face never moved, not a muscle twitched, and her steely eyes were as dry as her gunshot cough.

Oksana was standing outside, in the dusty yellow yard, smoking a Vogue.

---

[1] Rose and Oksana have a conflicted and tenuous relationship with men because their father abandoned them. Both need and want men, but at the same time are afraid to trust them. They keep alive the rescue fantasy that the older, kind man will appear and save them and set right their lives. When candidates for this role appear in their lives, they have a hard time trusting them and instead expect betrayal. It is common for abandoned daughters with trust issues to end up with **pimps, sugar daddies, and older husbands and lovers**. These relationships are never intimate and never between equal adults; they often disintegrate in disappointment and betrayal. Certain types of men, such as Colonel Alexandrov, are very good at spotting young women in search of a rescuer and using them for their purposes.

Interestingly, not only abandoned children search for a rescuing father figure; this tendency underlies the worship whole nations establish toward certain political father figures such as Hitler, Stalin, or Mao—or less frequently, a mother figure like Eva Perón. It is tempting to agree with Nietzsche's and Freud's idea that the roots of religion originate in this eternal search for the parental figure.

In that even, poetry-rapping voice of hers, rolling her *rrr*-s more than ever, Grandma Rosa said, "Oksana. Throw away the cigarette and come home with me. Now. Or never."

I could almost hear a metronome measuring the rhythm.

Slowly, Oksana threw her cigarette away into the sandbox.

"No," she said. "I won't."

Moving like scissors, with precise explosive steps, Grandma Rosa turned around and walked back home. Once inside the door, she didn't stop to take her grey jacket off or to wash her hands. She walked straight to the bookshelf, and pulled photos off the shelf: Oksana, high school graduation photo, laughing through tulips; Oksana the baby—same shining eyes, the lace of the crib; Oksana, ballet performance, white tulle of her tutu dress, clenched hand pressed to her flat chest. Her lips moved, and I guessed more than heard, "And there's no defense from fate…" Even then she had to quote Pushkin.

"That one was me," I thought, as she lingered over a gray, vague image of a little girl at the top of the Steps. But I never said anything.

After that, I saw Oksana often, met her under old chestnut trees on the boulevards, and we drank hot chocolate, ate éclairs and overripe cherries from a white paper bag, shooed away bees and laughed at passersby as if nothing had happened, as if she had never left home. I would lean over to touch her new golden necklace or diamond bracelet, and rich, sticky cherry juice would drip from my fingers onto her blue jeans and her tanned toes, and she would slap me and laugh and smoke her slim Vogue cigarettes. She brought Chanel perfume for me, and food money for me and Grandma.

I refused to think about any of that, until one lazy May afternoon I walked to an abandoned garage in the corner of the schoolyard, where behind a huge linden tree, girls would smoke, taking turns to make sure no teachers were coming. I remember golden flecks of dust floating in the sun's rays, and slow, aching time—minutes melting like ice cream.

"You, stupid bitch," said Masha, a loud, freckled girl whose father was a captain and brought her chewing gum and deer-skin purses from Germany. "Get out of here, you Jewish dirt-bag."

I gasped.

"Slut," said a skinny, short girl next to her.

"You're a slut," echoed Masha. "My father saw you at the hotel bar. I heard him telling my mom, I know what you are. You're a *valutnaya prostitutka*, a hard-currency prostitute."

Odessa loved rumors.

I didn't say it was my sister; instead, I hit Masha right in her open mouth.

"Hooker, hooker," shouted the skinny girl, running away, her cigarette drawing an arch in the air.

I hit again and again and would not stop, until her freckled face was all red and her nose was bleeding and the older girls who came to smoke pulled me away. I had my first panic attack then, doubled in half in the corner of the hallway, unable to breathe, my stomach in knots, the bronze bust of Lenin watching me with a loving sparkle in his eyes. No one wanted to speak to me after that.

Our neighbors were talking, too. I was buying pickled watermelons and éclairs at Deribasovskaya Gastronom one Sunday morning, when I ran into Aunt Ludmila. I nodded to her, but she just pressed her bulldog face into the glass window-case. And then I heard her whispering to an obese woman in slippers next to her.

"She works for KGB," said Aunt Ludmila. "Her apart-ment's bugged."

I knew they were talking about Oksana.

"I know; she's a spy."

"No, seriously, she goes to Moscow to report to a very important KGB general."

"No, she just fucks him."

"Whore."

I turned around. Two women held a dry fish in their hands, turning it around, picking at its scales with their red fingernails.

As I passed by, my head high, I heard, "Whore!"

To me, my sister was an angel, and *they* were monsters.

After that, I simply refused to think about Oksana's life. I lived in My Fantasy World, where she had no life outside of the chestnut tree's shade and I only came to life with a book in my lap, falling through into the bright parallel world of my mind.

Five years passed, and there came a rumor that her KGB lover had left her, and that she was seeing a lot of men. I remember that bleak November day, Oksana in her red rain jacket, without her makeup or jewelry, a bruise under her tear-shaped eye. She didn't want to tell me anything, just chain-smoked her Vogues and gave me a thick roll of dollars that smelled like Chanel.

"I'm going to America. You won't see me for a little while."

I remember staring at the small burial mound of lipstick-stained Vogues on the faded grass, by her stiletto heel, and crying. It started to rain. I had no umbrella. Mascara got smudged all over my face.

"Don't cry, Little Bird," said Oksana, lifting my chin up with her gentle finger.

She pulled me into the telephone booth, then fished a golden mirror and a tattered toothbrush out of her purse.

"Let's make up our faces," she said.

The mascara, the needle, the peacock tail's eye quivered in my brain.

She kissed me on the forehead, and whispered, "Don't cry. Tears ruin your makeup."

That was the last thing I ever heard her say.

SINKING BOATS

Two weeks after that, the black rotary phone in our dusty hallway rang, and Grandma Rosa, holding onto an empty stroller, listened to a husky Ukrainian speech, her face solid, unyielding. Oksana was dead. There was a fire, and the militia found only her teeth and bones. She was twenty-three.

I couldn't remember the funeral. Sometimes I thought I had a vision of three tall, strange pale blondes next to me, in elegant black coats and sky-high heels; smoldering Vogues; a closed white coffin; an emerald-green foreign-made car; and a deaf silence—the silence of a dead whale on a seashore.

I knew I wouldn't sleep that night. I went out swimming into a cold Misty Lilac and hopped on a late-night trolley downtown. It was empty, lit up like a church, and something in its engine sang and cried like a violin, so I stepped off, and walked down the boulevard to the Opera Theater where Oksana used to sell ice cream. It was dark, and it was raining. I went down the Steps, listening to my heels clicking on the granite.

My head was empty, and the cold Misty Lilac blinded me, sparkling like a kaleidoscope, spiraling around me.

I sat down at the bottom and looked up.

"I can never reach the top," Oksana used to say.

I wanted to cry but I couldn't.

"Grandma," I thought. "I need to go home to Grandma Rosa."

When I came home, Grandma Rosa was stretched on the bed in her steel-gray suit, her nose thin and pointy, Pushkin's volume by her side. I shook her by her paper-thin shoulders until the book fell down on the floor and her tight bun came undone and silver hair covered her face. Her eyes were open and stared behind my head at the slowly rotating fan, at the monstrous shadow moving around and around. I couldn't remember what happened later that day.

I couldn't remember the funeral. I remember hot-pink carnations and the long drive from the crematorium, alone in a fish-smelling taxi, the brass urn of Grandma's ashes strangely warm in my hands. I remember the smell of oily earth and wet rain, and the same three pale blondes by my side. They all went under the same gray granite tombstone—my mother, grandfather, grandmother, and sister. I could hardly breathe.

The next day, or maybe the next week, the meaty old man with the nutcracker jaw came to visit me in my communal apartment. He came in an emerald-green, foreign-made car, wore a salmon-silk shirt, and brought white roses.

"A smoke?" he offered me Vogues.

I took one, and looked at him through the smoke, my head empty. It all felt like a movie.

"My name is Colonel Alexandrov," he said in a shrill, womanly voice. "I'm so sorry."

He blew his nose into a white starched handkerchief, stared inside it with an air of mourning and remorse, then folded it in two. The bald spot on top of his head looked like a raw piece of ham, and as he put his crablike hand on my shoulder, his damp fingers looked thicker, shorter, and redder than I had remembered.

"I want to help you," he said.

He blew his nose again, examined the handkerchief, and folded it in quarters. Then his bloodshot swine eyes stopped at my neck. I had a dizzying sense of time repeating itself over and over again. It all had happened before, and not once. I stared at Pushkin's portrait on a bookshelf.

"You are the most beautiful woman I've ever seen."

He blew his nose so hard, I thought his head would explode, then stood up.

"Move in with me. I've rented an apartment at Deribasovskaya; you'll love it."

After that, I couldn't remember things clearly. It was all like a dream. The only details that stuck in my memory were the butcher knife in my hand, blood on his salmon-pink shirt, his crab fingers clawing the air and the gap[1] between his nutcracker yellow teeth as he hissed at me: *"Pozhzhaleyeshsh, blyadskoe otrodje…"* (*You'll regret it, spawn of a whore*), and the burst of the front door being slammed, like a gunshot.

I also remember a feeling of being two, being my own double. One was sitting on the bed, hands over her head, not moving, not breathing, dead. The other peeled off, stood up and said, "Run!" It was the second one that walked around the room, searching through the drawers, bookshelves and beds. I could almost hear my brain ticking—it worked like a clock, like a GPS system. It calculated my escape, and it gave me the directions.

Relatives?

No relatives left. Great-Aunt Rina's dead. Her daughter Inna, my only cousin, not dead, but in America, having emigrated to New York years ago. Grandma Rosa said Inna had written, many times. Sent a written invitation. America. Oksana had wanted to go to America.

Grandma Rosa didn't throw things away. Papers. Desk, second drawer. Third drawer. Secret drawer.

Two hours later, sewn in a worn periwinkle pillowcase,

---

[1] **"Gap"** is an interesting choice of words. There is a gap in Rose's memory relevant to the chain of events. It is also possible that she purposely conceals the whole truth from Mike.

stashed away in a trunk, I found a typewritten letter, in English: "To Whom It May Concern. This is to invite my great-aunt Rosa and my cousins to visit me and my family…" With the note was a bankroll of two thousand dollars.

I took our passports, all the papers, three pairs of underwear, and a toothbrush. I took Grandma's volume of Pushkin. I never forgot how I stepped out into the yard and sat on a bench in the shade of a cherry tree. Time stood still; nothing moved. Heat was everywhere—like a sleeping monster. Ripe cherries fell down on the blue asphalt of the empty yard. A red cat slept in a sandbox next to a broken doll. A radio echoed through the yard, a woman's voice bouncing off the walls, words blended, as if she was speaking a foreign language. I knew I would never come back.

"Rose," said Mike.

He was looking deep into my eyes. I noticed a dark line underneath his eyelashes, like eyeliner.

"Sweetheart. You said it was November? Is it hot in Odessa in November?"

My mind went blank again.

"Sometimes. I told you, I can't remember."

"I know, I know. Never mind, I'm sorry. Just tell me the rest. How did you get here?"

I was silent for a while. I'd never told this story to anyone. Luke knew I had a sister who died, and that my whole family had died, but that was all. He never asked more. He believed in privacy. Why did I never talk to Luke about it? Why did I talk to Mike the Motherfucker, and not my husband, about the darkest secret of my life?

I never talked about Oksana—to anyone. Ever. I couldn't. That's why I wanted to write a novel about her.

But to talk about her to a stranger? I was drawn to him; I wanted to tell him everything. I couldn't stop. His arm was around me, and I kept staring at his tattoo. *You must become who you are.*

"Tell me," whispered Mike, patting my shoulder. "Tell me all."

And I began again, in a voice that did not sound like mine.

I ran outside without ever looking back. I jumped into a cab and went to a crematorium-like building, the Visa and Passport Department. I've never forgotten the stale smell of wet dog hair in the taxi.

In the office, I didn't bother to stand in line. I knocked on the head of the Visa Department's office. Cold, formal, moving like a machine, I placed the letter from cousin Inna and my application for a tourist visa to the U.S. on the desk. I put Oksana's passport next to the papers. Then I put the cash from Grandma's trunk next to it. Then I said, "My cousin is deadly sick. I need to leave urgently."

A gray-faced man looked at me, at the letter, at the green bills. He switched off his phone. Then, without a word, he wrote something on my application, and took the cash. He put it in his pocket, and nodded. Then he switched his phone back on, and told me in a suddenly shaky, sweet voice, "We wish you and your family all good luck. Go to window number nine and they will issue you the visa today."

I took another taxi to the airport. I didn't stand in line there, either. I went through the line of screaming, sweaty women holding sickly children, ignoring them, and marched right into the head of the Ticketing Department's office. I placed Oksana's Chanel dollars on the desk, and asked for a ticket: Odessa-Moscow, Moscow-New York. A woman with a snow-white tower on her head took the dollars and counted them. She looked into my eyes. I didn't blink. Then she put them in her pocket and wrote me a blue ticket to Moscow and a note to Galina Nikolaevna in the Moscow International Airport office.

"Your luggage?"

"It's coming. Separately. My sister is bringing it. I'm fine."

In a trancelike state, I flew to Moscow on the next plane. I had my worst panic attack in the U.S. Embassy. I didn't remember how I ended up with a tourist visa and got to Moscow airport, to Galina Nikolaevna's office—she could have been a twin of the woman in Odessa, the same snow-white tower, same prison-inspector eyes—but I got a ticket, no one stopped me at Customs, and I slept all the way across the ocean.

I lived at cousin Inna's and was working as a waitress in Manhattan when I met Luke. We got married and moved to California for his job, and we've lived there ever since.

I FEEL YOUR PAIN

"Oh Rose... I feel your pain... You are talking to my heart... My poor little girl," whispered Mike. "You suffered. You are trembling—"

His voice enveloped me, it sneaked into the dark alleys of my memory like a snake in a basement. "Cry, Sweetie, try crying, you'll feel better... You have nightmares about it, don't you, Sweetie?"

I did. The Nightmare.

Was he a spy? He knew my dreams, and what I wanted to hear and how, and my deepest secret fear, my nightmares.

I longed to tell him about the part of the Nightmare that I never even thought about. Those cherries, those heavy and torn pieces of sweet meat, falling, falling, crashing on the blue asphalt. The bloody drops, the rotten smell, the buzzing flies, the churning of my intestines. And then, the emptiness. Then, all of a sudden I would discover myself all alone on the deserted beach. Standing on the cold rocks, frozen, chained and gagged. I looked up, and I couldn't move. I screamed so hard the blood rushed from my throat, but nobody could hear me. Like a fish. I didn't have a voice, I was invisible, I didn't exist. That was the worst part about the Nightmare.[1]

---

[1] It is possible that Rose's depressed mother was consistently unavailable to her child, failing to attend to Rose when she cried for extended periods of time. Thus, the mother created emotional trauma through neglect: That might be **the root of Rose's trauma**. It is widely accepted today that environmental parenting trauma has a tremendous impact on childhood development. In the 1970s, many parents rationalized their lack of empathy for their newborns by calling on the then-popular methods of Dr. Spock. Being attended by their mother during early

"Tell me your dream, Rose. You will feel better. You will be free."

I shook my head.

He was patting my hair, kissing my forehead with fleeting kisses, and humming a soothing tune into my ear. I was gasping, my eyes were burning, and my whole body, every cell of it was tingling warm, as if I were made of fireflies. The tender, festive heat was filling me, overflowing me, and suddenly I felt my insides going into a blue-and-red spasm. I was on the brink of a warm orgasm... The room in front of me trembled and swam in rose-gold rays, I felt tears gathering, and then Mike brought me closer to him, his perfume strong like acacia, and whispered into my ear, "You did it, Rose, right?"

I froze.

"You moved in with the colonel and worked for him, Rose, didn't you?"[1]

I sat down on the bed. Mike was observing me. My mind went blank.

"November to May, you worked for him, right?"

From shaking with passion, grief and remorse, I went to standing stock-still. I stared, silent, at a cupcake-pink dildo on the vanity table. I waited for my tears to dry up. I took a couple of yoga breaths. Then I turned my head toward him without looking at his face.

---

infancy forms the whole basis for the person's attitude towards the world and environment—depending on whether it is cold and hostile or warm and receptive.

[1] By telling the incomplete story, Rose repeats her pattern of partial exposure. Opening up through her narration is threatening, so instead Rose habitually uses her defense mechanisms and hides behind words and events just as way physically, she hides behind her outfits and hair.

"Do you want to do anything?" I said. "We have ten minutes left."

"Ha-ha-ha… You've given me everything I wanted, Rose."

He sat down, reached in his pocket and handed me a rolled twenty-dollar bill.

"This is for you… Thank you, Sweetie."

He got up and left the room.

I sat on the bed, looking at myself in the mirror. Did I just tell this total stranger, a client in a dungeon, my deepest sorrow? Did I just get tipped twenty dollars for it?

Mommy scrutinized me as I walked to the fridge and searched for my apple, but she didn't say a word.

"You okay?" asked Susanna. "Wanna smoke some pot?"

"I'm fine, thanks," I said, walking toward the bathroom to change.

"That's what he does," I heard Susanna's hasty voice. "Cracks you open, reads your mind, right? Forget about him, don't think about him, come smoke pot with me…"

I just shut the door, and sat down on the toilet seat.

Time stopped, and when Zoe came banging on the door, shouting, "I'm bursting, girl, get the fuck out of there!" I felt a part of me squeezing into the corner by the tub, and watching the other one standing up, unlocking the door, and walking out.

CLEANING

I kept watching myself going through the motions: starting the car, driving across the bridge, parking in the garage, patting Potemkin's warm head, and taking to cleaning. I didn't eat or rest. Instead, I scrubbed first the downstairs bathroom, then the kitchen, then the upstairs bathroom, and kept vacuuming every rug, every corner, dusting every hook in each closet despite the fact that Maria Lucia, our cleaner, had been there the day before.

In the living room, I moved Nick's paper puppet theater from the coffee table. The cut-out paper dolls hung over the edge of the paper dollhouse. I pulled on the string of a princess doll, shaking her limbs. Her fair face stayed still, but her arms were outstretched in such a desperate gesture that I shuddered and let go of the strings. I looked at myself in the mirror. In the dim light of the living room, I looked as if I were cut out of paper. I touched the mirror to feel that it was me. The mirror was cold. I felt flat and lifeless, as if I had to pull on my own strings to move the feathers over the shiny surface of the mantelpiece.

I organized my writing notes on my desk, and then looked at my wedding picture. My own image scowled at me. Suddenly, it seemed to me that it wasn't me. It was Oksana, holding my husband's hand with her gloved fingers, laughing at me from underneath the glass, faux pearls shining in her hair. I put the photo down, and kept brushing and polishing until I noticed that my hands had turned red from bleach and my skin was blistered, and then I took a shower, scrubbing myself until I had scratches on my legs and stomach. I threw away my jeans and t-shirt. I could have burned them.

"Yuck! My Transformer stinks likes Windex," whined Nick. "Why did you move my theater?"

I wanted to pat his hair, but I was afraid to touch him.

"You wanna go grab some margaritas?" asked Luke.

He scratched his neck, which he did when he was concerned. I was infamous in my family for being domestically handicapped. I never did anything around the house.

"No, I'm fine. Thanks," I said. "I need to go shopping."

Luke looked at my forehead.

"You hate shopping."

It was true. I got unusual panic attacks in big stores: I yawned. Every second. Would not stop until I stepped out of the store.

"C'mon. Let me fix you a drink instead," mumbled Luke.

I said no, and watched him heading for the garage.

"You need cash?" he looked at me over his shoulder.

I shook my head, and went to Target. I spent two hundred and eighty three dollars, pretty much everything I had earned[1] that day. Those dollars felt like a snake, a dead mouse in my purse. I needed a new purse. I grabbed stuff without looking, and ended up with three pieces of lavender soap, two bottles of Pantene shampoo, all-purpose cleaner, a box of All Free and Clear detergent, a new teenage-line perfume, Mickey Mouse pajamas, pink pencil sharpeners, and a new snow-white shower curtain. I didn't like any of their purses, but I bought a box of black oversized envelopes for no good reason other than fifty percent off.

---

[1] **Shopping** is a coping skill, similar to eating, which is designed to medicate psychological pain. The essence of both shopping and eating is consumption. Shopping is consuming with one's eyes and hands, and, similarly, it brings instant gratification. Buying new outfits is also a symbolic reinvention of oneself.

"No way I'm wearing *this*!" said Olga, tossing the pajamas aside.

"I want a shower curtain with *Transformers*!" said Nick. "And—*pink* is for *girls*! Girls are weird!"

"Weird yourself!" said Olga.

Roxanne went to her room without saying a word. Luke was in the garage, working on his robot.

MIRRORS

I locked myself in the bathroom and grabbed my old surgical tweezers. I always did that after a fight with Luke, or during bad PMS, or after sleepless nights following a flu outbreak in the family. I tweezed my eyebrows. They were barely there, and the arch was Greta Garbo-dramatic. Fortunately, I'd inherited my wild eyebrows along with the eagle curve of my nose from our half-Jewish Grandma Rosa, so they always grew back at ultrasonic speed.

I plucked out a hair and felt a slight prickle, both painful and sweet. I remembered pinching Mommy's client—was this what he enjoyed, too?

Potemkin jumped onto the pink toilet seat cover beside me.

"Do I look old?" I asked her.

I swiped my finger over the dark shadow underneath my eye, examining fine lines.

I saw my sister's face in the mirror.

It was her pinkish birthmark on the right collarbone, her flamingo-like flowing curves of the neck and nose, her bitten nails. She had Grandma Rosa's same unibrow and baby-eagle nose, which were hardly unique in Odessa.

What made us memorable, though, was the eyes. Slanted, almost Asian, the tear-shaped eyes were the reminder of Tartar-Mongolian rule in Russia and Ukraine. Along with the long legs, the mysterious eyes were the only gifts from our conflicted Ukrainian father.

I liked to argue with Oksana that I remembered him, and I thought I did remember a heartbreaking scent of sex, sweat, and sweet, cheap perfume, acacia maybe—or maybe it was Odessa's summer scent raging in my memory. I did remember every detail of his face and body; for hours and hours I'd scrutinize three black-and-white photographs that Grandma Rosa had wrapped in an old *PRAVDA* newspaper in a shoebox in her trunk. Tabletop hair, corn yellow and thick—I knew it!—Lenin's kind crow's feet, cobalt-blue shadows instead of eyes, a bulldozer lower jaw, a golden cross with a tiny golden Jesus around the sinewy neck of a lumberjack. Years later, my cousin Inna told me that he had considered himself a true Cossack—until he abandoned my mother for a much older woman named Rebecca Levitsky, emigrated to Israel, and became a Hasidic Jew.

The color of our eyes, though, came from Great-Aunt Rina, the opera diva. Sudden, ever-changing, impossible to pin down, that dizzying sea-blue-green with sunny speckles was Odessa itself, with its golden beaches, gentle waves and lusty endless summers.

I remembered Oksana in front of the dark oval mirror over the couch, Great-Aunt Rina's peacock feather fan covering up her high cheekbones, a sidelong glance lingering over the reflection of her bronze shoulder, laughter dying on her lips, fingers running through the champagne-silk hair. She had already learned her mascara trick, and as she fluttered her spiky ink-black eyelashes, her widely set eyes lived their own life, like undersea anemones swaying their tentacles or exotic forest butterflies landing on her face. Unlike me, she had that lazy eye, and it rolled away like a forgotten ball on the sand, so even I always got lost in that unreal vast space between her eyes, like in an ocean of dreams.

Except for the lazy eye and her Z-shaped scar, Oksana and I were almost identical. After that many years, the differences faded away from memory.

My head hurt, and I touched my fingers to my forehead.

I felt Misty Lilac seeping into my head again—and out of the fog came Europa Bar and Colonel Alexandrov. His swine eyes gleamed, his meaty chin jerked toward the bar counter. It was a signal, and like a robot I walked toward a jellyfish-like American. I was rocking my hips in a mermaid fluid way, and laughing. I sat down on the high stool, crossing my legs the way Oksana used to do, swinging my foot in her spiky-heeled shoe. I wore her venomous flamingo-pink dress, I spoke in her voice, and I smoked Vogues like she had. I sipped a cognac from a short-stemmed glass in a Deluxe Suite, and watched the client's cellophane flesh jiggle over me for a few minutes, my mind blank.

"Where are you from?"

"Washington D.C."

"You like Odessa?"

"I love beautiful girls from Odessa."

"Have you already visited the Ambassador's Restaurant? Yesterday? When are you leaving?"

I knew all the answers were being recorded. I never knew why Alexandrov needed all this stupid stuff and I never cared. I hated Alexandrov.

How had Mike known? Was he there, watching me from the high stool at the bar, one of many security guys, always in the shadows, always there, always watching you, the way I was watching myself? Was he hiding in the folds of the hotel room curtains, watching Alexandrov stashing dollars in my bra, making cocaine lines on my round golden pocket mirror, pinning me to the smelly carpet with his crablike hands—his cadaverous abdomen pouring over me—breathing garlic and vodka into my neck, calling me his little Oksana? Did he watch me sitting in the dusk, tweezing my eyebrows to bloody nothing, then picking at my skin trying to catch the invisible bugs underneath, picking at the already bloody skin and shaking with disgust?[1] Who was he? Who was I?

"It was me, me, me," I repeated aloud. "She's dead."

I felt dead myself. I didn't look at Potemkin, I didn't look at myself, but I talked to myself in a low voice: "She'd never get wrinkles. She'd never grow old. She'd stay beautiful."

Even though she had been dead for so long, my burning love for her was still tinged with bitter, poisonous jealousy. By choosing to die young she stayed young—forever. She was always my grandmother's favorite, always better at everything than I was, better dancer, better student, better even at death—just better.[2] She was a star, and I was not. But I could make it up to her, and I could write my novel about her, and she'd live on—and so would I.

Potemkin was washing her white whiskers, oblivious to my internal turmoil. I plucked out hair after hair. Time stood still.

"How you doin' there, Honey?" asked Luke by the door.

I hadn't heard footsteps, so I didn't know how long he'd been there.

"Fine," I said. "I'm—I'm going to take a bath."

"But you took a shower already," he said, very quietly.

"Well—I just want to relax," I said. "I won't take long."

I sat on the edge of the bath, watching the water filling the bath halfway.

I imagined Mike watching me from somewhere, watching me watching myself in the mirror, and I felt heavy inside, and

---

[1] **Self-harming behaviors** are common in individuals with **Dissociative Disorders**. The majority of individuals diagnosed with Dissociative Disorder inflict self injury. Experiencing sharp physical pain brings a person back to reality, ending dissociation and affording relief.

[2] Extreme sibling rivalry once again.

wet down there, and I remembered Susanna's hot mouth and trembling white-blue eyelids.

So I climbed in, and rested the showerhead between my legs. The water's strong stream was teasing and caressing me, making everything inside alive and tense, and I felt the warm wave going through the lower part of my abdomen, rising up, making me dizzy and breathless: I was plunging into one of my favorite erotic fantasies, Atlantis, unrolling in the underwater world.

I used to play it in Odessa since I could remember myself; I used to replay it in New York, when I had a crush on Ivette, another waitress from Eatz, a French music student with cinnamon-red bangs, a pale mouth, and a large star-shaped birthmark in the corner of her right eye. We would take long walks under a red umbrella, hand in hand, European style, and then sit on a bench, feeding croissants to fat squirrels, and then I would go home and drown in Atlantis, the aquamarine abyss, the brilliant beauty. Atlantis, my lost love. How many times I replayed it in my mind, I didn't know. It always played out the same way: I was a mermaid. My fish tail cut into my abdomen[1] like a sword: oyster colored, fish-fouled. I was there, but I was not me. I waited for my lover to swim toward me. It was maybe female, maybe male, maybe a mermaid, maybe a dolphin. We were entwined, limbs mingling, melting in a kiss—a hot, French kiss, mouths sealed upon each other…

I couldn't see her face, but I knew it was Susanna; it was her gentle mouth, her alive and dancing tongue. We merged into the primordial rhythm, and somehow we were inside

---

[1] In her Atlantis Fantasy, Rose is reconstructing events from her infancy: her mother or grandmother bathing her and washing her genitals.

of each other. The delicious tension in my tail[1] grew heavy. I watched myself[2] gasping, cringing, writhing, until I felt a sweet spasm and my body contracted sharply, almost painfully, and then released.

Those water spasms were always of a power almost indescribable, out of that other world. In the real world, in my real bed with Luke, I didn't feel anything akin to it. My body was almost numb and sex had nothing of this cosmic dimension and magic—it was more like lasagna: juicy, fleshy and filling.[3]

This night, everything proceeded as always—a mermaid watching a mermaid, a mermaid loving a mermaid.... A fan-

---

[1] This part of the fantasy might derive from experiences in infancy when Rose's mother would come into her room at night, turning on lights, changing and breastfeeding her. This mix of sensations—the comfort of the mother's breast; the warmth of the milk filling the stomach; the light playing on the ceiling; and the release from urination and swaddling—brought forth her first orgasmic sensations. During a time of frustration, anxiety, and stress, an individual may turn to the erotic satisfaction of infancy as a soothing mechanism. Such stimulation during infancy as diaper changing, kissing, and hugging, is stored in deep memory. Recurring memories bring a sense of security and pleasure.

[2] **Observing other people's sexual encounters** is the third most common fantasy for heterosexual men and women because they can sexually experience voyeuristic tendencies without breaking the rules and being punished.

[3] Possibly due to her dissociation disorder, Rose is unable to fully participate in lovemaking with her husband. Sexual irresponsiveness of this sort develops during sexual abuse as an intrinsic part of the array of defense mechanisms; it is possible that as a child Rose was sexually abused, but due to amnesia, another defense mechanism, she can't recollect the actual abuse.

tasy within a fantasy, a dream within a dream—lonely shadows floating through the ocean, a mere reflection of light[1]—until for the first time in my life I opened my eyes under the water of my dream and looked into my lover's eyes. The reality tore the fabric of my fantasy like a shark's fin: I recognized the eyes. It wasn't my ambiguous double, a nebulous mermaid without a face. It wasn't Susanna. It wasn't Ivette.

No. Plum-brown, sparkling, these were the eyes of Dr. Strong. He looked at me with lust and love, and my insides shrank and exploded—and still, I imagined Mike watching me writhing in my bathtub as I succumbed to the most powerful orgasm I had ever had.

---

[1] **Somatosensory fantasies** reflect early preverbal experiences. They refer to a time when no object relations and no object-related fantasies have yet developed, and no narrative as such yet exists. There is evidence for preverbal fantasies in children where no ego (self) has yet developed and therefore no self-object relation. These are fantasies of purely bodily experiences.

MISTRESS GRETA, THE PSYCHOLOGIST

That morning, Luke did not go running. When I woke up, he was propped up on his elbow, looking at me.

"Morning," I said. "No running today?"

"No," he said. "I'm worried about you. You were whining in your sleep, like a puppy."

"I'm sorry."

"Listen, maybe you've had enough of that research already? I'm worried."

"Honey, I'll be fine. I'm almost done. I promise I'll quit this month."

"Okay," said Luke, scratching his neck. "I'll take the kids to school. You just rest."

Before I got in the car, Joe, our neighbor, came into the driveway.

"Hey, have you seen Blossom?" he asked. "Vanessa's having a fit. He went missing yesterday."

"He was around," I said, thinking about Oksana, Alexandrov, Grandma, Dr. Strong—and for some reason, pistachio ice cream.

"That's what I told her," Joe shrugged. "I just flew in last night, and she's having a cow. Drive safely."

Usually, I stopped thinking about my "real" life once I crossed the bridge, but that day I wasn't even sure what was real and what was not. Oksana, Alexandrov, Grandma, Mike, Susanna flew through the Misty Lilac in my head; my temples were splitting. What was real, what was a fantasy, what was memory? Was memory real? Talking to Mike was all I wanted to do, and I hated him for that.

"Good morning, ladies. Another day, another dollar."

Like a broken record, the dungeon life repeated itself every morning, and I found it almost reassuring: Mommy frying her bacon, smoking, and scrubbing the spotless kitchen counter. The flies were gone, but the stench was still there.

Susanna smiled at me a little longer than usual, but I pretended not to notice.

"Rose, you've got cat hair all over your butt... Greta, you have an early morning session. Whipping and spanking. Read the card."

Potemkin had the gift of penetrating forbidden spaces through the tiniest openings, and she had apparently used it to spend the night in the driver's seat of my SUV. Her grey fur stuck to my jeans like a piece of my home. This trifling incident made a heavy impression on me. The magic of crossing the bridge had failed to work.

"Girls, who's on their period?" asked Mommy.

"I am," said Susanna.

"Save your tampons for Leo the Fish."

"Why?" I asked, my stomach turning.

"You don't want to know," said Susanna.

"He uses them as tea bags," answered Zoe, chewing. "He's not the only one, trust me."

"Gross," I said. "Why, why would they do that? And why is he 'The Fish'?"

"Looks like one, out of the water. You should see his eyes. It's easy money, anyway. He just stops by, gets the tampons, pays, and off he goes. I keep them in the freezer."

"Creative!" Zoe laughed.

"We had to be creative back home," I said. "We didn't have tampons."

"What do you mean?"

"I mean it. There were no tampons in the Soviet Union. And no condoms."

"You must be kidding me. What did you use?"

"Cotton wool. Sometimes there was no cotton wool, either; then, you really had to be creative."

When I was little, I refused to go to the public bathroom after I saw in a trash can torn pieces of cotton wool soaked in blood. I thought that a man-eating Toilet Monster hid in the Asian-style toilets. I imagined its toady head, not unlike Lucifer from a medieval etching, covered in black flies and excrement, emerging from the foul-smelling black hole. Those round openings were like black voids, like eyes into Hell. I trembled, convinced that the Toilet Monster would jump out of the hole and tear me to pieces with its shark teeth. I stopped going to the beach in summer, pretending I was sick, and stayed at home reading instead.

I was reading *The Three Musketeers* and eating cherries one stifling afternoon when my stomach cramped up, and I ran to the toilet with diarrhea—common in a southern town, like flies and homeless cats—and discovered cherry-red blood between my legs. I knew I was dying.

"I'm going to die," I told Oksana.

She had just come home from the beach, her white hat torn, cherry juice on her cheek, and she was taking her salty swimsuit off in front of the oval mirror, laughing as usual.

"You silly little bird," said Oksana. "You won't die."

Grandma Rosa came from the kitchen with a pile of towels in her hands, and Oksana pointed at me. "Bleeding!"

"Here, take some cotton wool, put it there," said Grandma, going into a long bout of her dry cough. "We all get it. You'll learn to walk with it. It comes every month. Don't ask."

That's when I knew the Toilet Monster had gotten me. I wanted to ask Grandma Rosa about it, but as I looked at her pursed lips, I felt the blood rushing into my cheeks, and I didn't say anything.

"Now that's gross. What about condoms?"

"No condoms. Abortions. My grandma had twelve abortions, and my mom had eight."

"And you?"

"Zoe," said Mommy. "Mind your own business. It's okay, Rose."

"I was a virgin," I said.

Everyone laughed, and Mommy patted my shoulder, and coughed for about five minutes.

"You really should quit smoking," said Zoe. "Listen to you, you're about to break down like an old car."

"No bloody way in hell," said Mommy.

"She's right," I said. "You remind me of my Great-Aunt Rina—she had emphysema, and had this machine and wires hooked up to her, and she still kept smoking."

"Then what happened?" asked Zoe.

"Nothing," I said. "She died."

"We all die, one way or another," said Mommy. "At least I'm having fun."

In an hour, while I was washing my hands, Greta arrived in the living room, placed her money on the table, and stood in the middle of the room, her chest rising and falling, her skin strawberry-creamy, chewing gum faster than usual.

"And?" Mommy raised one eyebrow.

"Oh! It was... it was very nice."

I recognized the twinkling in Greta's bulging eyes. I remembered the spy session.

She twisted her hair around her thumb for about a minute, looking toward the cuckoo clock. Then she sighed and talked in a voice even softer than usual.

"I once sent a newly divorced mom of three to a kickboxing class. I mean, a client. A therapy client. She came back so happy, I thought I should try it myself."

"Your point?" asked Zoe.

Greta smiled and kept twisting her hair around her thumb.

"This is like kickboxing. I should send my therapy clients here."

Mommy frowned, Zoe chuckled, and Susanna smiled her Mona Lisa smile, as usual. Greta turned to her.

"You know how you're always so nice to everyone? You are, really."

"Thanks," Susanna stopped smiling.

"Rose, you are always so contained, so European. We're all pretty polite here."

"Hell, not me, girl," said Zoe. "Screw that!"

"No, not you. But you're right about one thing: screw it! I mean it did feel good to whip that jerk! I wasn't told what to do, and could do whatever…"[1]

Mommy gave Greta a murderous look.

"Hey. You. Ms. Psychologist. You're a fool. It's a job. I specifically told you yesterday: You are submissive. No matter what happens in there. They top you—from the bottom. Listen: You get carried away, and you're fired. Stop catering to yourself. Just do your fucking job."[2]

---

[1] Greta externalizes her anger and shame by placing the responsibility on "bad" societal rules.

[2] Mommy does not want to be alone in her misery, and she will not allow other women to vindicate themselves. She needs to make sure that no one is exempt from experiencing the full burden of pain and shame for being a sex worker. She cannot rationalize or externalize this burden, and she will not let anyone else do it, either.

Greta sat down. The creamy flush gave way to milk-white paleness; her soft lips drooped. Mommy went back to the kitchen and started to paint. I could hear the brush slapping against the wall and her hoarse breathing.

Zoe stood up and scratched her elbow, stepping from one foot to another.

"Listen, girl," she said.

Then she walked over to Greta, slapped her heavy red hands with their chipped nail polish onto Greta's pillow shoulders, and worked them in.

"Good neck rub, and you're fine," she murmured.

"Thanks, but no," sighed Greta.

Zoe shrugged, her face ruddy, and went into the bathroom, slamming the door behind her.

"Want to smoke some pot?" asked Susanna, smiling with her lips only.

Greta just shook her head, her eyes closed, her jaws moving.

"I just want some privacy."

I followed Susanna to the porch and watched her roll a joint and smoke it. I didn't smoke with her, just watched her pink lips going through the motions, smoke rising, but my head was going round and round and round.

MOMMY,
THE LIFE STORY OF A REAL DOMINATRIX

"God, Mommy's mean," I said.

"Nah, she's a sweetheart."

Susanna kept a straight face. I looked for a twinkle in her eyes.

"I'm not joking. She's too soft inside, so she's being tough on the outside, you know?"

I knew.

"She's had a rough life. Really."

"I'd imagine. Do you know much? Does she ever talk about it?"

"That she does. When it rains. For some reason, when it rains, she smokes pot and tells you her whole life story. Her bones hurt, so she talks. I hear it every winter. Know it by heart."

"How did she get here?"

"From England, you mean? Not sure. Some things she never talks about. Like her Ph.D. in psychology. I don't know if she's lying. She's probably lying. But then, maybe not. I'm not lying. I'll have my Ph.D., soon."

She looked up at me, and I nodded.

"Of course, you will."

She sighed.

"I guess. She's been running the dungeon for the last thirty-five years, that's for sure. Her daughter grew up and left, went to Maui. Her grandson grew up and left. Her Jamaican boyfriend hangs out here sometimes."

"She's got a boyfriend?"

"On and off. Steals her money and smokes her pot."

"What's he like? A pervert?"

"N-no. He's in a band, his name is Tornado. He's thirty years younger."

"So she was married and had a kid and all that?"

"Yeah, she was. They say."

Susanna looked at the roses in the garden, frowning. I could tell she wanted to add something, but she didn't say anything for a while. I wanted to get all I could out of her. For my writing.

"Does she talk about her parents?"

"She was adopted. Her birth mom had postpartum depression really bad, tried to kill her right after delivery, wanted to strangle her."

"God!"

"Yep."

Susanna took a deep drag, "Still sure you don't want to smoke? You want me to blow it into your mouth?"

She folded her lips into a flower shape.

"No, thanks. So, what happened?"

"Well, her dad wasn't around, because he was in the British army, fighting the Nazis, and so the neighbors raised her."

"This was all in England, right?"

"Yeah. World War II,[1]" she said. "They didn't even tell her that she was adopted, because they were so prim and private, and swept everything under the carpet, so she never knew for a fact that she was adopted. She worked a lot as a kid. Her

---

[1] **Rejection by her parents** and **war** are two major childhood traumas that form Mommy's personality structure. Bitter and tortured, Mommy humiliates and dominates women and men alike, driven by her unresolved aggression and hostility against her parents. By nursing and torturing hundreds and hundreds of men—or the **Big Monster Father**, the **Big Monster Man**—she is fulfilling her wish to both possess and punish her idealized daddy in military uniform.

adoptive mother was a housekeeper at a boarding school. That is, mind you, an all-boys' boarding school. All Mommy did was cleaning, scrubbing, dusting, and playing with the boys."

"Ha! It hasn't really changed that much."

"Nope. You know that photo on the bookshelf? The faded out, black-and-white one?"

"Jimmy? The one who died young?" I asked.

"Timmy," she said. "She was twelve. She never really got over it, I think. She always talks about spanking and caning. It was still legal to do it, I guess."

"I still can't imagine her with a boyfriend, you know."

Susanna frowned again. She was still staring at the roses. This time she pointed her finger toward the garden, and then put it to her mouth. I looked and saw nothing, just rows of ivory and creamy roses, and some wisteria, and a grey bird sitting on top of a short olive tree and staring at us.

Susanna looked around. She had a paranoid look in her always-calm eyes, and I thought that maybe the pot was starting to affect her. She gestured for me to get closer, and whispered in my ear, "You know, there've been maybe hundreds of women who've worked for her, right? I don't know how many, but over thirty years, can you imagine? Well, there's a rumor that's been passed along, a legend."

She spoke even quieter, "Xenia told me that Mommy killed her husband."

She paused.

"Dismembered him, and buried him in the garden, over there, under the rose bush. The one with the bird on it now."

I looked at the bush.

Susanna kept whispering, "Zoe heard that it was a client, not a husband. Her friend told her that she saw a ghost with a rope around its neck, creeping around in the Dungeon."

I placed my palm on her chilly shoulder. "Well, you know. It's probably—well, not true. Where's her daughter now, did you say?"

Susanna closed her eyes.

"Who knows. Maui, they say. The daughter herself must be pretty old. Mommy had her at eighteen. She tells horror stories about it—there was no birth control, no legal abortion—sort of what you were saying. She's always telling this story about attempting a back-alley abortion. It gives me the creeps: she punctured the placenta, and pumped carbonic soap inside!"

"Ouch!"

"Then she tried a back-alley herbalist, but nothing worked, so she had the kid."[1]

She looked at me, her pupils wide, and went back to whispering.

"Sometimes I hear clinking in the closet in the Boudoir, and I freak out."

I saw her turning porcelain pale, and took her in my arms, patting her smooth hair and inhaling her clear, odorless scent.

"It's fine, Honey. It's just a rumor."

"I'd never sunbathe in the garden, ever," she talked feverishly into my ear. "This other girl did, and then she got a terrible skin condition, and the UV-rays are carcinogenic and clients prefer white skin, and—"

---

[1] Mommy identifies with her mother and attempts to kill her own child, and later repeats the mother-daughter murderous pattern by hiring young women and then getting rid of them.

THE MENOPAUSAL WOMAN

"Get back here!" Mommy screamed from the kitchen. "Enough gossiping! Carolyn is coming."

I let Susanna go, almost pushing her away. I could see our embrace from outside, like an observer, and it made me feel distant and cold.

"Oh, him," said Susanna, standing up. "He's old as fuck. His name's Carolyn."

Fantasy: menopausal woman, a servant, read the card. *Visits once a month. For thirty years.*[1]

"She'll do the dishes, clean the kitchen, and serve us tea," said Susanna. "Then she'll massage our feet, and polish our shoes if we want. She's a sweetheart."

The sweetheart was a tall, lanky man in his eighties, with white hair pulled back in a bun, white stockings, a white-and-green checked skirt and a white top with a ruffled collar. His shoes were conservative, plain-Jane, size 11. He looked and moved like a daddy longlegs or an oversized mosquito.

Carolyn swiftly put on a neatly ironed apron and gloves, and took to cleaning with even more ardor than Mommy. Mommy sat with us in the living room, smoking a joint. As usual, after smoking she softened up, and threw sideways glances at Greta.

"I think I'm getting stoned on your second-hand smoke," I told Mommy.

---

[1] This individual, who, physiologically speaking, is a male, chooses to wear female clothing (**transvestic fetishism**) and perform activities perceived as typically feminine (**behavioral autogynephilia**), to inhabit an imaginary female body and its functions (**anatomic** and **physiologic autogynephilia**).

"You complaining? You have the most gorgeous legs, Greta," she said. "You and Rose both will be so good for foot fetishists, only you need to grow your toenails longer... It just takes time. Everything takes time. You'll get there."

"Now," she whispered to me in a conspiratorial voice, "when Carolyn serves us tea, tell her you are from Russia, and you are going to take her back to the Kremlin Palace as your servant... She'll love that. But be gentle with the old girl. She's very sensitive. All the guys in his generation are like that, so bloody sensitive, so clumsy. They don't know how to handle a woman. Most of them just grab and pull you. I cuff their hands behind their backs when I work with them..."

Carolyn showed up with a silver tray, fine porcelain cups and saucers, and a teapot.

"Would you care for some almond biscotti, Madame?" she asked me, taking a low bow.

"Call me Your Highness. I belong to ze Royal Family," I said in the worst Russian accent I have ever heard. "Yes, My Highness carez for a biscotti."

I pretended to be my Great-Aunt Rina; the legend had it that Stalin once heard her sing and cried his eyes out.

"Let me have one, Carolyn," said Mommy. "Come here. Listen, when I was eleven, this boy Timothy and I used to play shoe shop. He was a salesman and I was the Queen of England. I was a mean Queen, just like my mother was when she was shopping. I slapped Timmy all over his face with my shoe ..."

She gently slapped Carolyn on the cheek. Carolyn bowed and turned to me again.

"Your Highness, may I comment on the noble line of your foot?" she lisped.

"You may, Carolyn," I answered, poking my chin forward and lifting my foot un-royal-like for everyone to see its noble line. "You are ze best American chambermaid, Carolyn, and I will take you wiz me to my Winter Palace, to snow-covered Siberia to serve bergamot tea to me and ze Great Princesses Anastasya, Alexandra, and Pulkheria. You will ride in ze back of my bearskin-lined sleigh through ze taiga and will carry ze train of my diamond-encrusted robe. I will put you in a cage with my tamed bear to show to ze Russian peasants."

"Enough," hissed Mommy.

"You may *rrrretreat* now, Carolyn," I said, not without regret.

"Go easy on the pot! You'll give her a heart attack. Too much excitement! The guy is fucking eighty-five!"

The tea party was over. Carolyn was taken to the Boudoir for her ob-gyn exam, administered by Mommy. The group of internists was invited to attend: Greta, Zoe, and Susanna crowded around the bed. To my relief, I was called to attend to the next client.

THE FOOT FETISHIST

The session was supposed to be just thirty minutes.

"I can't find his card," I said.

"What do you need to know? He's a foot fetishist. Use that creativity of yours."

I opened the door and gasped. The foot fetishist was Josh, my husband's best friend. Josh, a post-graduate Ivy-League student, a nice Jewish boy from the East Coast. I almost ran away.

"Good day, Mistress Rose," said Josh—and I realized he was not Josh.

I figured the second-hand pot was getting to me even more than I thought; but really, the guy could have been Josh's twin brother. He wore the same cargo shorts, a t-shirt with Andy Warhol's Mickey Mouse, and Woody Allen-esque glasses, and he had the same scared-bunny look.

"Hello, darling," I muttered. "Follow me."

We then descended to the Dungeon, passing by the group of mistresses in the Boudoir. The rule for a session interruption was to stop, wave and say something kinky, but everyone seemed to be too preoccupied with Carolyn's exam, so Josh and I took the stairs down to the Dungeon unnoticed.

"Are you here to have fun, dear?" I said. "You like beautiful shoes, don't you?"

"I—I'm extraordinarily visual. Sensual. I—I have an im-m-mense desire to let go. An urge to give away control, you know?[1] A terrible urge."

---

[1] In essence, **foot fetishism** is delegating the power of authority to the worshipped person, or more so to a particular body part, investing it with ideal qualities.

Two pink spots on his cheeks spread to his forehead and neck, as he stuttered in a breathless whisper, his eyes cast down, like that of a schoolgirl confessing a crush. "I do love elegant attire and sheer stockings. I love, love pumps.[1] Let me k-k-kiss your shoe…"

"Admire my royal feet, slave," I ordered. "On your knees. Unbuckle the straps. One by one. Slow down! Remove my shoes with your teeth. One by one. Faster. Massage my feet!"

Josh obeyed. He was rolling at my feet.

"I have to lie down and close my eyes for a second," he said in a trembling voice.

He flopped down on the bed in a heap, like a down blanket, and I wished I had read the card for this client. I hoped he wasn't having a heart attack; he couldn't be older than thirty, but what did I know? I sat next to him, placed my foot next to his face and started: "Once upon a time I had the best arch in the Odessa Royal Ballet Theater. I was a prima ballerina. Rose La… Rosetska. La Rosetska. You've heard the name? You see this arch? I still do special dancing drills to keep my feet strong…"

I waved my foot this way and that way, and wiggled my toes. The foot fetishist gave a low groan. The real Josh was a poet, and I decided that my client should appreciate my improvisation just as Josh would.

"Feet, feet, you see feet everywhere… Pumps, pumps, pumps… Feet, feet, feet… like white-white swans they land-

---

[1] **Wanting one's Mother is a taboo**. Josh's mother was distant and had no time or patience for him. The unconscious conveniently substituted a shoe fetish for the **Big Monster Mother**. In the same way savages worship wooden fetishes personifying their deities, the fetishist worships The Mother in a form of a shoe. The sexual energy was rechanneled from the breast to the foot, another body part symbolizing Mother.

land-land down-down-down on the white-white lands...
Snowflakes and feet, swans and snow, feet and flakes, down
and swan, down and up... Odette and Odille..."

I started to hum the swan theme from the second act of the
ballet. I thought of Great-Aunt Rina. The foot fetishist's body
jerked and I jumped up: a heart attack!

"I am sorry," whispered the fetishist. "You are so lovely, so
very lovely. I am so unworthy of you.[1] You make me feel like
no one has. I... I am... done... Can you please turn away? I
need to get dressed."

I went into the corner and arranged some ropes and chains
on a hook.

"I am so—so grateful to you," he kept mumbling.

"I should make a career change," I thought. "A foot-fetish-
ist Swan queen. Change names. Rose to Odille."

Odille. The air around me trembled. Misty Lilac was seeping through the creamy lace of the Boudoir curtains. Blue
shadows started their flying dance—Odessa Opera Theater,
Swan Lake.

"Odille—"

I heard muffled coughing and turned around.

"I'm ready," said the fetishist.

He looked even more like a scared bunny. I felt like giving
him a carrot to take home.

"Thank you, Sweetie," I said. "You are my favorite guest. I
love the way you appreciate my beauty."

The whole session took about ten minutes.

---

[1] One of the most common defenses against intrapsychic
conflict for sexual deviants is splitting thought-process
that lead to worshipping or demonization. The idealized
object is "good"; the worshipper is "bad."

On my way through the Boudoir I spotted a slight commotion by the bed. I led my client out through the door, "Come back soon, Hon." He gave me a hug, and looked at me with teary eyes.

ODILLE, ODETTE

I stretched out on the carpet, closed my eyes. Odille, Odille, echoed in my head.

"Odille," I whispered.

The slight beat of the tongue against the roof of my mouth sent me back into my childhood. I was eight, and it was the first time I saw *Swan Lake*.

That day replayed in my head in flashes of sunlight, steam, and marble: Grandma Rosa scrubbing us pink in a bath: steam and rosy patches of flesh; my hair being pulled tight, so tight my eyes teared up as Grandma braided it with her stiff, knobby fingers. All white ribbons and creamy lace, we marched to the Odessa Opera Theater. I remembered a golden flash of sun, like a razor cut—a coin in a dark crevice of blue asphalt, next to a cigarette stub. It glistened at me with its ribbed edge, and I quickly fished it out of the hole, pretending I was fixing my white sock.

"Stand up," said Grandma, and pulled me by my other hand. "Stand up straight."

She spoke slowly and quietly, as if she were reciting a poem.

"Today, I want you to look at the theater carefully."

I pressed the coin in my palm, and looked at the theater. I was thinking I could buy an ice cream with that coin.

"It looks like a cake," I said, just to say something, because I knew Grandma expected it.

"Or like a palace," said Oksana.

Grandma nodded, and smiled with the corners of her carefully painted lips.

"It is a palace. A palace of Art. When I die, I want you to remember that."

We stood in silence. I was clenching my twenty-five kopecks in my fist.

"This style is called *barrroque*. Remember: barrroque. Repeat: bar-rr-rroque."

She rolled her *rrr* with a special sharpness.

"Barrroko," we said in unison, catching each other's eye and trying hard not to burst into laughter.

"Over there, on the very top. See the chariot? It's Melpomene."

Oksana pointed her finger up, "I see it! Grandma, why have you stopped talking to Great-Aunt Rina?"

Grandma slapped her hand, "Don't point. It's rude. Look at the sculpture and don't ask about things that are none of your business."

Oksana didn't flinch, and we both looked at the marble woman riding a chariot.

"Why is she driving big cats?"

"These are no cats; these are four furious panthers."

I forgot about my coin and stared at the panthers. I wanted to be Melpomene, and tame wild panthers. I imagined myself riding in a golden chariot, pulled by harnessed black cats, my fiery hair flying behind me.

"Why are they furious?" asked Oksana.

"She tamed them. Melpomene is a Muse, and Art is the most powerful weapon."

"Stronger than panthers?" I asked.

"Much stronger. Stronger than death."

I kept looking up, but Oksana was already pointing at something else, and I heard another loud slap.

"Don't point, I said! You're in public. People are looking."

"I didn't! Look, they are dancing! Is it a mother and a daughter?"

I looked down and saw a marble woman and girl, the mother bent over dancing with a little girl our age.

"No, she's the Muse of Dance. She's teaching the girl. The girl will be a ballerina."

"Like me," said Oksana.

I looked at her behind Grandma's back, and stuck my tongue out. I was getting bored, and I wanted to buy an ice cream. I wanted to tell her I'd found twenty-five kopecks.

Inside, Grandma held our hands, and we climbed a shining marble staircase, with all kinds of lampions, candelabrums and lights blinding me. Everything was red and gold. I wanted to please Grandma, and asked, looking up at her, "Barrroque?"

"*Rrrrococo*," said Grandma.

"Rrrrococo," echoed in my head. "Rrrrococo."

Gilt blossoms, hearts and cupids, my head was going round from the shining light as I lifted my head and stared at the ceiling, brighter than a hundred suns. Then the curtains rose, and I saw white swans swimming over bright, violet water, and I kept thinking about a chocolate éclair or pistachio ice cream, feeling the warm coin in my palm.

"Can we go to a café, please?" asked Oksana during the intermission.

"We have no money for that," said Grandma, her lips pursed. "You came to the theater to enjoy the art, not to stuff your stomach."

"I have money!" I said triumphantly, and opened my palm.

The coin reflected the thousand lights from the crystal chandelier.

"Where did you get it?"

"Found it. On the ground."

Her steel eyes drilled into mine.

"Are you telling the truth?"

Suddenly, my mouth trembled, and I felt myself smiling, laughing and blushing, trying to stop myself, and bursting into even worse giggling.

"You're a liar. I'm ashamed of you."

She took the coin from my palm, and put it in her pocket.

"I don't know where you got it, but you are going to wait outside. No ballet for you."

"Grandma, I found it, I swear I did, I—"

"Stop screaming in public," whispered Grandma, practically hissing.

She pulled me outside the theater, and almost threw me onto a bench.

"Sit here and think. And if you leave, don't come home. Ever."

I cried and cried, until I was tired of crying. I looked at the ice-cream cart under its green umbrella. I looked at the panthers and the powerful goddess. I imagined myself being her, being strong, being a panther tamer, and Grandma was a panther, and I hit her with a whip. Then I imagined myself being Oksana, seating in the red velvet seat, watching the swans, maybe eating an éclair, bought with my coin.

I closed my eyes. I wasn't me anymore.

"Look at her," I heard Grandma's voice. "Now she's asleep. What a shame."

WHAT IS NORMAL?

"Rose! Are you asleep?"

Mommy was still in the Boudoir.

"Come join us."

I walked back slowly, first looking at myself in the mirror. Then I looked at the bed. Carolyn's breathless body was spread on the vinyl like a giant bug. Her face was blue. She looked dead. Her skirt was hiked up to her waist and I saw her lacy white panties, the type my grandma used to wear, a slight bulge in the front and the creepy bluish skin of her exposed thigh. Goosebumps crawled up my arms and every little hair stood on end.

"Forget Odille, forget Odette," I thought, "This is one sick Ophelia..."

Mommy was hunched over Carolyn's crotch with a giant vibrator in her hands. She held it with a miner's grip, as if ready to drill and crush rock; it appeared she was sawing the old lifeless body in two.

My stomach was all knots, as I watched Mommy pushing the grotesque purple penis underneath Carolyn's tilted back. Then there was a squeaking sound, as if a small animal was squished, maybe a mouse, and the session was over.

Carolyn[1] breathed heavily, then suddenly smiled and sat up on the bed, like a broken old doll whose spring triggered.

---

[1] Carolyn's preoccupation with surgical "treatment" and "hormonal therapy" might track back to a childhood trauma of illness or fear. I had a similar case in which the analysis revealed a castration fear leading to the menstrual blood-stained rags in a bathroom basket. My patient grew up during the 1940s in an impoverished environment where many family members shared the bathroom, personal hygiene standards were extremely low, and no

"Thank you, doctor," she said to Mommy. "I feel much better now after my paroxysm."

I held onto the wall as she shuffled out of the Boudoir, carrying her totebag.

"This box of almond biscotti's for you, girls," said Carolyn.

Greta was in the bathroom, pale and silent, washing her hands. For a while we took turns, scrubbing, soaping, rinsing. We did not look at each other.

"Take it easy on the water, girls. Or pay my bills," cried Mommy.

"It's a defense mechanism," Greta muttered.

"So, how was your first foot fetishist, Rose?" inquired Mommy.

She was at the desk, smoking, fidgeting, and editing the *YourFantasyWorld.com* website. She dragged a tabloid-worthy photo of Greta around the screen: bedroom hair, the milky whiteness of her breasts shining against the blackness of a disheveled prom dress.

"It was... easy... and strange."

"You don't say! Was he Asian? In his sixties?"

"N-no. Jewish, in his twenties..."

"Oh, my mistake. That other guy did toe and foot worship. With his teeth. Boy, did he like to have a spike heel

bodily functions were ever explained. As a result, the little boy developed a phobia of mutilation associated with bowel movements and developed a chronic constipation condition. As an adult, this patient perceived and presented himself as a female and wore pads once a month, imitating menstruation. Through psychotherapy and medication I successfully treated his phobia and his debilitating constipation. Eventually, this individual went through hormone therapy and a sex change and is at present happily married to a loving husband of twenty years.

jammed into his nipple! Try balancing on the bed in your heels. On one foot! His younger sister studied ballet, back in Hong Kong. Sure thing, she had beat the shit out of him with her toe shoe. That guy first would lick your heels.[1] He'd squeal like a puppy and then he'd stop and bark like a bulldog: "Pinch my breast!"[2] ... So, what was strange about your guy?"

"That's the thing. He seemed so... normal, I guess. I mean, he wasn't weird, or anything, and that was strange. You know what I mean? He looked like a friend of mine, as normal as it gets," I said.

"You never know what your friends are up to. What IS normal?"

Mommy roared with her haunted house laughter, then coughed. She rotated her chair and faced me.

"Are you normal? Or me? Who's normal?"

She raised her knobby finger.

---

[1] **Analytic Narrative:** This individual is **orally fixated**: He is fascinated with breasts, nipples, teeth, and the acts of **biting and sucking**. The most likely scenario would be a trauma during the first year of his life (oral stage), when he was abruptly weaned as his mother became pregnant with his younger sister. He had to soothe himself by sucking his thumb, a common autoerotic activity. Later, he and his sister engaged in eroticized games that included genital exposure and stimulation, such as pinching and biting. After puberty he masturbated while sucking his sister's ballet shoes. Every time he engages in sexual activity, he regresses to the oral stage of psychosexual development.

[2] This individual changes his voice because he is playing two roles in a session: that of a child being abused and that of the abuser. As Freud pointed out, "It can often be shown that masochism is nothing more than an extension of sadism turned round upon the subject's own self." In both cases, the 'self' becomes the sexual object. Also, this is a common way of being both the victim and the aggressor (child/parent).

"No one, honey. No such thing as bloody normal."

She coughed out a puff of smoke.

"You know what bugs me? You turn on the bloody TV and hear people being judgmental. What do they know? They know nothing. I heard that fat lady a year ago talking about perverts. She says, 'Monsters.' And I think, Lady, whadda you know? You're a monster, too. Just take a good look in the mirror. You're scared shitless, cause you're a monster, dear, just like everyone else.[1] And you leave my perverts alone."

Mommy was fidgeting in her chair. My brain sizzled and shriveled under her burning stare like her breakfast bacon... I wanted to go home. I craved feeling Nick's flattop under my palm, felt like hugging him to my chest, drowning in his boyish scent, unwashed, yet clean.

"I'd be good on TV. I'd tell them a couple of things about perverts. What they're made of and where they're coming from."

"Where are the perverts coming from, Mommy?" said Zoe.

She wasn't munching on anything, and her round face looked worn. With two deep lines running from her short nose to the corners of her lips, she looked like a prematurely aged baby.

"The same place as you. Moms. Nannies, teachers. Parents.[2] You know that. Your son wants you, but you're here, working. So he takes on loving your shoe—done. A foot fetishist."

---

[1] True. Growing up socially functional and compliant is always accomplished at the expense of repression of inborn sexual and aggressive drives. Not only boys, but all humans are born with instinctual drives that have to be partially suppressed in socialization, which causes mental illness. Modern American psychoanalysis in its abandoning of the ideas of instinctual drives shows a perfect example of a group neurosis.

[2] Everyone given the charge of socializing a child con-

"Fuck you, Mommy," said Zoe, her face starting to look like a crushed tomato. "You leave my kid alone. He's fine."

"Don't fret, pet," said Mommy. "Your kid's fine. It wasn't about your kid. I'm saying we all screw up our kids one way or another.[1] Get over it."

"Oh, bull, Mommy!" said Zoe. "My folks didn't screw me up—they were never around. My dad was a long-distance truck driver, my mom worked night shifts, and I was always on my own."[2]

"And look at you now, Hon!"

"Oh, you go to hell, Mommy," said Zoe, but without her usual aplomb.

Mommy took a deep drag on her joint.

"I will, baby, when the time comes... You know what hell is for me? Foot fetishists. I hate having anything touch my feet."

Everyone looked at her felt boots.

"My feet are a horrible mess—"

"My feet are a horrible mess..." echoed inside my head.

---

tributes to that child's neurosis. A human being has two alternatives: growing up as a functional but neurotic in-dividual—or being socially ostracized and developing a gross psychiatric disorder.

[1] Yes! We are doomed to inherit our traumas from our ancestors and transmit them to our descendants—until the superior man braves to abandon the concept of "morality" and thus break the vicious circle. In very simple terms, Mommy formulates the principle of transgenerational transmission.

[2] Zoe's lack of agency and low self-esteem stem from her having been neglected as a child.

MY FEET ARE A HORRIBLE MESS

"My feet are a horrible mess. Don't look at my feet!" Grandma Rosa used to say when we went to the public baths on Saturdays.

In summer, Odessa had no hot water. In fact, the whole Soviet Union had no hot water in summer. The whole country smelled like sweat, salt, sperm, blood, and excrement. The odors of heated human bodies blended with the aromas of cherries, herring, and sour cream, fermenting in the southern temperatures at a merciless pace. The overwhelming scent of the Black Sea—dead dolphins and salt—ruled over the lazy city. It was a kingdom of foul, pungent smells.

Once a week, Grandma Rosa took us to the public bath. It was no spa. In fact, I always imagined that Hell would look like our Red Proletarian Bath. In dense steam, naked women with watermelon breasts, barrel abdomens, and undulating folds of pale flesh threw tubs of boiling water onto each other. I was scared to look at their twisted red faces as they whipped each other with mops made from birch trees, leaves flying around, branches whistling through the air, slapping sour cream-white buttocks and backs. My head went round from screams.

"It's my tub, woman!"

"You stole my soap!"

I always cried at the harsh dish soap that Grandma Rosa used to wash my hair. It got into my eyes, stinging so badly I thought I would go blind, and it smelled of wet dogs and wood glue.

"Nobody ever died from a little soap," said Grandma Rosa, smacking me with the sponge. "Stop feeling sorry for yourself. Stop crying."

That was the only place where I got to see my grandmother naked. Her body reminded me of a torn cigarette: frail gray skin, empty breasts, fading shape. The only remarkable thing about her body was her feet.

Grandma had once been statuesque, and all these years later, she was still a real lady—a queen, almost—but her feet were the paws of an animal, of a faun. Every time I went shopping at Whole Foods and saw clusters of purple cauliflower, I thought of Grandma Rosa's bunions. Her toes were misshapen, clawed, like those of an ancient bird; her big toe and the next toe crossed over, intertwined like the roots of a wicked tree. Her toenails were eaten away by fungus, and stuck out like splinters.

Her feet were her dark secret, buried inside the coffins of her black pumps. She had three pairs of them, and that was all she wore for shoes, except in winter, when she would wear black boots that looked exactly like pumps. Black pumps and silk stockings worn at work, at home, and probably to her narrow bed. That was what one remembered about her: black pumps clicking like a military drum, chiseled ankles, red lipstick, and a razor-sharp voice rolling French and Russian poetry in cadence, a perfect woman with a dark shadow of monstrous physical flaws.

Grandpa made his living painting portraits of communist leaders and landscapes with curly birch trees and red tractors in front of an unnaturally blue horizon, but at home he sketched—feathery charcoal on yellowish paper—naked women, hundreds, thousands of them. He had a habit of pinning them to the wall by the window, piling them on top of each other. Caught on the water-green faded wallpaper, the women in his sketches looked like nymphs fleeing from fauns, their miniature feet hardly touching the ground.

"Beauty would save the world," he used to say, finishing a sketch and pinning it down on top of another, stomping his combat boot and coughing into his burgundy scarf.

He would pull his beret to one side, kiss the tips of his smoker-yellow fingers and send an air kiss to a charcoal nymph. I was wondering if he had ever seen Grandma's feet.[1]

The day of his funeral was the last day Grandma Rosa wore pumps. She put all her pumps into a coffin-like shoebox, covered them with Grandpa's burgundy scarf and suede beret, and packed them away into her trunk: neither Oksana nor I could fit into her doll-like size fives. Then she put on felt boots, just like Mommy's, and wore them day after day until she died. I missed the clicking sound of her heels on the hardwood floor of the hallway just as much as I missed Grandpa's tangerines and walnuts wrapped in golden foil—he used to hide them underneath the Christmas Tree, bursting into peals of laughter.

"I have bumpy bones on my feet," said Mommy, coughing, "Bloody hooves, I'm telling you. They don't fit in regular shoes. I've spent my whole life hiding my feet. It isn't silliness or paranoia. I went to see a podiatrist, and he said that my feet were the worst he'd ever seen. I can't believe guys would pay to lick them."

"How bad can they be?" asked Zoe, shrugging.

Without a word, Mommy took off her felt boots and then her cotton white socks.

Purple, blue, covered by a tangled web of veins—those were Grandma Rosa's feet. I shook my head and closed my eyes.

"Wow," said Zoe. "Mommy."

---

[1] Another example of transgenerational transmission: from her grandparents and parents, Rose inherited her denial skills and her inability to share and trust.

FANTASY CAKE

I drove across the Bay Bridge, blasting the Russian pop star Tatyana, Queen of All Sorrows. The bridge was so gray. My life was gray, too. Made of recycled cardboard, devoid of feeling. When I was little, the world had colors. My past burst with the bloody red of cherries, the rainbow brightness of beach umbrellas. It was smudged with the jet black of Grandma's pumps or Oksana's mascara. It was 3-D, alive. My dreams had even more vibrant, almost psychedelic, colors: A bacchanalia of screaming hues, transparent golden yellows and schizophrenic lilacs fused into a stellar shower, the brilliant blues and greens melted together into a polar light. Like my childhood world, the realm of my dreams was rich and alive.

My present life was a pale imitation, a black-and-white Xerox copy of my real world, Grandpa's charcoal sketches, the Bay Bridge of my daily commute, underlined by the shameless red of my stilettos. Suddenly, I thought that I was dead, had died a long time ago—with Oksana. I was dead, but I was still alive.

> *The foreign land will never be my own…*
> *The ship is gone and I'll never go home…*
> *I whisper your name, it comes out as a moan…*
> *My songs don't fly… In tears they drown…*

Tatyana's mournful voice had a melodramatic quality that could turn a wedding into a wake; listening to her made me want to fly off the bridge headfirst, straight into the ocean.

For a few moments, I saw myself jumping into the gray of the Bay. Then I saw Nick, biting his lower lip, drawing a green armadillo. I did not jump off the bridge.

Instead I went to Odessa, the Russian grocery store and bakery in the Richmond District, San Francisco's Russian neighborhood. I stumbled around the aisles, getting pushed by stern old ladies in elaborate glasses and hairdos reminiscent of Pharaohs. They busied themselves sampling putrid marinated cabbage and oily herring, sniffing smoked cheeses, and reading techno-bright nutrition labels in Ukrainian.

The line was never-ending. I'd never stood in a line like this in an American grocery store.

"Muni bus fares are going up fifty cents," I heard behind me.

"It's a nightmare," echoed another voice. "They are robbing us."

I piled up my purchases—a jar of pickled watermelon, two chocolate éclairs, a generous piece of multi-layered puffy sour cream honey cake, and a bottle of champagne, called "Odessa"—on the cashier's counter in front of a formidable saleswoman with a shiny red face and a solid pyramid of whipped cream for hair. She turned the piece of cake around with her lobster-like hands and frowned.

"Where's the price? Masha," she barked into the dark doorway. "How much is Fantasy?"

"Fantasy?" I asked.

"The cake," said an old lady in a white summer hat behind me. "Fantasy's good, but Bird's Milk is richer."

"Thanks," I said, and then turned back to the saleswoman. "Do you ever have pistachio ice cream from Odessa?"

She gave me a hateful stare and shrugged.

"Yes, when will you have the pistachio ice cream already?" echoed an old lady behind me.

She was clutching a glass jar of pickled herrings in one hand and dragging a little boy about Nick's age with the other. Her open mouth, round sunglasses, and wrinkled neck made her look like a turtle a storm had tossed on the seashore.

"Move on, women. Pistachio ice cream! Just to think of it! There was no such thing," said a man in a brown pancake cap behind the turtle lady. "Everyone's in a hurry."

"What do you mean, no such thing?" I asked.

"Look, lady. I worked at Odessa Cold Factory. You know what we made? We made ice cream. Crème-brûlée, vanilla, strawberry."

"What about pistachio?"

"There was. No. Pistachio ice cream. In Soviet Union. Understand?"

I shrugged.

"You must have dreamed it. Will you hurry now?"

The turtle-lady behind me turned purple.

"Young man, are you telling *me* what we had and what we had not in Soviet Union?"

"Whom are you calling 'young man'?"

The long line of people behind me came to life. Old and young men and women waved their packets of Canadian cottage cheese and Original Kiev Borscht made in Brighton Beach, sprinkling odorous liquids around, screaming, spitting, and stomping their feet as if their lives depended on pistachio ice cream. I looked behind me at the red faces, twisted mouths, and clenched fists, and my homesickness receded.

"Grandma, let's go!" whined the little boy. "I'm bored, I want a candy."

He looked like Nick and spoke English.

"Speak Russian like people do," said his grandmother.

"Don't want to," said the boy. "I'm American. We're in America. You speak American."

People in line stopped screaming. Everyone looked down and sideways.

"Mine is the same," said the man in the pancake cap. "What can you do?"

He opened his arms in a gesture of letting go.

"America."

Nobody else said anything.

"Four dollars ninety nine cents for Fantasy," screamed the invisible Masha from the doorway.

"Listen, consumers," spoke the saleswoman. "We have no pistachio ice cream, never had. I have work to do here. You are done, young lady. Are you buying the herrings, woman? They are three dollars ninety-nine cents."

I grabbed my bag and walked out of the store, thinking about pistachio ice cream. Oksana used to serve it under the chestnut trees. I knew it. I remembered the green, gooey sweet mass with golden speckles of nuts. I could still see it melting, sticking to my fingers, and hear the wasps buzzing around, drawn by its syrupy aroma. I remembered the rich taste, the velvety texture on my tongue, the crunchiness of the gritty pistachios on my teeth, the smoothness and sweet coldness filling my mouth, sliding down my throat, the intense nutty aftertaste on my tongue. I could not possibly have imagined it. Or... Could I? Was it my fantasy? If that was a fantasy, my whole life probably was a fantasy, too.

What if none of my memories were real? Weren't all memories fantasies, anyway?

THIS PURSE IS SHAPED LIKE A DREAM

On the way to my car, I stopped by the glitter-and rhine-stone-adorned window shop of a Paris Fashion store. A zombie-like mannequin had an oversized purse the color of a crimson rose. It was hanging off her pointed elbow.

I craved a new purse. I went inside.

"Hollywood stars on board!"

Raya, a matron in a tiger-print nightgown waved to me from behind the counter. She had fake diamonds in her nail polish. I knew Raya from peeking inside her store a few times a year after buying Russian food. Raya was a true Odessan woman. With the look of a transvestite diva and the talk of a stand-up comedian, she could host a show in Las Vegas.

"I'll tell you why you were born," said Raya.

"Why?"

"To own this purse. Look at it."

She turned the purse around. A tiny lock on the zipper gleamed in the darkness of the store.

"You see that shape. Do you know what it's shaped like?"

"A *varenik*?"

"Your mouth is shaped like a *varenik*. This purse's shaped like a dream. Three hundred dollars, discounted from five hundred and fifty, believe it?"

"I'm not sure I need a purse," I said.

"But of course! It is Italian! Designer! Alligator leather! Bjuteeful!"

"Alligator?!"

"Imitation."

I opened my wallet and looked at the rolls of pressed twenty-dollar bills: That day, I'd earned three hundred dollars exactly. I looked at the purse. It felt alive. I touched it. The soft leather crinkled under my hand as if whispering, "I am yours!"

Suddenly, Josh, the shoe fetishist, came to mind. A purse, I thought, is like a shoe. It would not talk back or hurt your feelings, and it would be there for you, no matter what. It was an ideal love and friendship. I then knew how Josh the foot fetishist felt.

"I'll buy it."

"You'll never regret it. Stilettos to match?"

"No, but tell me something, Raya."

"Anything, doll."

"Was there pistachio ice cream in Odessa?" I asked.

"You wish!" she whistled, and added, picking her teeth. "Why do you think we left?"

I clutched my treasure as I drove home, singing along to *Oh Odessa, the pearl by the sea...* and tried to shoo away the memory of my grandmother's pursed lips. Owning three pairs of Italian-made pumps was acceptable, and paying a professional cleaner in order to dedicate oneself to literary work was fine, but spending the equivalent of the weekly food budget on a purse was unworthy behavior. I had betrayed not only my grandma, but a whole army of Homers, Baudelaires and Gogols, and the Goddess of Art. I could hear her chasing me in her chariot, four furious panthers galloping, about to catch me and tear me to pieces.

I'M NOT GONNA CRY

At home, I unloaded the food on the table and threw a pizza in the oven.

"Dinner!" I shouted.

"What's for dinner?"

Nick was at the table, unwrapping the Fantasy cake. Olga picked on the éclair.

"Wait! Where's Roxanne?"

"Dunno. She hasn't eaten since morning," said Olga.

"Go call her."

"She's not going to come, Mom. She didn't eat lunch at school, either. She's in a zone."

I put the pizza slices on plates, and rushed upstairs with Roxanne's favorite—pickled watermelon and a chocolate éclair.

"Open the door, Sweetheart."

"M-m-m."

I knew by that short sound she had been crying for hours. It took me forty minutes and one hundred *sweethearts*, *honeys* and *milenkayas* to make her open the door. Inside, the heater was blasting on high, and Roxanne was rolled up on the bed, curled over her laptop, her winged shoulder blades sticking out from her black tank top.[1]

She had turned thirteen one month before, and ever since then she'd never let her new laptop—a birthday present from Daddy—out of her hands. I sat down next to her and felt like

---

[1] Roxanne's stubbornness and refusal to eat or to wear clothes recommended by Rose can be understood as a rebellious attempt to individuate from her mother. It takes on extreme forms because her anger at her mother is so intense. Instead of identifying with her mother, as would be appropriate of a girl in latency stage, she refuses everything that belongs to her mother's world.

putting my hand on her perspiring, suffering narrow neck, running my fingers through her ink-black hair, but I knew I couldn't do it. She was in pain: the pain of a baby bird with a broken wing, or a baby raccoon with a bleeding paw. I could not ask questions, either. I knew the answers anyway: The ruthless coming-of-age jungle of boys and braces, acne and betrayal, with its throbbing, longing, and loneliness.

I sat by her side and waited, listening to her soft sniffing. Finally, she handed me her laptop, without turning her face to me.

"Watch this," she said. "The words...Only don't say, 'You're about to have your period.'"

I watched a YouTube video of the Ukrainian singer Ruslana. I imagined Ruslana's picture at *YourFantasyWorld.com*. *Mistress Ruslana, fierce like fire, ruthless like a panther*. It was not just her straight, black hair, ferocious eyes, muscular legs, and black leather outfit; it was her intensity as she sang, in English:

> *You think you know me, think you control me*
> *The more you're feeling right, the more you're going wrong*
> *Don't say you got me, you don't know anything about me*
> *The more you make me weak the more I'm getting strong...*

Shaggy wolves with burning yellow eyes and terminator men snarled at Ruslana and tried to get her, but Ruslana just danced and sang:

> *I'm not gonna cry, I'll stay in the woods*
> *When my heart is aching*
> *I dance with the wolves*

"Here," I said. "We're not gonna cry. I like it. It is like my grandma's favorite poem: *'We, gypsies, dance—we don't cry—I press teeth into lips, won't cry.'"*

"He hurt my feelings, Mom. He... he cheated on me... with Lexi."

"Shh," I said. "We'll take your feelings, and put them in a little precious box. Lock it and hide the key..."

"I'm not a little girl, Mom," said Roxanne, sitting up straight as a violin string, her quiet voice vibrating with hatred. "Go away with your stupid poems and fairy tales! Can't you treat me like I'm a grown-up already?"

"The hatred only makes me love her more," I thought. It was so helpless.

"Okay then. Then I'll tell you one thing and I'll teach you one trick. Here's the thing: all men cheat. They are just made this way. Don't let it bring you down."

"You are lying," she said. "Daddy would never cheat."

Her black eyes shone, and she gave me the look of a little creature backed into a corner.

"No, not Daddy."

I grabbed a mirror and a tube of mascara from her desk.

"And here's the trick: if you feel like crying, just put your mascara on."

"I have my mascara on."

"Put more. Hold your brush at an angle, like this. See, they curl much better this way."

I thought about Oksana's needle. America was different. Men were the same, but American mascara was nothing like the old Soviet cake mascara of my youth. My daughter didn't need the needle, only the mascara tube with its own little brush.

"See, now you can't cry. 'Cause if you cry, it's all ruined."

"I have waterproof mascara, Mom," she said, finally smiling with one corner of her mouth only.

I started to laugh.

"Better than poems," murmured Roxanne.

She fished a spongy piece of a pickled watermelon from the sauce.

"Depends," I said.

THE TRUTH

Then we sat in the dark for a while, crunching the salty-sweet pulp and watching Ruslana dancing with the yellow-eyed wolves.

"You know, when I was your age I had a crush on the neighbor's son."

"What was his name?"

"Vladik."

"Was he cute?"

"I thought so. He had brown eyes, and he had this weird hair, coffee-and-milk hair. It looked like he had highlights, but of course he didn't, it was the Odessa sun. He was missing half of his front tooth, so his smile was all crooked and funny."

"Did you go out with him?"

"He once invited me to eat pistachio ice cream with him."

"Did you go?"

I shook my head.

"Why?"

"I can't remember," I said. "Was too shy, I guess."

I lied. I didn't want to tell Roxanne that at her age I wouldn't speak to boys at all, I was so scared. I was scared of all men, because of what had happened to me and Oksana.

When I was about twelve, every morning when I came to the kitchen to get my oatmeal, Vladik's father, "Uncle Oleg," sat at the table. I stared at the red poppies of the plastic table-cloth, at an open jar of pickles, or at his wife's hammock-like bras drying on the line, at the newspaper in his hands—any-thing—so I could avoid seeing his hairy knees and worn box-ers, the clusters of wiry hairs and folds of bluish skin on his stomach.

One morning, Grandma Rosa was out of the kitchen, and Uncle Oleg put his newspaper down.

"Come over here," he said.

The sight of his almost-naked body stooped on the chair filled me with nausea. It rose, churning inside, making my neck and head warm, and I could feel myself blushing, but I stepped forward. I read and reread the fat letters on the front page, without making sense. *PRAVDA* read the letters. *THE TRUTH.*

"Growing fast," said Uncle Oleg, grabbing my shoulder.

His hand reminded me of the crabs he caught at the beach and then boiled in a giant pot in the kitchen. It crawled down my shoulder, pausing on my chest, then kept crawling downwards, heading for my stomach. I remembered seeing everything from aside:[1] my protruding tummy with his red hand on it moving down toward my pleated skirt, the newspaper print from his fingers smudging over my ironed white shirt, the cigarette still smoking in his other hand. I never forgot the smell of pickles and vodka on his breath, mixing with the wet newspaper-print smell, as he pushed his fingers under my skirt and between my legs. I didn't feel anything, just kept watching it from outside myself, frozen.[2]

---

[1] **This is it!!!** Rose finally reveals the traumatic event that had caused her **Dissociative Disorder**. Sexual abuse victims often develop dissociation as a defense mechanism. This defense mechanism is often recruited in a situation of extreme danger or, in Rose's case, in reaction to trauma that occurs when neither fight nor flight—the regular means of escape—is available.

[2] Rose dissociates from her body, having the "out of body" experience of observing the abuse scene from aside and imagining that the abuse is happening to someone else. As an adult, Rose is unable to fully experience intercourse with her husband because as a child she had numbed her senses to protect herself from becoming aroused when her neighbor molested her.

Then I heard Grandma walking into the kitchen. She was holding a hot iron. I watched Uncle Oleg's hand jerking away and onto the table and grabbing the newspaper. He shook with his smoker's cough and read, "The 25th Congress of the Supreme Committee..." The words blended, but I could see my grandma's pursed lips and a frown.

"Go eat your oatmeal," she said.

Every night after that, I saw Uncle Oleg twice: in the dark hallway leading to the bathroom and in my nightmares. Every night I struggled away from his paws, while he panted, his vodka-pickle breath getting into my every pore, pinching me, getting under my bathrobe, crushing me against the wall. I never made a sound, fighting silently, and would end up snaking my way out of his grip and into the bathroom.

One night when Grandma Rosa handed me a towel—one end for your feet, one end for your face, middle for your butt—I refused to go to the bathroom.

"Girls must wash every night," said Grandma.

"I won't go," I whispered.

"Go stand in the corner until you're ready," she said.

I cried quietly, thinking about Vladik's golden hair, the cold wall of the hallway, and imagining the greasy tiles of hallway linoleum opening and the furious Black Sea rising from beneath the basement, swallowing Uncle Oleg forever. When dense Misty Lilac had obscured all thoughts, Grandma dragged me out of the corner by my hand, her arthritic fingers around my wrist like a vice.

"What's wrong with you, child?" she said, and slapped me on the back of my head.

I looked at the rows of books—they waited on the shelves like soldiers at attention—and didn't answer.

"She won't go 'cause she's scared," said Oksana from underneath her blanket.

"No mumbling," said Grandma and turned to me. "Speak louder. What are you scared of?"

I looked at Pushkin's portrait, praying to him to make it all go away somehow. He looked at me, all curls and dimples, his eyes laughing, as if saying, "Hang in there."

Oksana jumped out from her bed, ran to us, and threw her arms around me.

"Grandma, it's Uncle Oleg. He pinches. I punched him, but he still does it. He…"

I still remember the lack of color in Grandma Rosa's cheeks.

"Is this the honest truth?" she asked me.

I nodded and looked down at my slippers.

"You stay in your room," she said.

"What do you think she'd do?" asked Oksana, pulling me to her bed. "Hit him?"

"Kill him," I said.

"She'll tell Auntie Ludmila and then *she'll* kill him," said Oksana.

Grandma returned after ten minutes and said, "He won't touch you anymore. Go wash up."

The hallway was empty. All doors were closed. Uncle Oleg never looked my way again, but each time as I passed him in the kitchen, I heard his coarse whisper from behind the Truth newspaper, "Stinking Jews." Vladik never talked to me again, only threw empty tins at me in the yard.

All I could say to Roxanne was, "Things were different there."

"Why did you leave Ukraine? Things are better there," she said.

"It's not about the place," I said. "It's about us, you know."

THE LEMMINGS

When I left her room, squinting at the bright light in the kitchen, I heard unusual sounds coming from Olga's room. They were Toys "R" Us Squish Me Toy-quality sounds, only the music was *Swan Lake*.

I opened the door and saw Olga and Nick glued to a computer screen, fighting over the keyboard and the mouse, giggling and fussing. I walked in, stood behind them, and looked at the screen. Against a pitch-black background, ant-like rodents wobbled along cliffs and stairs in endless rows—then threw themselves down and dissipated.

"What is it?" I asked.

"*Lemmings*, Mom," said Nick, and elbowed Olga.

"You don't know anything, Mom," said Olga, and shoved him back.

"Daddy showed this to me," said Nick.

"Daddy showed this to me, actually," said Olga.

The lemmings marched the way the young pioneers marched during the parades of my childhood—joyfully, energetically, bouncing off the plank, clueless and invincible, only to perish in heaps, without any effect on their surroundings.

"Don't you feel sorry for them?" I asked.

"They're lemmings," said Nick. "They are supposed to die, Mom."

"Duhhh!" said Olga, rolling her eyes and shoveling half a cookie into her mouth.

"What do you do to win?"

"Even the website says it's impossible to explain," said Olga. "On that level."

"Bang!" said Nick.

I turned around and went to the garage. Luke was stooping over the robot.

"Honey."

"Yes?"

"The *Lemmings*?"

"What about them?"

"Don't you think it's a bit disturbing?"

He put a wrench down and scratched his neck.

"You are kidding, right?"

"They're self-destructive. They are brainless, sad little creatures. This elated march toward death—why, why do our children have to identify with something that dumb?"

Luke came toward me and put his large hand on my shoulder.

"You really need to rest. It's just a stupid little puzzle game."

"It makes me sick—did you—have you seen them jump off the cliff? Can't the kids read a book instead? Like *David Copperfield*? *Tom Sawyer*?"

Luke rolled his eyes, just like Olga, and went back to his robot. I waited for a while, but he didn't say anything and didn't look at me. I saw red patches coming up his neck.

I went back to Olga's room. The music changed. It sounded like an orchestra of gnomes playing "London Bridge Is Falling Down." Olga snorted and shrieked.

I left, sat on the couch in the living room, and stared at the amethyst light. It was cold and clean light with no heat.

Luke shuffled in from the garage and came toward me. His face looked like a sunken ship.

"Come here," he said.

The idea of being touched felt nauseating. Everything was nauseating.

"I... I have my period," I lied.[1]

He sighed. I wanted to talk to him, but by the time I opened my mouth, he'd stepped away, and said, "I'm going to go back out and pull a few more wires. I might sleep in the living room."

"Sure," I said.

I sleepwalked into the bedroom and climbed into bed, rolled on my side with the blanket between my legs, closed my eyes, and pulled out the fantasy that came to me when I was really anxious. It was The Female Warrior Does the Dying Beast, a fusion of *Jurassic Park* and Westerns I used to watch in open-air summer cinemas in Odessa. Some days I was an Indian, a Pocahontas, lilies and eagle's feathers in my braids, a necklace of tiger teeth and claws around my neck, a battle-axe in my hand.[2] Other times I was Melpomene, the Goddess of Art, riding a black panther, a whip in my hand; and sometimes I was the Amazon Queen, my bronze legs gripping a pterodactyl's flanks, its filmy back vibrating, pressed to my crotch. And sometimes, I would be all three, switching between one and another with the incoherence and inconsistency of a dream.

---

[1] Rose is becoming more affected by her work at the dungeon. She is starting to have difficulties compartmentalizing the parts of her life. She is starting to generalize her experience and her husband is gradually blending into the **Big Monster Man**.

[2] A double axe, or labrys ("lip") is the symbol of the female labia at the entrance of the womb. It was used as a battle and ritual weapon and an agricultural tool in the matriarchal societies. The labrys design is found in Paleolithic cave paintings, and later on murals, mosaics, pottery, seals, and jewelry.

That night, something was stamping behind me, and I knew it was going to rape me.[1] It was naked, rough, red-faced, covered with patches of black fur.[2] I raised my battle-axe high and sliced his body—like a knife slices butter—leaving him gasping, mouth twisted... down he fell, and I slowly, very slowly, inserted my fingers, one by one, inside his soaking wounds, deep, deep, deeper. Then I mounted his dying body, and rode it like a horse off the ground and up and up into the transparent sky into the blue lightness, my stomach, my pelvis contracting in orgasm.

I always slept well and had no dreams after my fantasies, but this time, as I slid into heavy slumber, the blanket still between my legs, I had a nightmare.

I was in Hell.[3] Hell was busy. Devils with Mommy faces and bleeding hooves were buzzing about, *Lemmings*-like, throwing clients into the blazing fire of a giant oven, chomping off

---

[1] Rose is stimulated by danger and the sense of conquest.

[2] **Fantasies of forced sex** are the second leading fantasy subject among heterosexual women. Such fantasies allow women to safely investigate their sexual feelings while not taking responsibility for them, thus staying guilt-free. It is also known that fantasies of forced is the first most common fantasy for homosexual women.

[3] **Hell** in Rose's dream is the representation of both the dungeon and her life. She has a choice: either to continue acting out her childhood traumas (penis envy and unresolved Oedipus complex) and violate her taboos, or to keep suppressing her conflict but remain torn and neurotic. In either case, she finds herself in Hell.

Rose's Hell is reminiscent of George Eliot's version of Hell:

What is hell? Hell is oneself.
Hell is alone, the other figures in it
Merely projections. There is nothing to escape from
And nothing to escape to. One is always alone.

the perverts' heads, sawing off their genitals and dancing in a primeval rite of passage, whacking around the severed body parts. Candles, dildos, and needles towered over sinners like Manhattan skyscrapers; merry-go-round-like pinwheels slowly churned, mincing sinners; tank-sized rattraps crawled after their victims, clicking and clacking.

A giant *Lemming*, no, a Rat raced after me, and I was not me anymore. I was Rose, an Amazon warrior clad in red vinyl. I had a razor in one hand and a whip in the other and I fought the Rat like a delirious porn-cartoon Nutcracker. Tchaikovsky's tired tunes boomed with a rave-party force. The Rat bit me, teeth like daggers. I felt piercing pain and I knew it was Rose's pain and the devils' pain the perverts' pain and the Rat's pain. I screamed, and slashed, and smacked. I sliced the Rat's throat and stood knee-deep in the boiling black blood and shit. The stench got so bad I could not breathe.

And as I placed my spike heel on the Rat, with one precise Zen move I cut out my red-red heart and pinned it to a blank page in an open book that was bigger than me. Million-dollar red, swollen, and shiny heart. I watched the blood flowing from it, forming vinyl writing on the white of the page. I woke up screaming, with a sharp pain in my chest.

I reached for Luke; I was dying to hug him, press myself against his sweaty body, dissolve in his heat and the powdery smell of his deodorant. I wanted to speak to him, to Mike, to anyone, tell them everything, cry and scream.[1] Luke's pillow was cold. I remembered he was in the living room.

---

[1] Rose consistently suffers from an inability to establish communication with people in her life. She fantasizes about speaking to Mike, a stranger, because such contact creates the illusion of interaction and allows her to remain in her pattern of secrecy.

I jumped out of the bed and ran to the living room. The tiger throw on the sofa still had Luke's body contour, smelled like him, but he wasn't there. Potemkin glanced up at me from the pillow, her green eyes sparkling at me, and went back to sleep.

"He must have gone running," I thought.

HELL

I knew I couldn't sleep, so I stepped out in the street to smoke. Through the smoke, I saw a bright spot approaching me. It looked and moved like a ghost in the morning twilight. Then I realized it was Blossom, walking slowly down the street in his lionlike manner. He sat down in the middle of the street like it was the middle of the bed and stared at Vanessa's door. His ears moved. The door opened and I saw Luke. He was looking at me, squinting.

"Hi, Honey," he whispered.

I didn't hear the words, but I saw his lips moving. I saw the whole scene from aside: a man in his running clothes and oversized, brand-new sneakers, a tanned woman in a black bra, looking at me through the white gauze of the curtain, the amethyst light flickering in the dusk, the rose-gold cat, in the middle of the road, and another woman in a ridiculous Chinese velvet robe embroidered with dragons, a cigarette in her hand slowly burning through her index and middle fingers.

I didn't look at Luke; I looked at Blossom. He stood up, jerked his tail, and walked off. He stepped like a retired king. For a split second, I wished I could be him: walking down the broad street, aloof and confident, little lies and treacheries foreign to him, above good and bad and all moral convictions.

I was still watching Blossom, but I knew Luke was standing next to me. I smelled his odorless deodorant. I also smelled Vanessa. I didn't want to look at him, didn't want to see his dry sweatshirt, his messy curls, his watery eyes. I didn't want to hear what he was about to say.

"I'm sorry," he said.

The cigarette started to burn my fingers, and I looked at my hand instead of the cat. It was shaking, but I didn't feel it.

"Honey," he said. "Please."

I closed my eyes. I didn't want to look at anyone.

"Give me the cigarette," he said. "You're burning yourself."

Potemkin rubbed against my leg.

I couldn't remember getting ready but just as I was heading for the car with Nick's Spiderman lunchbox and my Goodwill bag of dungeon clothes, I heard screaming from upstairs.

"...and you are dumb, and your friends are dumb..." screamed Olga.

"...*you* wore it yesterday..." screamed Roxanne.

I ran upstairs, stumbled over Potemkin, who was galloping by my side, almost fell down, and found both girls clutching the sleeve of an old green jacket. Nick skipped around them like a pagan dancer, sticking his tongue out and cheering. He was still in his pajama bottoms.

"Stop it! We're late! Nick, put your pants on, you guys, let go! Stop acting like animals!"

Ten minutes later, we were driving along the empty street in a grave silence broken only by Nick's crunching on dry cereal from a plastic bowl. Olga was wearing the green jacket, her face shining like a honey-glazed pancake. Roxanne was pretending to look over her math, her black hair hanging over her face like velvet blinds. As always, she gave up. I gave Olga a sharp look. Ironically, she was the one who took after my sister Oksana. My sister always won. She always had the jacket I wanted.

As soon as I dropped off the kids, I reached for my cell phone. I had a strong desire to call someone, somewhere, to scream, to cry, to hear another person's voice saying my name. The phone was missing. It was getting late, but I made a U-turn and sped up down the street toward home, not knowing why I was going there, who I was going to call, or what I was doing next.

At home I waved to Potemkin, who was on her way outside, found my phone on the desk (seven missed calls, all from Luke) and threw it in my purse without listening to the messages. I didn't feel like talking to anyone anymore. I rushed to the garage, then stopped. I knew I'd forgotten something on the desk, but I couldn't remember what it was.

I went back, shuffled papers around, opened and closed drawers. Then I saw it. My wedding picture. I suddenly saw Luke's smile. I threw it on the floor, and left without looking back.

I was late, so I backed out of the garage, speeding, brakes screeching. Then I felt a slight bump.

"Potemkin!"

I fell out of the car, my heart almost jumping out of my chest, unable to breathe, blood rushing away from my skin, and stared underneath the wheels. There, with the same look of royal calm, lay Blossom, his large body turned into a bloody mess.

My hands went to my mouth. Everything went dark before my eyes.[1] I pressed my body into the side of the car, shaking and unable to scream, to cry, to move. I didn't know how much time I spent like this, when I felt a gentle touch on my shoulder. I just shook my head.

"Here," said Vanessa's voice. "Here, come here."

She was crying, and grabbing me and holding me, and for a while we stood there, in each other's arms, crying without talking. I'd never felt that close to Vanessa, or to anyone else. Her breath smelled like tequila, mixing with the musky scent of her kimono.

---

[1] Dissociation episode. Rose "loses time."

We brought a shoe box, and placed Blossom inside. He was heavy as a rock. His torn orange fur was splattered with blood, and we covered it with Vanessa's quilt. We didn't speak. We dug a hole underneath an acacia in her yard, placed the shoebox in it, and covered it over with soil. A white petal fell down and rested on top of the tiny grave.

"Bye, Blossom," said Vanessa.

She put her spade down, her thin lips twisted, and went back to the house, signaling me to follow her. Without the bounce in her walk, she moved like an old lady.

I followed her into the living room, where she went for the bar.

I stood by the window, looking at the street through the white gauze—from Vanessa's side of the street. It was the exact same view as mine; I could see our oversized green recycle bin. Next to me, by a coffee table, stood a floor lamp, a bronze girl chasing a bronze butterfly around the stained glass globe. The glass was a milky-lilac color, gentle and brash at the same time.

I patted the smooth globe. The bronze girl's outstretched arm, her vain attempt to catch the butterfly, its frozen wings trembled through my tears.

Vanessa came back with a bottle of tequila and two shot glasses. She poured drinks. The glass danced in her tanned fingers. We drank it without a word, our faces twitching from alcohol.

"I'm sorry," I said.

"I'm sorry, too," she answered.

I put the shot glass down and walked out of the house and down the street to my car, without looking back. My head was empty now, and my body warm from tequila. I started the car and drove to the dungeon.

Crossing the bridge, I listened to the news, trying to focus on fires in the San Fernando Valley, and smoked my Vogues. In the background, I kept the *Lemmings* orchestra playing, "London Bridge is falling down, falling down, falling down," like a broken record, again and again and again.

IT'S JUST A CAT

The morning was quiet, and I curled in my armchair opposite Greta. She was immersed in her book, her shoulders rounded, her smooth hand supporting her cheek, but she wasn't reading. The gentle sun poured onto the caramel hair that fell over her tired face and lit the peachy fuzz above her soft upper lip. Mommy was munching her bacon in the kitchen, mumbling; Zoe was smoking on the porch; and Susanna was asleep on the floor, a Catholic saint statue, her pale virgin hands crossed over her chest.

"Greta," I whispered.

She looked up at me. Her bulging eyes shone with helplessness and kindness, and I wanted to talk to her. I wanted to tell her what had happened that morning. Instead, I said, "What are you reading?"

"Michael Strong... Have you read him?"

I knew I blushed.

"The **DEVIATIONS** guy?"

"Well, yeah, this is his early work, scandalous stuff. He writes this really controversial philosophy-psychology stuff, sort of like social Darwinism with a Nazi flavor..."

She was chatting away, chewing her gum, turning the book around in her soft hands. *Should I tell her?* I thought.

"He considers himself Nietzschean-Freudian, go figure. Kind of really extreme. I once took his lecture at Stanford, and that was something else! He's from San Francisco, and Susanna said he might be one of the clients here,[1] right, Susanna?"

We both looked at Susanna, who didn't say a word and didn't move.

---

[1] Wrong!!!

Greta switched to a whisper, "Who knows? He's a hottie, great body, and he speaks well, but then there's something really creepy about him, don't you think?"

"Screw Strong, Greta," I said quietly. "I—Can I tell you something?"

"Sure."

She put the book down. I stared at the gold-and-green lottery ticket she used as a bookmark.

"Rose?"

"I just killed somebody."

"What?!"

"A cat."

"You killed a cat?"

"My neighbor's cat. My neighbor, she—I don't like her. But I didn't want to kill her cat."

"Why—I mean how did you kill her cat?"

"I don't know. I had bad, bad dreams. I dreamt that I went to Hell, only it was also here, in the Dungeon, and we all were there… It was horrible, and I couldn't sleep, and then—"

I stopped.

"Then?"

"Then I ran over Blossom."

"Blossom?"

"The cat."

"Jesus, Rose. I'm sorry."

"Yeah."

"Sorry, girl. You need to take a nap, or take a shower, or a drink?"

"I just had a drink. I already can't think straight. Tell me, do you have bad dreams?"

Greta sighed, her chest moved up and down.

"All the time. Bad dreams, always falling down. Down, and down, and down, into the darkness, every night."

She wrapped her arms around her chest, as if she were cold.

"Like *Lemmings*," I said, covering my eyes with my hand.

"Look, I mean it's not that horrible, it's just a cat. I ran over a pigeon a year ago, and it just happens, but—you know, you look weird. You sure you don't want to—I don't know, call your husband?"

I shook my head.

"It's just a cat."

I felt tears coming, but I didn't want to cry. We didn't say anything for a while.

"Better to forget," I said finally.

"No," said Greta. "Better to talk. Tell me."

I looked down and bit my lip. I really wanted to tell her and Susanna about Luke, and Vanessa, and Oksana, and Mike, and my whole life, but as usual, I could not force the words out of my mouth.

"It's okay, you'll feel better," said Greta. "C'mon."

I took a deep breath and started to talk. Once I started, I could not stop. Only instead of my life, I talked about a dream, at the same time knowing there was something else I wanted to say, something I was leaving out, forgetting.

"About a week ago, I had this other terrible dream: lots and lots of girls and women, all naked, all thrown together like in a concentration camp, only it was a boat. Some were young and beautiful, some were pregnant, some were bleeding, some were giving birth or breastfeeding, some were old and dying, sagging breasts, ugly bodies—"

"Ugh," said Greta.

"Yeah, all in a crowd, together, suffering, quarreling and complaining, like at a wake. Some were crying, and some were silent. Mommy was there, she was a captain, an old pirate, a black patch over her eye, a parrot on her shoulder, and she had a hook in her hand, and she was hitting other women with

232

this hook. She gave me a key and ordered me to go down, into the bowels of the boat. Get a hook for yourself, she said. And you know what I found there, when I opened the door? Men. Crammed together in the filth and the darkness, also naked, chained to the walls. They were slaves, and they suffered even worse than the women, only they could not cry like we did. Oh, they were awful—none of them were quite right, they were blind, or mute, or deaf, or deformed, or retarded, or something, and I saw my son there... And then Mommy ordered me to torture my son with a hook..."

I stopped and we stared at each other for a while without saying a word. The silence crept in on us, and I had to say something—anything, just to break it.

"What does it mean?"

"Don't know. I was never good at interpreting dreams, you know."

We looked at each other again.

INTERCOURSE WITH A CENTIPEDE

"I have a dream, too. I see it a lot."

Susanna's voice rang like a bell. Greta and I looked at Susanna's motionless body. She was still lying on the floor like a dead princess in her invisible crystal coffin, all light and air, her transparent eyelids shut, her face still.

"I have intercourse with a centipede. Every night."

Greta and I didn't look at each other.

"You read Kafka? That type of bug. Well, I've never, ever had an orgasm with a guy. I sure have them in my dream…"

Nobody said anything for a while. Then Susanna opened her eyes and stared at the ceiling.

"You've never had an orgasm?" I repeated.

I couldn't focus on anything; thoughts were fleeting through my head like wind over a snow-covered field.

"Not with guys. Or with girls," she said. "Only when I'm by myself. I fantasize a lot, and I can come without even touching myself, but of course it's better if I do."

"Lucky you," said Greta, sighing. "I have a low libido. Even with a vibrator."

"I just imagine something," said Susanna. "Not sexual—just stealing a necklace from my mom's jewelry box,[1] or sometimes

---

[1] Susanna doesn't feel that she is worthy or deserving of her mother's expensive jewelry—or an orgasm. Susanna's mother never allowed her any **privacy to masturbate** and so she began doing it in secret, in the bathroom, binding her libido to urination or defecation. For Susanna, excretion and sex are equally exciting. Her interest in enemas, brown showers and other excrement-related fantasies stems from that early taboo. Instead of taking openly what is hers and belongs to her, she secretly and silently steals from her mother in her desire to take her mother's place.

walking naked down Telegraph Avenue, just in my heels, and the cops are staring at me and instead of catching me, they get erections, so everyone can see, and everyone is laughing at them.[1] So I make them masturbate, and I just watch. Or sometimes I'm a guy and a girl at the same time, fucking myself and watching at the same time."

"I have bad fantasies. Someone is running after me, but I can't see his face. I don't think he has a face. He jumps on me—"[2] said Greta.

She sighed and rubbed her elbow.

"And?" asked Susanna.

"Can't remember. I also had a fantasy about my supervisor, when I was in school," said Greta. "I wanted to be a mouse and live in his old shoe."

---

[1] In order to enjoy herself, Susanna must conceal her desires. Law enforcement—authority—is ridiculed by eroticizing the cops, and the risk of punishment increases her enjoyment and the thrill of her stolen reward.

[2] Sexual abuse victims often fantasize about **rape, bondage, abduction, domination**, and **forced sex** because during their first sexual experiences, sexual arousal was initially associated with the abuse itself and with the ensuing emotions of fear, disempowerment, and loss of control. In such cases, a **victimization fantasy** might be necessary in order to achieve orgasm. The experience is defensively sexualized; the libido is attached to the abusing object.

The rapist in Greta's fantasies is faceless and anonymous. She might be protecting herself from memories of physical and emotional pain. It is also a way of making possible coping with sexual guilt: She is a victim of an unknown environment and would not be held responsible for any pleasure she receives. Rape fantasies without violence can occur in women with no history of child abuse; for them, forced sex is a ticket to guilt-free sex. It is not associated with pain and violence.

"Sick," said Susanna, not looking at anyone. "Rose, you have any fantasies?"

"No," I said.

She sat up, and stretched, her arm almost transparent, arched toward the ceiling. I just watched Susanna's slow moves. She caught my look and laughed, "Catness?"

I looked away, blushing.

"No fantasies. You're funny, Rose. You guys want to smoke some dope?"

I felt a chill crawling up my arms and legs. Susanna and her outstretched arms, Greta and her trembling hair, the mantelpiece with Timmy's photo, the **DEVIATIONS** book, tossed on the carpet—everything lost its color and volume, looked fake, flat, two-dimensional, a paper cutout. Susanna's voice was distorted, "Just don't tell Zoe, she's so loud."

SEX EDUCATION

The silence was broken by the phone. We all listened to Mommy's voice screeching the familiar, "Yes, honey. Sure, dear," and waited for her to shuffle into the room.

"Greta and Susanna, a client for you. Greta, check Joseph, the sex education card. Susanna, fill her in."

She shuffled back out, limping, muttering, "My back's killing me today; it's all out of joint—boy, I can't handle this anymore."

Susanna stretched again.

"Easy one. We cuff him to the cross in the middle of the floor, he's a middle-school student, we are two teachers. You point at my breasts and say, 'These are breasts, you can't touch them, they are for babies...' He looks, you spank him. He shouts, 'Mea culpa, mea culpa...' He's a Latino. I show a tampon, 'This is for girls, don't look.' He looks, I hit him. You point at me, 'She is a virgin, don't look.' You whip him. I show a dildo, 'Masturbation,' and so on and so forth.[1] You get the idea. Just repeat after me and feed it back. Some sex education!"

"We had no sex education at school," I said. "Nobody ever talked about sex. Nobody ever talked about anything."

---

[1] **Analytic Narrative:** This individual was most likely brought up in a repressed family; for example, an extremely religious Catholic family, where sex—and body parts related to sex—was taboo. The sex education classes at school broke these taboos but were highly arousing. He learned at home that the sexual excitement he felt in class was wrong and punishable. At the same time, his libido could not be entirely repressed. As an adult, he resolves this conflict in a typical compromised solution and gets sexual gratification but is immediately punished for it, thereby receiving **absolution of sins**.

"So, you want to smoke first?"

"Thanks. On the porch?"

I didn't want to smoke pot. I watched Greta rising slowly, her shoulders rounded, her head low, following Susanna to the porch. She bumped into Zoe, who catapulted into the room, her face tomato red, cell phone clutched in her square hand.

"Little jerk! Just like his goddamn father! 'Mommy this, Mommy that!' Won't leave me alone! Left me ten voicemail messages this morning! And you'd think something horrible happened, right?"

"What happened?" I asked.

"Well, he got all freaked out 'cause there was a big bug in the kitchen. The guy's eight years old—grow up already! He claims he can't squish the stupid bug—it makes him all queasy.[1] He feels sorry for the bug! Anybody feel sorry for me?"

"Is he at home alone?"

"Of course he's at home alone. Do you think I get paid enough to get a babysitter for an eight-year-old? He had a fever this morning, so he couldn't go to school."

Her phone buzzed again, and Zoe collapsed into the armchair, creating a small earthquake.

"I'm not picking up this time. Let him cry all he wants!"

Zoe—powdered sugar stuck to her chin, her nose glistening—looked like Rudolph the Reindeer. I hated her and her son.

The land line rang, and Mommy moaned, "This place is like fucking headquarters... 'Oh hello, Sweetheart! Today

---

[1] Another example of externalization. Internal danger, possibly the fear of unacceptable sexual impulses, is translated into **a fear of insects**, a common phobia. It begins in children around the age of three as a fear of monsters.

we have Greta, Rose, Susanna and Zoe... Oh very nice... Oh you are disgusting... Oh please. You are welcome, Honey.'"

She hung up, slamming down the phone.

"Bloody Hell... Cocaine Jack... He has to make at least three phone calls before he gets his ass here, and he's only made one so far... They get off on this. This is part of their fantasy."

"Why 'Cocaine Jack?'"

"Snorts cocaine, obviously. Rolls up hundred-dollar bills and snorts like a pig, then bounces off the walls—in his panty-hose. Shimmies all around the place. He might like you, Rose, and will offer you some, but of course nobody takes any. He's easy. You sit in the Boudoir in front of the mirror and change clothes, put on your makeup, do your rollers, and keep telling him 'You are disgusting!'"

"Why?" I asked. "I mean, why does it get him off?"

"Can't you see? It's all about the mother. You can almost see him watching his mother getting dressed and ignoring him. He would try to get her attention, cry, dance, play, grab her clothes. She would tell him he was disgusting.[1] Get it?"

"Got it."

---

[1] **Analytic Narrative:** Cocaine Jack had a **Tantalizing Mother**, who alternated between seducing and punishing him. After exciting him sexually, she punished him fiercely for being aroused. The mother's reaction to his arousal (horror and disgust) was her own defense; her **Internal Morality Police** penalized her for provoking her son and for her incestual wishes. Incapable of admitting her own incestual desires, she would project them onto her own son and then punish him severely for it. The horror of incest is at the root of the mother's reaction. Cocaine Jack was overwhelmed as a boy and sexualized both watching a woman apply makeup and being verbally crucified for the excitement he obtained from it. **It is a common phenomenon for mothers to punish their sons for their own incestual provocations.**

A scene flashed back into my mind. My son had peed all over the floor in the bathroom like he always did.

"You are dishgusting!" said Olga, one curler in her mouth, another in her hand.

"Dishgusting yourself!" he yelled. "Get your hair out of my toothbrush!"

It was still morning, and I was ready to leave the dungeon. I was desperate for some sleep, but instead I went to the kitchen and got out a plastic container of pickled watermelon.

Mommy whistled. "Nice purse!"

"I bought it yesterday... I shouldn't have, I couldn't really afford it."

"Oh, you had to! Look, girls, Rose got herself a new pussy!" she said. "What are those?"

"Pickled watermelon."

"Where on Earth do you get those?"

"In a Russian grocery store."

"Ew. How revolting. Why would anyone pickle a watermelon?" asked Mommy. "You're not supposed to do that!"

"You're not supposed to suspend men from ceilings by their dicks, either," I said.

I reached to take the container back off the table.

"Oh, listen to her. She can talk, after all," said Mommy.

"Wait, let me try it," said Susanna. "Sounds interesting."

"Don't bother, Susanna" said Mommy. "Zoe will eat it; she eats everything."

I didn't say anything, just made myself a very strong coffee.

THE PSYCHOTHERAPY FANTASY

"Rose, your twelve o'clock is a psychotherapist fantasy, a Boudoir client, but you will have to take him in the Dungeon."

"Why?"

"We have an animal in the Boudoir at twelve. I can't move him to the Dungeon."

"Animal, animal, animal."

I thumbed through the cards looking for an animal fantasy. I had made my coffee too strong; my hands were shaking.

Disturbing ideas came to mind. Tortured kittens? I had Blossom's royal death mask in front of my mind's eye. Human cockroaches? Circus bears gone wild? Saber-toothed tigers? Cages and chains? The card was missing. Susanna and Greta were back from the porch, stoned, laughing, Greta giggling, her voice losing its softness and becoming a squeaky cheerleader chuckle. I turned to Susanna.

"Hey, what's animal fantasy? Can't find the card."

"Enema! She said 'enema,' not animal," laughed Susanna. "You didn't even smoke any, did you? Rose never needs pot, she's always high. Seriously, you look like you're high right now,"[1] she took a breath. "The enema fantasy, older crowd, sixties and seventies. When they were kids they were treated to enemas for constipation..."[2]

"You do it?!"

---

[1] A vacant, trance-like stare is typical for a disconnected dissociative state.

[2] **Klismaphilia,** the love of enemas, is often observed in older individuals or in cultures where enemas are still used for constipation relief. **Phallic Mother with enema** is a classic Freudian Mother.

"Sure. It's one of my specialties.[1] I'm actually producing a porno movie about enemas. You have the psychotherapy guy, anyway."

Susanna and Greta kept laughing. My head was about to burst.

I read the card for my twelve o'clock: *Name: Dean. Fantasy: a psychotherapy session. Wear open-toed shoes, a short skirt. Long toenails. Listen to his fantasies, and play them out. Will ask you to squeeze his balls—just say no.*

I once was in therapy. My shrink always brought back memories of my elementary school teacher. Just like the math-and-spelling Napoleon of my childhood, my therapist wore a uniform pleated ankle-length skirt, a baggy gray blouse, and no makeup. Her shoes looked orthopedic. I never could figure out her age.

We spent most of the time talking about my 'childhood abuse.' I stared at her shoes, and told her about Uncle Oleg, the hallway nightmares, Grandma Rosa.

My therapist explained to me that the history of sexual abuse in childhood often leads to promiscuous behavior in adult women.[2] I kept looking at her orthopedic shoes—two brown tanks, ready to attack—and wondered what she really thought about me, my Ukrainian past and my behavior. She always knew when my fifty-five minutes were up, without

---

[1] Susanna is fascinated by enemas both because she likes to be transformed into a powerful phallic figure and because her own control over the taking in and expelling of bodily matter is an issue of conflict.

[2] High-risk sexual conduct is another example of self-harming behavior, symptomatic for individuals with **Dissociative Identity Disorder**.

ever looking at the clock. I decided to copy her almost invisible frown—one eyebrow crawling up just a bit.

The Psychotherapy Patient arrived at twelve sharp, with a rolled manuscript. He didn't look like he'd stepped off the conveyer belt, as he had a porcupine mane and no facial hair. I knew this session was going to be different.

"A script," he smiled to me.

He undressed and sat down at the torture table. I was standing next to him, my hair pulled back in a French twist, glasses and no lipstick, secretly wishing my shrink and my teacher could see my lace and leather.

Dean was looking through his notes. He was naked except for the glasses on the tip of his nose, and he looked like the father of a big family at a nudist beach, reading to his kids.

"I have a fantasy, doctor. An obsession. I am obsessed with feet and short skirts. Toenails, too. Long, long toenails. Can I see your toenails, doctor?"

"No," I said. "What makes you think about toenails, Dean?"

I pushed my glasses up, trying to look professional, yet playful.

"They are sexy, doctor. Seductive…"

"I see. Try to think of a childhood experience that could have triggered this obsession, Dean. Did your mother or sister have long toenails?"

"You are good, doctor! I don't have a sister. But when I was sixteen, I used to mow the lawn for this lady… Mrs. Stapleton used to sit in her chaise longue, chatting with me, her feet curled under her. She had pretty, white feet and moved her toes all the time as she spoke to me. Her toenails were long and red. She was very kind, and she was a single mother, in her forties. She gave me candies. I would go home, eat candies, and jerk off... I had a fantasy that Mrs. Stapleton would catch me and punish me."[1]

"Very good, Dean. Tell me more about it, Dean. How would Mrs. Stapleton punish you?"

"She would pull my ear, hard... Pull my ear, doctor."

I slipped on a pair of rubber gloves. I figured a doctor would do that. Besides, I could not, would not touch anyone. Not after my nightmares. Not that day. Then I squeezed Dean's ear. It looked like raw hamburger and felt like a kitchen sponge. He winced.

"In response, I would kiss her feet and legs..."

He kneeled in front of me and started smacking his lips all over my short toenails. They felt like two giant slugs. I shuddered, hit him slightly with my foot and stepped away.

"Keep talking, Dean."

"Then she would twist my balls and slap my dick, hard. Doctor, will you do it?"

"No," I said firmly. "I will ask you embarrassing questions instead. Try to go further into your childhood. Think feet. What comes to mind, Dean?"

"I see a forest of legs, doctor. I'm a little boy, maybe three or five, walking next to my mom in a supermarket... I see those tall heels, and pumps... Those feet are big... When you are little, everything looks bigger... Will you squeeze my balls, doctor?"[2] he whined.

"No!"

---

[1] I would like to quote Freud's mention of a man who remembered "that he used to employ the idea of being beaten by his mother for the purpose of masturbation, though to be sure **he soon substituted for his own mother the mothers of his school-fellows or other women** who in some way resembled her."

[2] Dean tortures Rose by exposing her to his suffering. Every masochist is also a sadist.

And so it went for an hour. I got really tired of him. I finally understood why I had paid one hundred and twenty dollars for my one-hour therapy session. Therapists have a hazardous job.

"Dean, go into that corner and punish yourself."

"You are too kind to me, doctor."

While he busied himself, I tried to be positive and remind myself of the purpose of my being in the dungeon. I wasn't that sure anymore.

"Think hard! This is what you wanted. This script and the story are invaluable for the writing," I tried to convince myself.

Then a clever trick came to my caffeinated mind. Meanwhile, Dean had finished punishing himself, so he laughed and winked at me.

"You got the psychological part really well."

"I am actually a Ph.D. in psychology," I said.

"You are funny," said Dean.

"You are getting a homework assignment today, Dean," I said. "You will write me an email describing Mrs. Stapleton's toenails and your emotions associated with them."

"You really are funny," said Dean, tying his shoelaces. "Can't do emails. Or anything like that. I have children. I'm actually a really good parent."

"I understand, Dean. No problem. You can be a good parent—cover your identity but keep your personality," I answered, removing my rubber gloves.

"So funny," said Dean. "So good. So diplomatic. You are fantastic, you know that?"

He didn't tip me.[1]

---

[1] Dean is playing out his sadistic part; he compliments women at the end of the session, leading them to believe they will get a reward, and then he punishes them by withdrawing the monetary reward and violating their expectations.

FANTASY IS REALITY

As I stood in the bathroom, examining my face in the mirror, Zoe walked in and stood next to me.

"What's with the face?" she said. "You're okay? Girl, you're too hard on yourself. You need to take care of yourself, I'm telling you. Eat something. Smoke. I don't know—call your mom, whine, something!"

"My mom's dead."

"But you do have a sister, right?"

"My sister's dead, too."

Before I knew what was happening, Zoe's heavy arms were around me, and my head was pressed to her oven-like chest. It smelled like donuts, cigarettes, and sweat—and felt like home. Zoe was sobbing and patting my hair and rocking my head as if it were a crying baby. I felt tingling inside my nostrils, my lips shook. I fought my way out of her bearish embrace and worked hard on keeping my face calm.

"It's okay, Zoe," I said. "Thanks. Really. They died a long time ago. I'm used to it."

"You never get used to it," said Zoe. "Here, let's go. I'm PMSing so badly, girl, I know that, but I do feel for you. You're a freaking orphan. I need some chocolate. Where's my purse?"

Greta was in the living room, the book in her lap closed. The shadows under her eyes had gotten much darker.

"Here's another one," said Zoe. "Girls, have a Tootsie Bar. You need one."

I shook my head. Greta took her candy and put it next to her book.

"How's your book going?"

Greta looked up at me, smiling. She brushed her caramel hair from her eyes, throwing a quick, apologetic look at the book.

"Oh, I'm so pathetic. Reading, reading, even when I can't focus," she said.

Her hair fell back and covered her eyes.

"I know," I said. "You know, I was really down the other day, and grabbed this poetry book, sort of like a bible for Russians. The book doesn't matter, it just made me think: Susanna smokes pot, Mommy paints... I read."

"Yeah, and perverts? Come to see us."

She smiled, her bulging wet eyes looking at me from underneath her soft hair, the tame look of a beautiful cow.

"Oh, man! Greta! That's hilarious. Literature, the ultimate *YourFantasyWorld.com*."

Greta giggled, covering her mouth.

"Hey, I made you laugh," she said. "Literature *is* fantasy."

"Fantasy is reality," I wanted to say. "Reality is fantasy."

Instead, I said, "I have a cake called Fantasy at home, and it's *sooo* good. I tried reading **DEVIATIONS**. I got even more confused. If you listen to him, the perverts are about to liberate the world, they're like an underground movement, or a secret army..."[1]

---

[1] Rose misinterprets the following abstract from *DE-VIATIONS*: "There are two types of deviants. In some individuals, the ability to function is impaired by their powerful **Internal Morality Police**. They must pay the price for breaking social norms by accepting temporary compromises, and some become mentally ill. [...] Rarer is the type of men and women whom, following Nietzsche, I will call 'superior.' Those individuals rise above the Law. They are above and beyond society, religion, and morals. They are 'beyond good and evil.' They have no boundaries. By breaking the Law, **Superior Men** challenge the tribal fathers and follow their own instincts. '**God is dead**,' they repeat after the great teacher, and they burn

"It's more complicated than that," Greta said.

"Did you bring the cake?" asked Zoe, looking up from her book.

"I will, Zoe."

I turned back to Greta.

"You mean you understand what he's saying? Then, tell me: the desire to feel pain? The urge to experience horror? Why? I hate pain. Did you get an epidural when you gave birth?"

Greta nodded.

"Those guys want pain, they pay for it! How sick are they? Makes me sick to think of it."

"Oh, that. Physiologically speaking, when the body is hurt, the brain releases endorphins, the body's natural painkillers. They work like opiates. You basically get high. And as with any high, you need more and more…"

Greta was moving her hair back and forth as she spoke, and I stopped looking at her, just listened to her murmuring voice. Nothing made sense anymore.

"Psychologically, there are many theories. Strong is trying to prove that Freud was right about suppressed sexual instincts leading to neuroses. But I believe it's a way of defeating death anxiety…"

"Huh?"

I tried not to scratch my dry, itchy hands.

"Let's say John is afraid of dying, right?"

"We all are," I said.

I thought about Blossom's dead body in the shoebox, in the cold ground.

---

themselves on the fire of the old morality and rise from the ashes like the Phoenix, born anew."

"Sure. But John thinks, 'If I can stand the pain and fear, I'm special, I can resist death, I won't die.' He doesn't know he thinks this, obviously. You tell him this, he'll deny it."

"Oh, bullshit," said Zoe.

She sat in the armchair, eating her Tootsie Bar and holding a paperback like a baseball bat. Greta walked up to her.

"I'm sorry, may I see your book?"

She waved the book at me. The blue alien on the cover looked like my new robot.

"What's it about?" Greta asked.

"Fantasy," Zoe yawned. "Some aliens steal a girl, or something."

"See, aliens, monsters. You're doing it, too."

"Doing what?"

"Flirting with death."

"Like how?"

"Fantasies, novels about death make death unreal. You see a horror movie, and you don't die, right?"

"I hope not."

Zoe grabbed her book back, frowning.

A TOURIST

"You suck, Greta," said Mommy. "A tourist, that's what you are!"

She appeared in the doorway of her dark bedroom.

"Your Dr. Strong is way sicker than my Weird John! Stop the death talk and go clean the bloody bathroom."

Greta squinted, then said softly, "You are afraid of death, too, Mommy."

"And you think you're a fucking genius," said Mommy.

Greta grabbed her worn, brown purse and hid her face in it, searching for something.

"Fuck psychology. Fuck Freud. Fuck you, Greta."

With each sentence, Mommy chopped air with her right hand, pipe between fingers.

"I…"

Greta stood up, and her purse slipped off her lap and landed on the carpet, opening like a sandwich. Out of it spilled lottery tickets. Dozens of them. Maybe hundreds. There they lay, their silver strips glittering in the dusk of the room, like the bellies of dead fish, alongside chewing gum pieces and wrappers.

Greta covered her head with her hands, ran to the bathroom and shut the door. I heard water running.

"You don't know shit, Greta," said Mommy to the bathroom door, loudly. "Listen to me: Eat your sausage and stay out of the sausage factory! That's about how much you need to know. I don't need this. Rose!"

She turned to me, darting dirty looks at me.

"Mommy."

"Dean called. Did you use gloves to work with him?"[1]

---

[1] Dean further devalues Rose by complaining after the

"I did."

"This is not going to work," she said. "You know what I said to the girl who refused to do cock-and-ball torture? I said, it's like applying for a job in Starbucks and refusing to do coffee. You guys are here to work, not to run a freaking research lab. Susanna! Where the fuck is that airhead? A new client, bondage, for tomorrow at nine-thirty. She has to be here.[1] Rose, you too. Zoe, you clean up the bloody lottery. And then get out of my place. Enough for today—To hell with all of you!"

I drove over the bridge blasting Ruslana. I looked at my phone, but I didn't read any of eighteen text messages from Luke. I picked up the kids and didn't answer to Ms. Jenkins, who waved at me from the yard. It seemed to me that Ms. Freckle pointed at me, her face turning into one giant freckle, quivering in the air.

"Keep quiet," I told the kids. "I have a migraine."

---

session and punishing her as the object of the shame and humiliation he had experienced. He derives sadistic pleasure from victimizing Rose.

[1] I want to share with readers my own Freudian slip (typo, to be precise). In 2001, while working on the infamous "DSM Project," the group effort of licensed psychotherapists who advocated the removal of the Paraphilia Chapter from the *Diagnostic and Statistical Manual of Mental Disorders (DSM)*, I copied the following passage from the manual: "...the masochistic fantasies usually involve being raped while being held or **bound by mothers** so that there is no possibility of escape." DSM original text reads **others**. Notably, **bondage** (swaddling) becomes sexualized by infants during nocturnal erections that come with the need for urination. The link might be genitally associated and reinforced in childhood games at a later stage of development.

I probably didn't look well. The kids sat still without a sound, and ate the frozen pizza.

"It's not cooked through, Mom," whispered Nick.

"Shh," whispered Roxanne.

I went to the bedroom, turned the lights off and rolled into bed, under the blanket. Torn pieces of thoughts, memories and fantasies floated through my mind.[1] I kept going back to the Cleopatra Fantasy. Only things went wrong, as if an invisible director was drunk and mixed up the pages of the script. I saw an orgy: a crocodile-beast, hippo hindquarters wide apart, moaned as a squirming cobra rubbed against her swollen vagina, millions of scarabs fornicating, moving, hissing. And then a Sphinx with vermillion lips and red pointed nipples towered over me.[2] I recognized his almond-shaped eyes, his aquiline nose, his capricious and cruel mouth, a predator with a smile of a child —Mike! — and he pierced me with his monster phallus[3] as I opened inside out, moist and cramping, in a convulsion of an earthquake orgasm.

---

[1] During a time of frustration, anxiety, or stress, an individual turns to the erotic satisfactions of infancy as a soothing mechanism. Stimulation in infancy (**diaper changing, kissing, hugging**) is stored in the memory and revisited on multiple levels—fantasy is created.

[2] **Rape fantasies** in sex abuse victims may indicate an early onset of original abuse, while **sexual orgies** and **group rape fantasies** often suggest long-term childhood abuse.

[3] Rose's desire for **a monstrous phallus** should not be misconstrued as a desire for a larger sized penis in her sexual partner. "Golden phallus" here is a representation of pleasure. By wanting more of it, she wants more pleasure, more feeling, more excitement than she is able to feel.

LOVE

I woke up and saw Luke's watery eyes.

I just blinked, staring at the fluff of his eyelashes and the beads of sweat on his forehead.

"Honey, wake up," he said. "Honey, I need to tell you the truth."

Those fat letters, *TRUTH*, crawled slightly, like spiders in a jar, before my closed eyes. I kept looking at them, without saying a word.

"I never told her 'I love you,'" he kept whispering. "You are the only woman I ever loved. You are the love of my life."

I watched the spiders as they scattered across the blank field of my mind.

"I killed Blossom," I said.

"What?"

"Ran over him. He's dead. We buried him. Vanessa and I. You should talk to her."

I rolled over and listened to Luke's heavy breathing. Then I felt his hand on my hip.

"Don't," I said, sitting up in bed. "Didn't you hear what I said: I killed Blossom."

"He was just a cat," said Luke, sitting up next to me.

"You're driving the kids tomorrow," I said, grabbing my blanket.

I wrapped the blanket around me and went to the living room.

"Honey! Don't!" I heard him saying.

In the mirror, I looked like an angel or a person in a hair-dresser's chair. I felt dead.

I went upstairs. The door to Olga's room was open, her Barbies on the floor, and her bed was empty. I tiptoed into Roxanne's room. Another empty bed. Then, I saw them. A dark shape on the carpet. A comforter, and underneath, asleep—like little babies—in each other's arms lay my daughters, their hair mixed, ink-black straight locks and blonde poodle mane, Olga's face in Roxanne's clavicle, her plump hand over her sister's body. Next to them, like a dead soldier, was my old green jacket.

Tears ran down my cheeks, and I felt like falling down on my knees and holding my girls in my arms, never letting them go, kissing their mixed-up hair, their closed eyes puffy from crying together, the intermingled arms and legs that were once inside me, protected from pain and death by my own skin and flesh.

Instead, I picked up the worn-out green jacket and pressed it to my cheek. It smelled like cherry vanilla and sweat. I knew I was helpless myself; I knew I would lose them one day.

I put the green jacket on, and went down the stairs—up and down, ascending and descending, descending and ascending the endless Steps all my life—my eyes blind with tears, my brain numb, my heart bursting with pain, I wandered to the kitchen in the dark and fished for a vial of Vicodin that Luke kept in the fridge for the times when his dislocated shoulder hurt too much. I got three pills out and placed them on the kitchen counter. Then I opened the freezer, and took out an unopened bottle of vodka. I swallowed the pills and, the bottle in my shaky hand, went back to the living room. The pill got mushy in my mouth, bitter, and I tore off the seal, opened the vodka, and gulped straight out of the bottle. The vodka smell hit me like a fist, my grandfather swimming in the back of my brain in his suede beret and burgundy scarf. I drank more. Then more. Then more.

Before I passed out, I kept looking at the wedding picture, face down on the floor where I'd dropped it. I rolled down into the couch, my face pressed into Potemkin's purring warmth.

THE BONDAGE FANTASY

My alarm clock went off at six, and I couldn't wake up. I couldn't remember who I was or why I was in the living room. Then I saw the empty bottle of vodka next to me, and remembered. I didn't want to see Luke. I grabbed my dungeon bag, and left the house in the old green jacket and sweatpants.

It was drizzling outside. I stopped by the gas station and walked inside the station to pay in cash.

"Hola!"

The Latina gas station attendant smiled and waved at me as if I were her long-lost childhood friend.

I moved my lips into a smile, and gave her a hundred-dollar bill. While I was waiting for her to count the change, I looked around.

On a green shelf covered with foil, between a tall candle in a glass and a plastic rose, shone a golden hologram of Jesus.

Surrounded by hologram butterflies, glitter, and rhinestones, Jesus gazed at me with his sad, understanding eyes from a Hallmark background of frosting pink and baby-boy blue, luminous rays radiating from his tilted head. His bleeding, feminine hands juggled a shiny red heart. I couldn't take my eyes off that heart—it was bouncing in the hologram space like a beach ball, dripping with ruby blood like a bottle of a million-dollar-red nail polish, and flaming on the top with poisonous yellow like a racecar. His facial expression was too blissful for a person in pain, a hint of a smile in the corners of his girlish mouth.

"Gracias," the woman said, her blood-red nails pushing dollar bills at me.

I didn't count them, just threw them into the purse.

At the pump, I dropped the gas nozzle on the ground, spilling some gas. The transparent liquid mixed with the rain water, creating pale rainbow doodles on the blue asphalt. I stood there, watching the snaky lines fusing and molding, undulating. My thoughts worked in the same sidewinding, rolling manner, coiling together, moving, evaporating; I heard vague voices calling my name, echoing, asking me endless questions:

"Why? Why the dungeon?"

"Because you are a writer."

"But why am I a writer?"[1]

"Why Blossom?"

"Vanessssssa, Vanessssa, Vanesssa," hissed one of the voices in the background.

"You good?" asked the gas attendant.

She was standing in the doorway, looking at me, her hands at her chest, her nails red like Jesus' heart.

"I've been better," I said.

She smiled, nodded, and went back inside.

In the car, I blasted Tatyana to silence the voices. I sang along:

> *The foreign land will never be my oooown...*
> *The ship is gooooone*
> *I'll never go hoooome...*

Tears rolled down my cheeks. I had a hard time driving; I couldn't see the bridge.

> *I whisper your name,*

---

[1] Rose's writing is the rechanneling of her sexual and aggressive instincts through **sublimation**. Freud believed that **sublimation** — "the diversion of sexual instinctual forces from sexual aims and their direction to new ones" — was the ultimate coping mechanism, our best and only hope. Clearly, it does not fully work for Rose.

It comes out as a mooooan...
My songs don't fly...
In tears they droooown...

I drove on autopilot; I don't know how I made it to Mommy's house.[1] Finally, I switched off the CD player, and put on jeans, but left my green jacket on. Its collar was wet with tears. Wet through. I used a sleeve to dry my face, and pulled out my makeup kit.

I spent about an hour painting my face. When I was done, I looked like a Japanese geisha. My face was paper-white, my eyeliner made my eyes look like an etching of butterflies. I combed out my eyelashes with Oksana's needle.

Mommy let me in, and gave me a look. Then she whistled, said nothing and went back to her bacon.

I stretched out on the carpet in the living room, using **DE-VIATIONS** as a pillow, and closed my eyes. I might have fallen asleep again, because next thing I knew, Susanna was shaking me by the shoulders.

"Wake up, Rose," she said. "Wow. Cool Cleopatra eyes. Jesus, Rose, wake up, we have a British Lord waiting for you in the Dungeon!"

I sat up and looked at her. It took me a while to remember who she was and what she was talking about. Mommy was standing in the doorway.

"You look even worse than yesterday," she said. "What are you, PMSing eternally? So your new client is an Englishman, here on a business trip. You'll know he's British—his teeth are all rotten. Treat him well."

She giggled.

---

[1] **Highway hypnosis** is another common disassociation episode.

I got up and felt the fog creeping inside of me, trembling all around me, and next I watched myself sliding outside of my body like a foot out of a stocking. I watched myself following Susanna to the Dungeon and smiling to a tall man with wisps of gray hair on his biceps and a sad penis hanging between his vein-covered thighs. The feeling of not being present never left me anymore.

"I would love to be suspended from the ceiling, from my dick, please," said the man, with a dense British accent. "Can you do it, love?"

I watched Susanna tying the white rope all around the man's pasty body, and then neatly ornamenting his penis with a cute red ribbon. Then she tied the whole package up to the ceiling as requested.[1]

"Christmas present," Susanna whispered.

I watched myself watching Susanna purring, brushing her warm body against me, then against the client. She let him lick her arms and breasts, smiling and winking to me.

I saw myself: a flat paper face in the mirror. I wore my faces like masks. I had many masks. I had many women inside of me, dead and alive, and each me had her own mask—I didn't know the woman in the mirror; that mask was new, scary. The cherry-red mouth on white skin, like a murdered body in the snow.

---

[1] The desire to feel suspended is rooted in erections experienced by boys during movement games such as swings, climbing bars or being thrown up high in the air by fathers. Fear and sexual excitement become one.

Freud stated that **"there cannot be a single uncle** who has not shown a child how to fly by rushing across the room with him in his outstretched arms, or who has not played at letting him fall by riding him on his knee and then suddenly stretching out his leg, or by holding him up high and then suddenly dropping him."

"Mistress Rose? Will you join us?"

Susanna raised her pale eyebrows.

I walked around the client like a robot, going through the motions, rolling a rope around a hairy wrist and pulling on it. Susanna put her hand on the small of my back, and arched her back, pressing her firm breasts to my chest, but I removed her hand and walked to the other side of the client.

"Oh no," said the client.

Susanna pinched me on the elbow, raised her eyebrows again, and said in her fake musical voice, "Thank you for helping out, Mistress Rose. You can attend to your business now."

"Thank you, love," said the client. "You Russian brute."

I nodded and left, listening to my stilettos clicking on the steps.

On the way back, I had to pass through the Boudoir. Zoe was blindfolded, gagged, and tied to the chair. Her client was standing in front of her with a big club in his hand. All I could see was his muscular back, covered in black, curly hair. I had a flashback from my recent Academy of Sciences trip: a Neanderthal hunter butchering a prehistoric cow. The red gag in Zoe's mouth was attached by black straps, cutting into her cheeks, smashing her baby face into a grimace of crazy laughter. I could almost feel that gag splitting my own mouth, pulling my lips apart, smooth plastic filling my mouth, pressing on my tongue. I looked down at my painted toenails and hurried out of the room.

THE SECRETARY FANTASY

Mommy was scraping paint from the windowsill in the kitchen as if she wanted to erase the whole house from the face of Earth.

"What's Zoe's session?" I asked.

"Oh, the secretary. Very popular fantasy. Stephen. Go read his card. Greta, you, too."

Greta read aloud:

"*Stephen. Fantasy: beating, bondage, wax. Body mutilation. Golden shower on the injured spot. Very high pain threshold. Addiction. Submissive, but dominates you from the bottom.*"

"That's not the secretary stuff. Must be the wrong Stephen. How about this one: *Fantasy: 'urge' to be fucked with a big dildo by a secretary or, better, a chauffeur.[1] Will repeat 'I'm not gay.'[2] The response: No, we are just having fun.'*"

Mommy grumbled from the kitchen, "And the real response is: 'Of course, you're gay! You want to suck a dick

---

[1] This fantasy suggests another case of negative Oedipal resolution, as with an absent or neglectful father. The libido is invested in the father figure, hence the desire to be submissive. This individual is most likely a latent homosexual, raised in a strict, upper-class family. His shame at desiring men is so immense that he imposes self-punishment by being dominated by a person from a lower social class. "In the male fantasy [...] being beaten also stands for being loved (in a genital sense)." The beating-fantasy also has its origin in an incestuous attachment to the father. The boy, who has tried to escape from a homosexual object-choice but nevertheless feels like a woman in his conscious fantasies, must endow the women who are beating him with masculine attributes and characteristics.

[2] Primitive defense and denial.

and be fucked—so what do you think you are? You're married and have children? So what? Who isn't?'"

A door slam, followed by heavy stomping. Zoe burst into the living room, grabbed her bathrobe, dropped her shoes and flew out to the porch. Her client slowly walked through the living room toward the exit, dissecting every girl with his washed-out blue eyes.

"Ladies. Have a wonderful day," he said.

Greta and I hurried out to the porch. Zoe was shaking, trying to light a cigarette. Her formidable frame seemed smaller; her ruddy face had lost its color. Her teeth were chattering, her right cheek was swollen, and her right eye was all purple and puffed up.

"Asshole! Jerk!"

Greta lit a cigarette for her.

"So, at first everything was fine. He was the high-powered man. I was his secretary. I spilled the coffee on his pants, he tied me up and blindfolded[1] me. Cool. Then he was supposed to get off. Normally, they blindfold you so you don't see them.[2] This fucker went for the club. It hurt like hell. He beat the shit out of me! And he gagged me, so I couldn't cry for help, or anything. I think he broke my ribs... A fucking crazy Nazi... I thought he would kill me."[3]

---

[1] **Blindfolding** is important to the sadist, not just because it adds to Zoe's fear but also because it prevents the aggressor from seeing her eyes so that he can fully distance himself and objectify her.

[2] Zoe's experience with the sadist has its roots in what is clinically referred to as **lack of agency**. The sadist picks Zoe because she is an ultimate victim.

[3] I believe that this man is not a *sexual* sadist. In fact, I want to clarify the common misconception: **violence, control, and domination in such cases are not about sex**.

Zoe lifted her bathrobe. The cottage cheese-white skin blossomed with bruises and exploded blood vessels. Her eyes were glistening, but she didn't cry.

"Jerk!"

MONSTERS

It was quiet. Zoe was lying on the carpet, her eyes closed, head in Greta's lap. Greta was holding an icepack to Zoe's eye and stroking her forehead and her hair with light, motherly motions.

"He's not coming back, Zoe," dropped Mommy.

She wrote something on the card. She coughed and cleared her throat. Then she kept talking.

"Hey, Zoe, forget it. Shit happens. You know who I ran into in the butcher shop last night? I'm buying my ground turkey, and then I see Philip the Baby. Remember Philip, Zoe? A really nice guy? Remember, from a couple years ago? He bloody used to bring you cookies. And you swaddled him and he had a pacifier and a diaper and you sang songs to him?[1] He's a good kid. I see him at the butcher's now and then, he loves steaks.[2] They all love steaks. They all do; just love that raw meat. Cocaine Jack told me that. He told me, 'Mommy, life is short. You gotta have fun. Eat steaks, snort coke, fuck whores. Have fun.'[3] But Phil, he's a nice kid... You know, I

---

[1] Freud noted, "No one who has seen a baby sinking back satiated from the breast and falling asleep with flushed cheeks and a blissful smile can escape the reflection that this picture persists as a prototype of the expression of sexual satisfaction in later life..."

[2] **"Love and hunger meet at mother's breast,"** said Freud.

[3] **Eating, sex, and drugs** are all about consumption and pleasure. Note how these activities are connected in our everyday language: "you are so sweet, I could eat you up," "cow" for a woman, "meat-market" for a nightclub, and so on. Both eating meat and having sex are about penetration and aggression, and both can be called the closest socially accepted imitation of cannibalism.

ran into him and his family a while ago. He and his wife had just adopted this baby. Phil was so sweet, he told me, 'I'm so happy that you got to meet my son!' Man, was he happy! Of course he was happy: he wasn't able to have any children of his own—and I know why! He couldn't come inside a woman."[1]

Mommy laughed, waiting for us to join. Nobody laughed.

"And listen—I guess he did learn to come inside a woman, because he and his wife had another baby. Hear that, Zoe?"

Zoe didn't answer. Mommy sighed and went to the kitchen. We heard her grumpy mumbling, "To hell with you, I've got a wall to paint here..."

"Why do you think they do it?" I asked Greta quietly. "Did you study those things?"

"I did... Everything is rooted in infancy..."

Greta almost whispered, so that Mommy didn't hear.

"People regress. It's soothing. Going back to the womb, it's comforting. Back to being a baby. Babies don't have responsibilities. Just suck on a big breast..."

Greta sounded like my older daughter preparing for her Science exam.

"No! I mean bondage, sadism, violence..."

Greta shrugged.

"Oh... Bondage was swaddling. Gags were pacifiers. Authority figures were sexualized... Listen, I don't know anymore. I don't know if I can work here..."

"Me, neither..."

The English bondage session was over and Susanna emerged from the Dungeon, naked and radiant. She hovered over the

---

[1] Phillip the Baby is a severely developmentally traumatized individual whose primary trauma most likely occurred during the first month of his life or even prenatally. When he is in the grip of sexual anxiety he regresses to early infancy or even fantasizes back into the womb.

client, seeing him to the door and sending him air kisses. Then she came back into the living room, gave me a sidelong look and whispered, "You should try smoking dope more often, really, it'll relax you. You were no good in that session, you know that?"

For a moment we just looked at each other.

"Why do you always undress, Susanna?" I asked.

"Because I feel like it," said Susana, "I get more tips that way. Plus, it feels good. Just me—as I am. I look good. What's wrong with Zoe?"

"She was submissive, and the guy overdid it…" said Greta.

Susanna's fake smile vanished.

"Oh, Sweetie… You want an avocado and alfalfa sprouts sandwich?"

Zoe didn't answer.

"This British guy told me, 'I wish I had your job. So much fun!'" said Susanna. "Fun."

She threw on a bathrobe and hid her face behind her *Directing Documentaries* book, the sandwich in her lap, untouched.

I stretched out on the floor next to Zoe and closed my eyes. It was the middle of the day. I didn't want to walk, sit, read, eat, drink, or shop—not even clean. I wanted to be locked in a room with no windows, all alone. I wanted to sleep with no dreams.

And then he finally showed up, when I wasn't thinking about him at all.

THE UNBEARABLE PAIN

"Rose, Mike the Motherfucker for you at four-thirty."

My stomach felt as if a red-hot wrench was slowly churning inside.

"He wants you to wear the red vinyl bodysuit this time. Warrior-queen rubbish. Remember, be careful," said Mommy.

I felt more than ever that my life was a dream. It wasn't me. Someone took over my body, over my life. Soft voices echoed inside my head:

"He's back! He's back!"

"Red suit?"

"Why not?"

"Don't!"

My mind was still, the gas-station puddle with its bleak rainbow of half-thoughts. I was sweating; the wrench in my stomach started to rotate faster. I'd had too much coffee, too many sleeping pills, too little sleep. I was about to break like a string pulled too tight.

"I don't know," I said. "I don't want to hurt anyone for real. I don't want Mike."

"Oh shut up," exploded Zoe. "I'll take him. I want to hurt someone for real—really badly."

"C'mon, Rose. You'll be all right. We all have those moments. You want some dope?" asked Susanna. "It'll help."

"I do," I said. "I want some dope. How much?"

"You'll pay me later. C'mon."

And so I ended up putting on the red vinyl bodysuit—like a glove on my body—grabbing my new purse, and going to the porch. There, all of us, Susanna, Greta, Mommy, Zoe, and I, sat in a silent circle, smoking.

It was the first time I'd smoked weed since Alexandrov's parties.

As I pulled in the skunk-smelling hot smoke, I departed further and further from my body. Everything around me became a surrealist movie.[1] The camera lingered on strange women, who sat like Indians by an invisible fire, tribal warriors, their faces painted, eyes blank, passing a joint around. For an endless moment, the camera lingered on a hummingbird hovering over a withering rose, then floated over to the haunted bush. There was no fog. Reality sharpened to its naked self. It shrunk, leaving no covering, not even the skin. My vision became a monster artist, a mad scientist, a maniac sculptor with a scalpel, slicing weightless objects and vague figures with the precision of a surgeon, transforming a comatose still life into a documentary film. A basketball game on the neighbor's TV faded away, and a heavy silence enveloped the world.

Every single detail of what followed stayed engraved on my memory, like a movie scene you watch again and again, like an episode from a recurring nightmare.

I remember opening my new purse, the leather crinkling, the tiny lock dazzling, and pulling out my lipstick, blood red and shiny. I remember the smooth feel of it on my lips; I remember the doorbell ringing with the loudness of a locomotive pulling into an empty train station.

I remember hearing menace in Susanna's laughter and her "I'll get the door," echoing in my head, "The door, the door, the door—"

---

[1] Rose chooses to self-medicate because her array of defenses is not working anymore. She is trying more direct ways of achieving detachment and disconnection from her anxiety-provoking feelings.

I remember passing through the empty kitchen, feeling ravenous, craving cheese, or something hot and greasy, bacon, maybe, or borscht, and not finding any. I remember grabbing the open champagne bottle left over from the spy session. I remember the warm and sour champagne taste in my mouth and in my throat, and I remember clicking my heels on the hallway floor, purse and lipstick still in my hand, "Click, click, click..."

MIKE THE MOTHERFUCKER

He appeared silently in the distance, in the darkness of the hallway, dreamlike, a train at the horizon, motionless, but moving toward me at a supernatural speed, closer and closer, growing bigger and bigger, Susanna floating in his wake, sending me air kisses.

I stepped forward, an equilibrist, wire dancer, walking an invisible rope, moving toward him, balancing on my own stretched nerves to the drumbeat of my heart.

I recognized his scent before I made out the triangle flag of his tangerine silk scarf. I could feel the animal-like odor of sex and danger seething from underneath the acacia aroma of his French perfume. That scent had imprinted itself on my nostrils, on my brain from the moment I saw him first—or maybe long before that, and now I knew it. He smelled like my father.

I was struggling for breath, my head pulsing with blood like an empty church, bell tolling.

"I missed you so much, Rose," he whispered.

I gazed into his almond eyes, looking for an answer: he smiled, like a patient at a dentist.

And once again, I slid outside of my body like a snake out of molting skin, leaving myself in the hallway, watching my body in its red vinyl suit going through the motions, watching my life passing before my eyes, like water through fingers. I was following my red vinyl-clad avatar down the endless stairs, a couple of steps behind, and for a second it seemed to me that the stairs shifted and moved like an escalator.

He started to undress. As he slowly removed his fine, velvety jacket, his menacing fingers playing with buttons, I sat down, crossed my legs, set my purse on the floor and put on my lipstick again. Each of my moves was slow, deliberate, meant to provoke and tease, and yet I was dead. I was there, but really I was hovering just below the ceiling.

"Oh, how I missed your eyes, this alien look of yours," he spoke, his massive muscles twitching under his skin like those of a slightly overweight bodybuilder, "That way you look at me through your hair—"

Each word was like the silent step of a panther—heavy, soft, and dangerous.

"I thought about you all the time. Let's play today."

His voice was smooth, yet tense with passion, a python swallowing his catch. "Will you play with me, Rose?"

I was spying on his every gesture, and I had the strange feeling that he was observing me—the way I was observing him—noticing my reactions, my every move, as if I were a lab mouse, as if he had a secret video camera installed somewhere on his body.

He towered over me, stark naked. I avoided looking down, between his legs. I stared instead at his torso, covered in tattoos and scars, but I knew he was getting more and more aroused.

I read the tattoo, "*Kill me again or take me as I am, for I shall not change,*"[1] snaking down his powerful shoulder all the way to a shockingly small hand, noticing that he was stealing an oblique glance at my chest, his eyes cast down. It was half-lust, half-shame, the lust of a prisoner, the shyness of a toddler.

---

[1] An incomplete quote from Marquis de Sade's self-description: "Imperious, choleric, irascible, extreme in everything, with a dissolute imagination the like of which has never been seen, atheistic to the point of fanaticism, there you have me in a nutshell, and kill me again or take me as I am, for I shall not change."

It occurred to me that we mirrored each other, two snipers, hiding behind our bodies, focusing, meditating, getting ready to kill—in cold blood.

"Punish me, Rose," said Mike. "I feel so guilty, so bad, so sad. Order me, order me to do anything you want. Anything. Command me, Mistress Rose. I want lots of pain."

He paused, then whispered, "And a rope."

I took a black slick rope off its hook. Shame, disgust, fear mixed in me with a piercing physical longing; I shook with the desire to be crushed by him while crushing him.

"I'll give you lots and lots—" My voice broke. "Of pain."

I took his feminine hand with care, the way I'd take a new-born baby. I stroked his fingernails—meticulously manicured, glistening—and felt as if I'd gotten shocked, as if his body was electrified. He groaned like a woman, and I wrapped the rope around his wrist, over a tattoo that read: *Du sollst werden, der du bist.*[1] Underneath the black Gothic letters was a hardening of his soft skin, and I felt a thick, jagged-edged horizontal scar. I dragged my finger over the scar, indulging in the smooth visceral helplessness of the torn tissue, my fingertip tingling. His blood throbbed in his veins, making my pulse quicken.

"Motherfucker," I whispered, my mouth dry.

I tied him to the cross with the same extreme care, as if he was a hospice patient, and I was a nurse, a nun, a mother.

"Allow me to pray to your beauty, Mistress Rose," his words were reaching me as if from underwater. "It's the beauty—" a hiss interrupted his whisper, saliva drawn in, a gasp, "the beauty in you that I always need to discover and pray for."

Each word echoed inside my head, "You ignite passion. Days and nights I'd crawl at your feet—"

---

[1] A quote from Nietzsche: "You must become who you are." (German)

My red vinyl suit was squeaking, and cold sweat poured down beneath it, gathering around my crotch, which was getting all wet, and my hands shook, but the spinning wrench inside came to a halt.

We moved as if entranced, in a deadly dance, meeting each other's moves halfway, guessing the next motion, knowing it without words. I wrapped the rope around his neck—he reached for the ends, I tightened it—he pulled it tighter, so tight his knuckles got white. I stepped back—he threw his head back. Spread-eagle on the cross, he looked like a crucifixion—at the centerfold of a pornographic magazine.

"Punish me, Mistress Rose," he whispered.

"I will."

We stared at each other in silence.

I pulled handcuffs off the shelf. Leather straps. Clothespins. Padlock.

Then I crossed my arms and just looked into his forehead.

The silence was bursting.

"What did you do, Motherfucker?" I finally asked. "What evil did you do?"

"I gang-raped my bride."[1]

"Your bride?"

---

[1] The rape and abandonment of a bride is a symbolic resolution of the **"Madonna–whore"** complex that many men like Mike possess. Usually, such conflict originates from their inability to integrate the image of their mother as not only pure and good, but also the sexual object of their desires. Similarly, one cannot possess a virgin, as the act of possession puts an end to the virginity. By possessing her, Mike turns her into a whore. By humiliating, torturing, and sexually abusing the body of his beloved, Mike simultaneously punishes her for her sexuality and for his own existential loneliness and the impossibility of a real union and real purity. "'**If I cannot have you, I will destroy you,**'" is the thought-work of a killer-lover." *DEVIATIONS*, Chapter 3, p. 176.

"Yes. Me, and other soldiers, my buddies, we survived a battle,[1] she was my sister, my little sister, a virgin, and I fucked her again and again, and I killed her, I killed my sister—"

I grabbed a black leather whip off the hook, and whipped him as hard as I could until my shoulder hurt. His body arched, then fell.

"My queen," he whispered, his schoolgirl eyelashes fluttering like captured dragonflies, a rose blush tingeing his face.

"Why? Why, Motherfucker?" I said, not recognizing my voice. "Why, I asked you—"

The whip whistled and landed on his face, leaving a red mark across his nose.

"Ahhh— I was drunk, I was stoned, I wasn't using my brain—"

"Bad. Bad, bad, bad."

With each word I whipped him over his chest, stomach, groin.

"Yes, I'm bad, I abandoned her, tied to a tree, naked, bruised and dirty, alone and miserable—"

I flung the rope away, and just looked at him.

"What—" Mike gasped. "What are you going to do to me?"

He was definitely watching me closely out of the corner of his eye.[2]

---

[1] **War and rape** motifs are common incestuous and aggressive elements. A victorious fight is a symbol of aggression, dominance and ultimate destruction. Mike's reward is his "bride," who is also possibly his Mother.

[2] Mike's fantasy is as multi-layered as a wedding cake. It is a show. He is both the actor and the audience. Mike makes himself both an object and the subject of his experience, while others are mere tools essential to his manipulation. His "soldier-friends" are multiple reflections of him, both spectators and accomplices. He needs others to watch him in order to make his experience real. However, those witnesses still are not enough, and Mike recruits

"Will you kill me?"

I waited. He watched. I could hear the voices in my head again, my thoughts racing, mingling, fusing:

"Hurt him bad? Hurt him more?"

"Hurt him. Hurt him. Hurt him."

I felt a yearning emptiness in my stomach. The voices raved: "Run, run, run, run! Out! Run!"

And then he said, "I killed my sister, because you killed your sister. You did, didn't you?"

My double in the mirror leaned down, painfully slow. It was me, and not me. I had stepped out of my body, I was an observer. Blue arrow of a shadow between the wax-yellow breasts. Plastic smile—lips only. Hypnotized by my own eyes—my pupils widened so the eyes seemed black—I watched both Mike and a strange woman that was me. Our faces multiplied, overlapped like a madman's collage.

I peeled off my shoe like a band-aid. I lifted it midair, in front of his face, twirled it—a spark of light dancing on the spike heel like in the stem of a champagne glass. I didn't look at Mike, but I knew his gaze followed my red lacquered fingernail as I traced it along the heel. I stuck my tongue out—its tip pointed up, with a tiny blue vein pulsating—rolled it over my upper lip, from right to left, then left to right. Pressed it into the edges of my front teeth. Touched it to the shoe heel. Licked it. Looked at him.

"Kill me, Oksana," he said.

Rose as an additional observer. Ironically, Rose's book serves the same purpose: Mike's fantasy here gets replayed again and again, reflected at multiple angles, as if in a room with mirrored walls, and the readers of her book are dragged in to deepen Mike's satisfaction, intensifying his orgasm to such a degree he cannot breathe anymore.

I froze, my tongue still on the heel of my shoe, feeling the miniscule scratches on its fake leather.

"Kill me the way you killed your sister."

He pulled against his rope. Not a strong pull. Light, almost playful, but enough to pop out purple veins on his neck. His face contorted. It turned into a mask of horror: swollen temples, bristled mustache, spasmodic mouth, sharp teeth. Bulging, terrified eyes. I saw blood vessels exploding in the whites of his eyes.

He let go of the rope, his lips softening, his eyes back to their almond shape, and whispered, "You never had a sister, Oksana. It's all in your head.[1] So kill me, kill me now."

He waited.

I saw the scene reflected endlessly in the mirror, I saw it with a hallucinatory clarity: a naked man tied to the cross, red nipples hard, pointed, a woman in red vinyl, a stripper shoe shaking in her raised hand.

The air trembled like cellophane. I saw the heel frozen midflight. It halted, shifted, and then collapsed and struck like a real stiletto, like a carving knife—or more like a lightning bolt, piercing the skin just below his cheekbone, stripping it off, sinking into the raw bloody pulp that just a fraction of a second before seemed so intact, so seamless, so indestructible, his

[1] Mike implies that **Oksana is an alter personality created by Rose's mind**. He might be right: studies of **Dissociative Identity Disorders** demonstrate that the abused child imagines the abuse is happening to someone else and thus experiences dissociated aspects of herself as other people, *alters*. Mike believes that Oksana is Rose's alter, created to carry the pain. Oksana later self-destructs by committing suicide, or, in other words, is killed by Rose. This theory can be confirmed by the way Rose describes her mirror encounters: she often does not recognize her reflection, which is one of the symptoms of **Dissociative Identity Disorder**. She switches to her alter and starts to see her other personality: Oksana.

face erupting into the bright-and-dark red of ground beef. I stopped breathing.

The Mist boiled in me, blinding me... All I saw was crushed cherries, yellow-pink stones, and dead flies shoved into the bleeding mash. Ripe. Juicy. Alive—and already rotten, sick through, sweet like a deadly poison. Like death itself.

Did I see the corner of his lips trembling—a child struggling not to cry? Did I see the heel sink—into his neck, into his chin, into his earlobe? Again, and again, and again, his flesh contracting, recoiling, and bouncing back? Did I hear a strange coarse voice coming from my own mouth, "You, monster!"—crash!—"You, beast!"—crash!—"You, Motherfucker!"

I didn't know. I didn't know how long I was at it:[1] Time stretched and melted and bent and evaporated, like a puddle of gasoline, like a vacuum of our own.[2]

I don't know what happened. I looked around and I saw blood on the silver lining of my shoe. I tried to loosen my grip, to straighten my spastic fingers, to wipe the blood off my shoe, off my fingertips. I couldn't.

Then I saw his face—the blood-soaked mass that used to be his face.

He wasn't moving. The rope cut into his throat.

---

[1] Rose's shame, guilt, and fear are so overwhelming that she protects herself by dissociation once again. Her pent-up frustration and rage are finally let loose. Mike becomes the target of her aggression. She punishes him for all the internal suffering she has endured.

[2] Rose's defense mechanism switches from being disconnected from her internal world to full disconnection from the external world. The experience is so traumatic that Rose's psyche needs to defend itself using extreme tools. She "blacks out," or "loses time," and **her alter takes over**.

This time he stuck out his tongue at me as if teasing me, like an evil clown, his lips distorted in silent laughter. I looked at the black hairs inside his nostrils—they didn't move—at a bluish vein at the tip of his tongue. The shoe slipped out of my hand. I undid the rope, smacked his cheek, poured some water down his forehead. I shook him by the shoulders. Blood smudged my fingers; I still didn't understand where the blood had come from.

"Wake up, you motherfucker," I whispered. "Wake up, you goddamn freak!"

Mike did not move. I let his body slacken, and looked at the meaningless heap of bleeding flesh, spread on the cross.

Did he move, just slightly?

No. I killed him.

I had no feelings left, but I could think clearly.[1]

---

[1] Because her old defenses are useless, she dissociates. She needs to save herself now, and she can only do so by cutting off her emotions. Therefore, Mike is just an object for her; she feels no shame or guilt and can make rational decisions.

NO EXIT

My first thought was: "The kids!"

In a flash, I saw an amber waffle crumbled on a red tray; a wasp digging into a pond of raspberry jam; lilies in a rainbow-hued vase; a yellow soccer ball on the dinner table; the amethyst flicker in the dusk... I saw the kids kneading dough on Sunday morning, Nick laughing, flour-covered cheek with a dimple. I could not die, I could not go to jail.

I looked at the mirror. This time I saw myself, and myself only. Not her. Me.

I grabbed my purse, my shoe, wiped the blood off the heel with a towel, found the other shoe, and shot through the back door and into the backyard—barefoot. My heart was pounding, but I could hear the muffled voices on the porch. Mommy was saying something about painting.

I ran to the garden gate, unlocked it, slammed it, ran to my car, pulled the keys from my purse, started the engine, and backed up from the alley. I saw Zoe running after me and then turning back, I saw her mouth distorted, her red neck tensed in a scream. I did not stop.

I was still wearing my red vinyl bodysuit as I crossed the bridge.

Blood was pulsing in my head, my hands were cold, and I moved fast.

I drove to Golden Gate Park, stopped my car in a desolate alley under an enormous indifferent eucalyptus, next to a pond, and stripped naked, peeling my red vinyl suit off like a skin, ripping it off, off with my black lacy underwear—wet through, smelling like a butcher shop—shaking, my teeth chattering. I pulled on my old jeans and a white cotton T-shirt, and the clean cotton felt good, but for about a second. I threw my red shoes—one still covered in dried blood— my lacy underwear, my crinkling suit into a black garbage bag. I wiped my hands with another cotton T-shirt and tossed it— into the bag. I lifted the bag and it seemed weightless.

"It must be heavy to drown," said a cold voice in my head.

A rock. I needed a rock.

I looked around and didn't see anybody, so I unlocked the car and stepped out, in my bare feet. A moss-covered rock sat right in front of me. I picked it up off the wet grass; it was covered with ants and old cobwebs. I blew on it and shook it off and then threw it—into the bag.

An old Chinese lady passed by, red umbrella in her gloved hand.

"Hello," she said, smiling and nodding.

I looked at her hat with hatred and moved my lips in a smile. *Does she know?*

"Nice day," I said, my voice throaty and coarse. "Nice day for a walk."

Her penciled brows moved up and she stopped smiling, but nodded and quickened her step.

"She knows," I thought.

I couldn't throw the bag into the pond. I locked the car from inside and wiped my forehead.

"Sutro Baths!"

Up the hill and along the ocean I drove, all the way up to Lands End, without stopping to think or check directions. I locked the car, looked around—nobody—and, bag in my hand, in my bare feet, I ran down the steps to the Sutro Baths.

With every step I took, I heard footsteps behind me. I looked behind my shoulder, one, two, three, five times—nothing. I thought for a minute that cops might be hiding behind the bushes and following me when I wasn't looking.

"Nobody's around. There are no cops, no one knows I'm here."

Down the endless steps, "No looking back, no looking back, no looking back."

Down an empty path, "No looking back."

The path snaked around ruins. Low, angular light hung over the monstrous rocks, casting deep irrational shadows at barren soil and still puddles of water.

"Crash!"

I felt a sharp pain in my foot and stopped—I'd stepped on a stick in the middle of an ant trail. For a second I examined my bleeding heel and smashed ants—the rest of them froze, then scattered sideways. I started to run again. I had no time.

The footsteps behind me resumed. I tried not to look back, then looked—nobody. I stood still, cold sweat on my forehead. The footsteps stopped. The menacing silence was deepened by the rolling of the ocean, and then pierced by the scream of a seagull.

"Like a woman," I thought.

Suddenly, I realized the footsteps were nothing other than my blood pulsing in my temples, my heart beating madly.

I stood at the very bottom of the Sutro Baths ruins. Above me was the enormity of the empty sky, below was the ever-moving ocean, and all around, on every side, cold rocks cut the horizon. A chain mounted into the rocks hung at the entrance to the grotto, and the red sign NO EXIT dangled from it, dancing in the wind. Everything moved, and then everything seemed to come to a halt.

DEAD

I felt so shaky that I grabbed onto a rock before stepping over the chain, and I entered the dark tunnel leading to the grotto. The ocean stench—salt and decomposing flesh—hit my nostrils. Sharp pebbles cut into my feet. The tunnel was endless, the footsteps echoed behind me, and I ran, ran, ran, the bag pulling on my shoulder, cutting into my fingers.

In the grotto, I stopped and looked around. No one. No loving couple hiding behind a shapeless rock. No kids setting off fireworks in its shade. Plastic-green plants swayed in the wind, and the waves crashed against the black rock. No one. The fading sun shed an eerie light on everything around, and it all seemed fake, like a cardboard backdrop for a high-school musical in an empty gymnasium.

I shuddered. Someone was watching me. I knew it. I felt it. Right above me, in the crevice of gray rock, a large pelican looked at me, like an old man, royal in its ugliness. It looked like it was carved, like it was not just a part of the landscape, but its owner, a deity of the rock. Its unblinking stare was heavy, like the rock in the bag. I knew the bird was judging me.

"It knows," I thought.

It knew the woman on the rocks was dead, and it knew that I had killed her—again and again, over and over; or maybe, she killed me. I was only a ghost of the murdered girl.[1]

I was dead.

---

[1] Inner conflict among alters is common for individuals with **Dissociative Identity Disorder**, and can even lead to suicide.

I looked at my hand clutching the bag. A dead hand. The skin was bluish from cold; the white gold of my wedding band was shining so much it didn't look like my ring. My hand didn't look like my hand. I noticed it was shaking, I noticed a tiny spot—blood? lipstick? ant?—on my index finger.

Then, I swung the bag and threw it into the ocean. The black plastic ballooned on the surface of the grey waters, moving, shifting, changing shapes, making evil faces at me. It floated for a while, the thin film rippling and trembling in the wind, and finally disappeared in a foam vortex. I stood shivering for a bit longer, unable to unglue my eyes from the moving water.

The water was turning red. It wasn't water. It was steaming blood. The ocean turned into a world-sized cauldron of nightmarish borscht, boiling and bubbling and pouring over. Blood was licking my feet like a dog. Blood ran down the cliffs and slopes and the pine trees. Blood soaked the air. Blood was everywhere, on my fingers, on my feet; I could feel its sultry odor, the odor of salt and nauseating sweetness. I turned around and ran up, but I felt the raging blood following me even as I made it to the top of the cliff, and looked back.

The desolate beach down below.

One step and it would be all over.

One step, and I would break free from the world with its plastic bags, ants, and motherfuckers. I would become one with death, one with eternity, one with this terrible and glorious abyss. Would I? Or would I be just another dumb Lemming in a dumb game, where even death is preprogrammed?

Did Vicky feel that way before jumping off the bridge? Did my mother—?

One step. NO EXIT.

I couldn't do it.

WHAT IS GOOD? WHAT IS BAD?

I returned to the car, my feet and ankles bleeding, weak and numb, and drove along the winding busy streets, up and down the hills, left and right, and up and down again.

Never had I experienced such a chaos of senses combined with such clarity of mind as during that long ride. All along, I could see myself from the side. I could not breathe. My hands shook as if I'd just drunk another tank of coffee, but apart from that I moved with the precision of a robot. Voices, questions, and answers buzzed in my head like flies in Mommy's kitchen.

"Did Mike die?"

"Possibly."

"If he did, should I return and get rid of his body?"

"No, Mommy can do it. She's done it before, I know."

"Is that police car behind me following me?"

"Should I drive to a police station, turn myself in, and plead guilty to homicide? Or should I plead 'not guilty by reason of insanity?' Should I spend my lifetime in an asylum or in jail?"

"Do you want to do this?"

"No."

"What do you want?"

"I want to live. I want to go back to Luke and my kids. To write. I want things the way they used to be."

"Is the police car still there?"

"What are the odds of being discovered?"

"Next to nothing. Mommy'd never call the police. Neither would Susanna, Zoe, or Greta. I wasn't observed in the commission of the deed. There was no evidence. No one in the dungeon knew my real name, my address, my occupation, my telephone number or anything about me. No one knew I worked at the dungeon, except for Luke."

"Should you tell Luke about the whole thing? Could you?"

"I don't want to lose him. Ever."[1]

"Would he leave you if he knew?"

"Possibly."

"Could he understand?"

"Possibly."

"Could he do the same?"

"Possibly?"

"Could you keep a secret from him for the sake of your life together? Could you lie to him?"

"I'll try."

"Could you keep a secret from the whole world? Lie your whole life?"

"I've done it before."

"Did you leave fingerprints?"

"Where is that police car?"

"Did you really kill him? Or did he kill himself?[2] Or is he alive?"

---

[1] Based on her childhood trauma (being abandoned by both parents), Rose expects to be deserted and anticipates indifference. Therefore, when her husband neglects her by showing no interest in her true self (her writing), agrees to share her sexually with other men (the dungeon job), and cheats on her with her friend (Vanessa), Rose does not question his choices. His presence is compensation for his lack of care.

[2] Could Mike commit suicide? Psychoanalytically, suicide is the killing of an internal poisonous object, essentially the only way to destroy the "bad" part of oneself. More likely, **Mike would never commit suicide** because he is capable of turning his erotic choices into ethical principles. He demonstrates that chosen individuals can reach beyond commonplace morality, "beyond good and evil" objects, beyond shame and guilt. Mike dares to become a

"Am I bad? What is bad? What is good?"

"Who am I?"

I pulled into my driveway and shook off an ant crawling up my ankle; it had been bothering me all the way home from the ocean. It didn't work; a couple of ants had crawled underneath my jeans, so I rolled up the cuffs and looked for the ants, but couldn't find any. I still felt the tiny feelers and legs tickling, irritating my skin, making me dirty, infested. I pulled the jeans higher, I scratched my shins and ankles with my fingernails until blood showed, but couldn't catch any ants. I started to feel them all over my body, on my back and neck, creeping inside my crotch.

I was suffocating. Ants, thousand of ants scattered in my head, inside my brain, blackening everything before my eyes, covering the world, gnawing at me, devouring me. My mind was teeming with ants. I put my fingers through my hair, and dug my nails into my scalp, scratching. I wanted to scratch through to the brain, scratch my brain until it bleeds, scratch out Mike, voices, faces, and this dull sweet smell that followed me.

It was not a smell like any other—lilies were sweet, but you sensed them in your nostrils, then recognized them in your head. This smell distorted my vision; it felt like a rock in my stomach.

I sniffed the car seats, looking for Olga's cream puff, or for pepperoni from Nick's pizza, a gob of chewing gum, Potemkin's shredded mouse—something material, something to explain the violent odor. I found a broken pencil, two Six Flags

---

Nietzschean Superman, an **Ubermensch**, and choose his own path in life—or in death.

stickers and a draft of a love letter, "Dear Charlie, I like you (crossed out). I hate you. Guess who," in Olga's curly writing.

Nothing that might smell. I went into the house and took three tranquilizers, washing them down with coffee. The smell followed me around the house like a dog. It seeped through the coffee. I started to sniff my sleeves, my clothes, my hands... my hands.

I looked at my right hand. It shook. It didn't like look mine at all.

There was a tiny spot on my index finger.

"Ant?"

"Blood?"

"There was no blood."

No, I shook it off, I scratched it, but the spot stayed. I noticed that my wedding ring had darkened and looked almost black. I pressed my hand to my nose and pulled the air in with my nostrils.

There was no doubt.

My hands smelled like blood.

I flew to the bathroom, tore off my jeans, my T-shirt, and stepped into the bathtub, turning the shower on. I stuck my hands under the warm water, lathering with lavender soap, washing between the fingers, under the nails, all the way up to the elbow, and then my whole body. My bleeding feet wouldn't stop bleeding. Blood was streaming into the tub. The water was pink-red. Blood was everywhere on the white tiles, blood and ants, and the sweet smell of death.

Fifteen minutes later, I dried my hands and rubbed a lavender lemongrass lotion into them, then pressed my knuckles to my nose again. They smelled like blood.

I stopped thinking. I cooked meatloaf and steamed broccoli for dinner—it smelled like blood. I picked up Luke's gray suit from the dry cleaner's—it smelled like blood.

I drove to Nick's school and walked down the schoolyard.

I avoided looking around, but I knew that kids stopped playing and stared at me, Ms. Jenkins and Ms. Freckle stared at me. Ms. Freckle pushed her glasses up her nose and squinted. Ms. Jenkins chewed her lips. Without a smile, her jowly brackets hung loose, and she looked like a bulldog about to attack and pierce her teeth into my leg.

"Hello."

"Oh, hello. I know you are in a hurry; however—"

I tried to look relaxed, and brushed my hair back.

"However, I will need to talk to you. I've sent you a note. Please take some time to think it over. I will not take any further action until I talk to you tomorrow."

Ants crawled down my neck and between my shoulder blades.

They knew. The freckled woman turned her back to me, puffing. She looked like a steam train.

"I'll talk to you tomorrow, Ms. Jenkins. Goodbye—"

I WILL NOT HURT OTHER PEOPLE

I listened to Nick's voice and heard, "Lucy, bad, didn't—" but couldn't focus on what he was saying. As I picked up Olga from her ballet practice and Roxanne from her ceramics class, I tried to hold my breath and not to inhale the smell, and all that time I had ants crawling over my body, but I did my best to ignore them.

I didn't look into Luke's eyes when he came home early, just waved my hands at the kids and shook my head. He grabbed a bottle of beer.

We sat down to dinner in silence. Only Olga and Nick talked and ate.

"I want to replay American Idol," said Olga.

"Wanna play *Lemmings*, Daddy?" asked Nick.

"Roxanne, eat your meatloaf," I said.

"Why don't you eat it?" she snapped. "I don't see you eating anything."

"Did you get good grades today?"

Luke sent Nick a cowardly smile, as if he couldn't really allow himself to smile, but was doing it for Nick. I looked down into my plate.

"I don't have grades, and I was almost all good."

"What do you mean? What was not good?" asked Luke.

He was slouching more than ever.

"I want two pieces of cheesecake, Mom," said Olga.

"What happened?" I asked Nick.

"Nothing," he said. "I told you in the car!"

"What is it," said Luke, finishing his second beer.

"Just this note from Ms. Jenkins. She's mean."

"Finish your cheesecake, and let's talk."

"Hey," I heard Olga's whisper. "Nicky. I'll play *Lemmings* with you."

I couldn't remember doing the dishes and moving to the living room. Luke was sitting in his armchair. I stood up next to him. Nick dug through his backpack for a long time, then produced a note, and handed it to Luke, without looking at us, and scratched his right calf with his left ankle. The note from Ms. Jenkins said: "Write twenty times: '*I will not hurt other people. I will not hurt other people.*' Discuss with parents."

"What did you do?" I asked flatly.

"Nothing," he answered. "Just screamed into Lucy's ear. I don't know why she cried. I pulled her ponytail. Ben did it, too, but he didn't get in trouble because Lucy only told on me. Ms. Jenkins got mad and she was mean, she didn't let me play knockout during recess."

Red patches covered Luke's neck and cheeks. He pinched Nick's little pink ear.

"Don't!"

My voice was hoarse. I did not sound like me. It wasn't me. I saw another ear, raw hamburger ear with black coarse hairs. Doggy eyes, pleading. Dean, the psychotherapy session.

"Don't," I hissed.

Everyone looked at me. Luke let go of Nick's ear.

"I'm taking *Lemmings* away," he said.

The little ear turned crimson. I looked at the robot standing next to me. I felt like a robot.

Nick rushed to his room and dove into his bed. He covered his head with a blanket.

"A kiss?"

"Nn–nn."

"A story?"

"Nn–nn."

290

I stood by the door. He sobbed and sobbed, then sighed. Then it was quiet. I tiptoed into his room. I pulled the blanket off his red face. I wanted to kiss his ear. I knew it would feel like a seashell. A sun-warmed seashell.

I couldn't. I was dirty, I had ants, my hands were bloody.

He shuddered in his sleep, sighed again and mumbled something. I kneeled down. His breath smelled like almond cookies.

"Mommy…"

I couldn't kiss him.

I curled up next to his bed on the floor, wrapped my arms around my chest, and stayed like that for a very long time. I felt blank. Ants were climbing under my pajama bottoms, I was afraid to move, I didn't want ants in Nick's bed. My hand shook. I tried to stop it, but it shook worse. I wanted to tell Nick a story. I didn't want to wake him up. I whispered quietly.

"Once upon a time, there lived a little Armadillo. Little Armadillo was brave, and he always launched on a journey without knowing what was going to happen to him. But he simply couldn't stay at home, for he was restless. And so he embarked again on the ship and sailed into the open ocean, all alone, for Little Armadillo was a lonely traveler. When the moon and the stars came out, he always stood on the deck and looked out into the horizon and winked at the magic lighthouse… for he knew that a storm would come one day and free him…"

I walked out of his room, and went to the backyard.

I wanted to smoke.

An amethyst light twinkled in Vanessa's window.

Was it the wind stirring my hair around? I touched my hair; my fingers were cold, inflexible—was it me? Who was it?

I once was a little girl and hopped down Potemkin Steps. I ate pistachio ice cream. I had sunny hair. I had no breasts, no pubic hair. I had no wrinkles. Was that me?

When I was pregnant my hair was blonde, or black. My breasts were large and my ankles were swollen. Was that me?

I looked at my hands, covered with ants. Bitten nails, red cuticles. Was I my sister?

I would be old, my skin would be like an elephant's, dull and creepy. I would look like Grandma Rosa. Would that be me? Or would I turn into her?

Which me?

I grabbed my hair at the temples. My mind exploded—all of me couldn't fit inside it. We were countless Russian dolls nesting inside my mind and my body, ants swarming inside my brain. I just kept their memories, their ice cream, their tears.

Who was I?

I didn't choose my name. I didn't choose my body, my face, my life.

I was a Lemming, a cheerful and blind slave of circumstances, a mindless ant in the intestines of the Universe. The amethyst light twinkled at me, teasing me, mocking me, and there was no way out.

I didn't smoke; I didn't want to; I went back to the living room.

I couldn't remember falling asleep. I only remembered The Nightmare. The cherries, the blood, the empty beach. I screamed. Nothing. I tensed my every muscle. I pulled at the invisible ropes. And then I heard my own voice. A train arriving at a station.

"Honey!"

They all stood around me. Luke was holding me, Nick was crying, the girls stood in the doorway in their pajamas. I knew I was awake, but I couldn't stop screaming. I didn't know what sound I was making. Then I heard it. I was screaming like a child. Sick child.

"Maaaaaamaaaaaa...."

I couldn't remember what happened then.

SOMETIMES I WANT TO BE BAD

I slept a long time. I woke up and saw a note: "Took the girls. Nick's asleep. Have a quiet day with him, I will see you after lunch. I love you."

Nick was at the table, eating cereal.

"Mommy, you look different," he said. "You were sick last night. Did your tummy hurt?"

"Just no makeup," I said. "I'm all better. It was my tummy."

"You should eat," said Nick. "Cereal."

"Nickie. I want to ask you something."

"I like you with lipstick more," said Nick.

"What were you thinking when you hurt your friend? Yesterday?"

Nick scratched his neck, then put too much cereal into his mouth, and chewed for a while. Finally, he said, "I didn't shink, Mama."

"Well," I said. "See what happens when you don't think? It always comes back to you, and you feel bad. What's the point?"

He shrugged.

"It's silly to do that. You don't want to feel bad, do you? It doesn't feel good to feel bad, does it?"

"Sometimes," he answered after a pause. "Sometimes I want to be bad and I want you to punish me. After that I'm good again, even much gooder than before. Do you know?"

I drove him to school and stopped by Head to Toe Beauty. The Buddha lady greeted me at the door, smiling and nodding her head like a Lucky Cat beckoning to me from the counter.

"Hi, Lizzy," I said. "Hair, dye, black, please."

She smiled and shook her head, looking even happier.

294

"No understand."

"Red hair, bad hair. Want black, black hair, like—raven black, oh forget it, like, like you!"

"I? No, no," she said. "Lady pretty. Me not pretty."

"You pretty," I said. "I bad. Me want you. Please."

I watched her fixing a dirt-like substance in a small dish. The fumes were toxic. Slow poison. It felt good. I closed my eyes. She worked the brush over my head, and I almost fell asleep.

"Finish," she said.

I opened my eyes. I couldn't see myself in the reflection. A pale stranger with short, black hair and no makeup stared at me. A changeling, a cold girl, a killer.

"You like?"

"Yes."

"Twenty six dorrrars."

The Lucky Cat bobbed his orange head at me, lips distorted in a smile. It was mocking me. It was dead Blossom.

At the door, I bumped into Ms. Freckle. She gave me a blank look, then frowned and swiveled her head on her shoulders, like Nick's toy army tank, trying to figure it out, to put together the resemblance, the physical notion of me and the changeling, and then she recognized me: "Oh, Oksana…"[1]

---

[1] **Here Rose/Oksana finally exposes the truth.** It is common for developmentally normal children, especially girls, between the ages of 3 and 10 years to create imaginary friends to cope with negative emotions. However, children with **Dissociative Disorders** experience imaginary companions as real; the imaginary friend becomes an alter. Thus, for little Oksana an imaginary nameless sister became helper, comforter, and protector, and eventually a self-destroying alter. "Big sister" is first created during the childhood abuse situation: Oksana leaves her body and watches Uncle Oleg hurting another person.

Developing a suicidal alter is common for individuals

I didn't wait, just ran to my car, leaving her there, stupefied. There was no escape. I knew she knew I was a killer.

I took two Goodwill bags of dominatrix clothes and dropped them at the Salvation Army, looking over my shoulder. In the doors of the store I saw Ms. Freckle again. I thought of the insulation in the Academy of Sciences, made from recycled jeans. Her grey hair moved in the wind. Her eyes narrowed behind the metallic frame. She pulled the cell phone out of her shapeless overalls and started to dial a very short number, without lowering her eyes, staring at me. I knew she was calling 911.

I turned around and left.

I came back to the empty house and poured myself some coffee. My hands were still shaking. I had little time left. They were coming for me.

with **Dissociative Identity Disorder**. After the imaginary sister dies, the waking self "Oksana" moves on with her life: She goes to America and establishes a new life with Luke. The nameless angry and self-destructive alter "Rose" is reactivated following extreme stress; she emerges to protect the waking self from memories of abuse. When the memories are brought to consciousness by the conversation with Mike, this alter is ready to self-destroy in order to save the whole from pain. Oksana is left behind once again when Rose disappears on the Bay Bridge in an episode of **dissociative fugue**.

WE ALL ARE MONSTERS

I opened my laptop and Potemkin sat down next to me, then sniffed the air, stood up, and walked away, wagging her tail.

Letters looked like ants. They tried to run away from me, but I caught them. I caught them, but lost my thoughts. I looked around the living room. I forgot what I wanted. My living room looked like a prison. Dust on the robot's head. I needed to clean. The green couch. An empty beer bottle on the coffee table. I thought they might be talking to each other. Voices raged in my head.

"What was it?"

"You killed a man."

"Who was he?"

"The book! Get the book!"

"***DEVIATIONS*!**"

I pulled **DEVIATIONS** out of my purse.

Mike stared at me from the back page. He looked like an assassin. I hated that forehead, that pout, the forehead of a philosopher, the pout of a princess. He was smirking and teasing. No, it wasn't him.

It was Alexandrov.

No, it was Lenin.

Gas Station Jesus.

My Father.

I flung the book on the floor, red blood on black, on my bluish carpet. I knew he was trying to trick me again.

"Strong, Strong, Strong. It was Strong."

I had to send it to him. I had to mail my book to him, so he knew.

I Googled "Michael H. Strong."

Next workshop in August; working on his next book, *Abnormal Psychology and Sex Education*. San Francisco-based. Mysterious scholar of darkest secrets. The plumber of human souls. Part-time professor at the Institute of Human Sexuality—there! Contact Us.

I opened Word. A blank page stared at me like a blind eye, like a void, a white hole. It contained the Universe. I opened my book. It had the ending now. I wrote down what happened, and how I killed Mike.

I pushed the Print button. Little James's piano drilled into my head. I closed my eyes. Pages rustled, flying off the printer.

The print job was done. James stopped playing. I typed:

"Mike, are you…"

I deleted it; my fingers were dancing so bad that I could hardly type at all.

"…you are a monster."

My eyes were running around the room. Things looked familiar, but they were not my things. I looked at myself in the mirror. It wasn't me. It was the changeling.

"… and so am I. We all are monsters."

I looked at Nick's puppet theater, flat paper dolls dead against the empty cardboard.

"So, no one is a monster; there are no monsters."

My eyes scrolled to the book stretched on the carpet. I wanted the world to know. I wanted to save the world.

"Publish my writing, Mike. Mistress Rose."

I printed the note.

I'm sending it to you, Mike. Publish my writing.

THE END.

AFTERWORD BY MICHAEL H. STRONG

On the day I received Mistress Rose's envelope, the Bay Bridge was closed to traffic while the highway patrol worked on retrieving an abandoned vehicle. The driver had attempted to jump off the bridge. She climbed the upper deck of the span linking San Francisco and Oakland, and due to dense fog no one was able to see the final plunge, but the woman had disappeared.

I made no connection—not then. I began reading Mistress Rose's story every morning, and after a week I knew the sad truth, and thus decided to publish these materials.

Readers familiar with my major work, **DEVIATIONS**, know that I have dedicated two decades of research and literary work to propagating the freedom of sexual expression. Publishing *We, Monsters* continues my lifelong effort. Art at times is more powerful than science; "the tygers of wrath are wiser than the horses of instruction."

Nobody is a monster. Rose philosophizes with her murderous whip; I analyze with a surgical scalpel of science. Together, we cut through the dead skin of reality, through the bondage rope of morals, through the frills of superficiality, and into the raw meat, into the essence. We open the abscess and bring out pus. Do not fear to see the mess or feel the pain. This mess is mind-clearing. The pain is liberating. So is the knowledge.

Scientific research is not the only goal of my comments. By adding my notes to the story, I translated the ethical choices of an individual into a political program of a social movement.

Created by chance, conceived by error, *We, Monsters* is a political manifesto.

I add here a *Glossary of Deviations* and relevant facts for those readers who are eager to explore further. For more in-depth information, read *DEVIATIONS* and *SURVIVAL AND PROCREATION*, by Michael H. Strong.

ABOUT THE AUTHOR

Zarina Zabrisky started to write at six. She wrote traveling around the world as a street artist, translator, and a kickboxing instructor. Her work has appeared in over thirty literary magazines and anthologies in the U.S., U.K., Canada, Ireland, Hong Kong and Nepal. She is a three-time Pushcart Prize nominee and a recipient of 2013 Acker Award. Zabrisky's short story collections, IRON and A CUTE TOMBSTONE, are available from www.amazon.com. You can find more about Zabrisky and read her published work at:

www.zarinazabrisky.com

ACKNOWLEDGEMENTS

This novel would never have happened without Katherine Zubritsky, a brilliant psychoanalyst, scholar, and life-long friend, who edited the footnotes and helped me wade through Freudian theory. Special thanks to Sammy Dwarfobia, the graphic designer behind the cover for sharing his talent and all the emotional and logistic support during this journey. Many thanks to Tarin Towers, my first editor, for her patience and tact. Deep gratitude to my first readers—Talila Baron, Olga Beregovaya, Rachel Bernstein, Yanina Gotsulsky, Larisa Idlis, Anatoly Molotkov, Eugene Ostashevsky, Luba Ostashevsky, Simon Rogghe, James Warner, and Anastasia Zakharova—for their invaluable contribution in shaping the manuscript.